cOMEWHERE IN ENGLAND

CAROLA MARY ANIMA OMAN was born in 1897 in Oxford, the second of three children of Sir Charles and Mary Oman. In 1906 she was sent to Miss Batty's School in Park Crescent, Oxford, where she eventually became head girl.

In World War One Carola Oman was a probationary VAD nurse at the Radcliffe Infirmary in Oxford. After various nursing appointments during the war, she was discharged in 1919. Her first book, *The Menin Road and Other Poems*, was published later that year.

On 26 April 1922, Carola Oman married Gerald Lenanton, and subsequently devoted most of her writing in the 1920s and 1930s to a series of historical novels, influenced in part by her close friend Georgette Heyer.

In the course of a writing career of more than half a century Oman published over thirty books of fiction, history, and biography, among them several historical works for children, and *Ayot Rectory* (1965), set in the village where she and her husband had settled in a Jacobean manor, Bride Hall. In later years she specialized in historical biography. 1946 saw her prize-winning biography of Nelson, the book on which her reputation as a biographer rests. She was appointed CBE in 1957.

After two strokes, Carola Oman died at Bride Hall, Ayot St Laurence, on 11 June 1978.

FICTION BY CAROLA OMAN

For Adults

Princess Amelia (1924)
The Road Royal (1924)
King Heart (1926)
Mrs Newdigate's Window (1927)
The Holiday (1928)
Crouchback (1929)
Miss Barrett's Elopement (1929)
Fair Stood the Wind (1930)
Major Grant (1931)
The Empress (1932)
The Best of His Family (1933)
Over the Water (1935)
Nothing to Report (1940)
Somewhere in England (1943)

For Children

Ferry the Fearless (1936)
Johel (1937)
Robin Hood, the Prince of Outlaws (1937)
Alfred, King of the English (1939)
Baltic Spy (1940)

CAROLA OMAN

SOMEWHERE IN ENGLAND

With an introduction by
Sir Roy Strong

DEAN STREET PRESS

A Furrowed Middlebrow Book
FM31

Published by Dean Street Press 2019

First published in 1943 by Hodder & Stoughton

Cover by DSP
Cover illustration shows detail from *Buscot Park* (1938) by
Eric Ravilious

ISBN 978 1 913054 19 9

www.deanstreetpress.co.uk

INTRODUCTION

By Sir Roy Strong

"LADY LENANTON, last Friday I eloped and married your niece." With that telephone conversation Carola Oman (1897-1978) entered my life more forcefully than before as the aunt of my wife, the designer Julia Trevelyan Oman. Carola was by then a formidable grande dame in her mid-seventies, whom I had first encountered as a Trustee of the National Portrait Gallery, of which I had become Director in 1967. What I only discovered years later was that she first woman trustee of any national collection, the other being the National Maritime Museum, the consequence of her acclaimed biography of Nelson (1946).

The Omans were a Scottish family from the Orkneys which had sought its fortunes in India in the late eighteenth century. Ann Chadwick (1832-1907), one of the heiress daughters of the builder of the Great Western Railway, had married one of the numerous Charles Omans, an indigo planter in Bengal who died early. She returned to England with her only son who became the great historian Sir Charles Oman (1860-1946), Fellow of All Souls and Chicheley Professor of Modern History. In 1892 he married Mary Maclagan (1866-1950) and Carola was their second child, the name a reflection of her father's frustration that their second child was yet another daughter.

Much of her childhood was spent in Frewin Hall, Oxford in a household which still had maids and morning family prayers down to the death of her father in 1946. She was educated at Miss Batty's and then Wychwood School, Oxford, although denied knowledge of Latin by her father. She grew up to be a striking young woman with an abundance of flaxen hair and blue eyes. Already by 1914 she had taken part in the long series of Oxford pageants which were such a feature of the Edwardian period. With the outbreak of the First World War that idyll came to an end and she became a VAD nurse serving in both this country and France. Her contribution to a book of verse, *The*

Menin Road (1919) is increasingly recognised as significant as female writers of the twentieth century are reappraised.

In 1922 she married Gerald Lenanton (1896-1952), a timber agent who was knighted for his services in the Second World War. His wounds, sustained in the 1914-18 conflict, curtailed any possibility of children. Carola inherited a fortune from her Oman grandmother enabling them to settle at Ayot St Lawrence close to Bernard Shaw in an Elizabethan red brick house, Bride Hall. She lived there until her death, apart from the war period which was passed at Flax Bourton near Bristol.

Carola had close links with two other female writers. One was Joanna Cannan (1896-1961) whose father was Dean of Trinity College, Oxford and whose literary fame depended on a steady stream of books for children focusing on ponies as well as over thirty adult novels. The more significant friend was Georgette Heyer (1902-1974), the creator of the historically accurate dream world of the Regency romance novel as well as a steady stream of thrillers. Carola too was prolific, writing over thirty children's books, historical biographies and fiction. She was hugely patriotic responding fully to the challenge of the Second World War with novels, *Nothing to Report* (1942) and *Somewhere in England* (1943) among them, and more fully in historical works like *Britain against Napoleon* (1942) and culminating with her prize-winning biography of *Admiral, Lord Nelson* (1946).

Already in the 1930s she had begun to write historical biography working through a succession of Queens, Henrietta Maria, Elizabeth, Queen of Bohemia and Mary of Modena. After the war came larger, more ambitious biographical projects including Sir John Moore, David Garrick, Eugène de Beauharnais and Sir Walter Scott. Although well researched, most would strike the modern reader as ponderous and lacking a sharper critical insight and analysis. She was awarded a CBE in 1957.

The Omans had a strong sense of identity and belonged to that group we now designate as the intellectual aristocracy but whose life was not in her case passed in academe. Her brother Charles (1908-1982) became Keeper of Metalwork at the Victoria & Albert Museum and a distinguished antiquary. The furnishing of the mind with an abundance of historical fact and wide reading in terms of literature was taken for granted. She wrote during a period when, for women of that class, servants were a given and 'work' in the sense of what happened after 1945 was totally foreign to them. Right until the very end Bride Hall depended on a cook and a butler-chauffeur. The world of Bloomsbury would have been also totally alien to her as indeed what we now categorise as that of the 'bright young things' and the smart set of the twenties and thirties. Much of Carola's life can be explained as demonstrating to her father that she too was capable of writing history. She inherited from him too his deep Conservatism. In his case so extreme that as an MP for the University he was nicknamed 'Stone Age Man'.

What of her papers that survive I have given to the Bodleian Library, Oxford. Some of her travel diaries, I am told, are of interest. She left me half her library and in the dissolution of Bride Hall following her death I came eventually to inherit the desk at which she wrote. For over forty years I have written all my books at that unpretentious Victorian partner's desk which I remember so well in what was her writing room off to the right as one entered Bride Hall. Carola was also a formidable needlewoman and her memory remains encapsulated here in one of a series of tapestry chairs that she worked. On the back she has etched a view of Bride Hall against which, in the foreground, one of her beloved Dalmatians scampers after a bird. It is a tiny vignette recording a once secure world that has gone.

Roy Strong

PART I
PIPPA'S POINT OF VIEW

CHAPTER I
"A CHANGE OF BALLOONS"
(March 2nd-3rd, 1942)

I

AT THE CORNER of Kidderpore Road, Philippa-Dawn Johnson said to her best friend, "I must now break it to you that I am going to desert you at the 'bus stop. I'm going to the Public Library." She added without much hope, "I suppose you wouldn't like to come too, and wait downstairs in the newspaper-room while I just look up a few facts?"

"No, thank you, Musty-Fusty," said her friend with decision. "I've had enough for one day of reading newspapers while I wait for you. While you were getting the fish, I read the whole of the sheet your aunt had put into the string bag to wrap up the dog-biscuit. It was a front sheet too, with nothing but ladies ready to sell scarcely worn mink coats, and urgently needing other ladies (over calling-up age) to give occasional help in light housework in exchange for happy home life in old-world country cottage; two toddlers. I even read Alcoholism Cured, and Unwanted Art. Teeth."

"You see," explained Philippa-Dawn, following her own train of thought, "just as they were closing the Library the other day, I discovered they've got a simply super book, full of photographs and descriptions of famous country houses, and I'm almost certain that I'll find Woodside in it."

"I can't see why," objected her companion. "There's a house called 'Woodside' here, in Outram Avenue, and it's not in the least famous or beautiful."

"Well, I don't know about famous," admitted Philippa-Dawn, "but my Woodside is definitely a Seat. The little modern Barsetshire Guide which I have managed to see, says so. I copied out what it said." She began to burrow in the string bag.

"Why you should want to spend your last evening here, looking at photographs of a house which you'll be seeing with your own eyes, for better for worse, to-morrow by tea-time," said her friend, "beats me."

"Of course I didn't mean to leave it till my last day," mumbled Philippa-Dawn. "Ah, here are my notes. I looked up Went, because the address is 'Woodside, near Went.' Actually it turns out to be eight miles, even from the Junction. I change there, and they're sending an ambulance to Westbury to meet me. The Sec. says so. Listen. It begins about Went—'an agricultural and manufacturing city, an Assize town and the see of a bishop, possesses large hosiery and aircraft factories . . .'"

"And a very large aerodrome," corrected her friend. "When was that Guide published."

"'To the north of the bridge,'" continued Philippa-Dawn in a high chant, "'lies the old and centre part of the city, in which there still remain a number of gabled houses of the fourteenth and fifteenth centuries.'"

"I expect you'll find that was the part that got blitzed," suggested her comforter. "Still, it sounds as if it had probably got a cinema or two and a Smith's and a Woolworth's. You'll go in there for your afternoon out."

"That's what I thought," nodded Philippa-Dawn. "And, as a matter of fact, old Went never has been blitzed, only the suburbs. That's why it's packed. 'Its prosperous but comparatively uneventful history begins about 1220. . . .'" Her voice trailed off. "'The Cathedral, originally the church of an abbey, is attractively situated amongst level water-meadows. . . .' Well, we needn't go into all that." Her voice rose again. "'A short branch line runs hence up the valley to Westbury. A little to the north of (1 m.) Went Junction, is Went Park (1600), the seat of Lord Merle of Went, with many portraits (grounds open Wed., Aug. and Sep. 2-5).'"

"It's a Maternity Home now," stated her friend. "Two women had gifts of sons at it in that sheet of the newspaper while you were getting the fish. They had both put in their pet-names in brackets, and one of them was 'Cockroach.'"

"By the way," said Philippa-Dawn, "I was such a long time because I discovered that they'd got some sweets in at Columbine's Cake Shop. They gave me two slabs. As the 'bus doesn't seem to be coming, do you think we'd better have them now?"

"What are they like?" asked her friend.

"Well, they're chocolate on the outside, and I should think it's a sort of Turkish Delight inside."

"We'd better have them now."

In not quite so clear a voice, Philippa-Dawn presently continued. "'Amongst the interesting monuments in St. Nicholas' Church, Westbury-on-the-Hill (5 m.) is that of the eccentric Lord Merle, friend of Charles James Fox and leading Whig statesmen (d. 1823), one of Chantrey's best works. The church, mainly Perp. with Norman remains, contains the burial chapel of the Morrisons of Woodside (see below) and altar tomb of Abbot Wayne (d. 1465), best seen. from the S. choir aisle. On the opposite wall are fifteenth-century frescoes. (Temptation of St. Anthony. Incredulity of St. Thomas.) The miserere seats should not be overlooked. At the Pheasant Inn, Hazlitt wrote several essays and was visited by the Lambs. The old Mill House (3 m. deep ford) has remarkable tithe barns. Close by is a field traditionally called Conqueror's Meads, popularly reputed to be the scene of some ancient battle.'" She broke off to ask, "Isn't it absolutely thrilling?"

"Does it ever get to Woodside?" asked her audience.

"It's just getting there. You can't hurry things in the country," said Philippa-Dawn. "There's another super grisly bit first. 'The villages of Upper and Lower Merle are unusually picturesque. Dead Woman's Hill (1¾ m.) on the main Went road may be ascended with advantage. View.* Its name recalls the brutal and mysterious murder of Janet Clarke in March, 1820. Sir Walter Scott, then upon a visit to the 1st Baron Merle, undertook a carriage drive to inspect the scene of the tragedy.'"

"I wish he'd put it in *Ivanhoe*," said Miss Johnson's unintellectual companion. "I wonder what the food'll be like at Woodside."

"Well," said Philippa-Dawn, arrested, "I'm nerved up to its being pretty awful. Auntie Prue—you know the way she can never stop telling one about the last War—says that she once got a rolled-gold chain in her pudding, in a hospital."

"Did she eat it, and have to be operated upon?"

"No, she didn't eat it, because the woman who was serving out the pudding—they were all dead tired, owing to dressing ghastly wounds, lucky brutes—said in an exhausted way, 'Will you have some pudding, nurse? There's a rolled-gold chain in it.' Auntie Prue took the helping, fished out the chain, and ate it, being hungry. It turned out that the kitchen-maid had taken it off her neck when its clasp broke, and put it in the scales, and forgotten it, and put the ingredients for the pudding on the top. The point of the story was that the kitchen-maid had then left for a week's leave, and everyone in the hospital knew that she was accustomed to wear on the chain a weighty locket, engraved 'Mizpah,' and everyone else had gulped down their helpings, so had to go about for a week feeling apprehensive."

"Perhaps you'll get fresh veg. and Heggs as it's the country," suggested Philippa-Dawn's friend. "Does your aunt mind your leaving?"

"Well, at first she was a bit inclined to be peeved," recounted Philippa-Dawn, "and talked about Loyalty to the Post—you know, the old F.A. Post in Nicholson Road, where she's been sitting since 1939. But I think she saw that I couldn't stay there much longer, polishing up the handle of the big front door, and then, by a stroke of luck, her cousin May wanted to come and live here, bringing her Free French cook—marvellous!—and her whippet—not so good. . . . I spent this morning doing out my room. By to-morrow night it'll be Cousin May's and the whippet's. At any rate," ended Philippa-Dawn, staring up at the garland of silver monsters gently swaying above them in the evening sky, "at any rate, it'll be a change of Balloons."

"There isn't much more," she continued, returning to her battered manuscript, and opening in more cheerful tones—"'At Woodside, to the south of Westbury-on-the-Green, built about 1721 by F. Smith for Sir Crosbie Morrison, whose great-nephew and successor Sir Barnaby Morrison, made considerable additions and alterations, we find many chimney-pieces in the purest style of Robert Adam, and a collection of classic sculptures. The mansion, which contains also a particularly fine staircase, with balustrading composed of S-shaped wrought bar iron, with crinkled leaf ornaments and several plaster ceilings in the Rococo and Chinese Chippendale style, has descended by inheritance to the present owner, Sir Thomas Morrison, Bt.'"

"I shall look forward to thinking of you alone on night duty among the busts," considered the auditor.

"What I can't exactly make out," said Philippa-Dawn, wrinkling her fair brow, "is how it now belongs to Mrs. Christopher Hungerford."

"Quite simple. Sir Thomas Morrison, last of his line, now inhabits a flat in Hove. Mrs. Hungerford has bought Woodside, and filled it with shot taffetas pouffes and cocktail cabinets. Or, again, sweet Mary Morrison has married the poor but honest Christopher Hungerford. You might let me know. And if you can get a picture postcard of the Seat at the village shop, on one of your muddy walks, you can send it to me, taking care to poke a pin through to show me which is your bedroom window. But don't dare to send any stories of grateful patients returning in a blaze of glory to say, 'Nurse! Nurse! yours was the arm that brought down the three Messerschmitts.' I'd prefer, too, not to have to hear that Mrs. Hungerford is a perfect rock of strength, with something of the angel in her tired eyes."

"I won't," agreed Philippa-Dawn, "because it's not hospital etiquette to tell any stories about patients. And I don't for a moment expect to find Mrs. Hungerford angelic. I'm a bit terrified of the sound of the secretary, too. Mrs. Bates, Auntie Prue's old Poona pal who lives at Westbury-on- the-Green and got me the job, sent Auntie Prue an Annual Report, or something, of the Barsetshire War Organization and it said that at Woodside,

Mrs. Christopher Hungerford (owner) had an invaluable Sec. in the Hon. J. Pratt."

"Perhaps he's a retired naval officer, with bushy white eyebrows and a quarter-deck manner," suggested her friend hopefully, "or, again, invalided with gastritis, and permanently pale yellow, although not much past middle age. Helping hospitals, invaluably, is just the sort of thing retired service people take on. I must say, grim though it is to be what is called 'the eighteen-year-old class,' I'm thankful that I'm not 'over calling-up age,' aren't you?"

"Um—yes," nodded Philippa-Dawn. "I shouldn't like to stay on here anyway, though."

"Oh, it's not so bad, in a few weeks' time, when there are flowering cherries and mays in every front garden . . . and tennis. . . . And of course I simply couldn't go anywhere where I wasn't allowed to take my piano. Perhaps the war will be over by the time I'm calling-up age. Perhaps I may marry and never have to raise a finger."

"I don't care for prisoned trees in front gardens," said Philippa-Dawn, sounding morbid. "Do you know, it was while I was washing up in the scullery in Auntie Prue's house, and looking out at a poor tree which had once stood in fields, that I suddenly realized I needn't stay. I sort of realized in a flash that I was a Person and could go where I liked. Have you ever felt like that?"

"Oh, often."

"When you say 'often'," said Philippa-Dawn, still morbid, "it just shows me that you have never felt what I'm trying to describe at all. It's a thing that only happens once in one's life, I should think. I suddenly realized that I was grown up, and that I must live in the country. And there's another thing, I've decided. I'm not going to be 'dear little Philippa-Dawn' any more."

"I've always thought it rather foul," agreed Philippa-Dawn's contemporary. "What are you going to be? Natasha, or Tatiana? Topical? You'll have practically a free hand, since nobody at Woodside will ever have known you existed."

"Mrs. Bates will have known," said Philippa-Dawn heavily. "I haven't absolutely a free hand. I've decided to be 'Pippa.' But you needn't put it on envelopes."

"Here's my 'bus at last," said Pippa's best friend violently. "Don't forget to let me know about Pratt, and the postcard. But you will be seeing me again, all too soon. What time did you say, to-morrow morning?"

"I've got to catch the 8.50," cried Pippa. "It's awfully decent of you, but honestly you needn't trouble, and anyway, you'll never make it."

"Oh, yes, I shall," floated from the crowded equipage, which was rapidly carrying Pippa's best friend out of the Kidderpore Road and, as things fell out, out of her life.

I I

Miss Pippa Johnson did not sleep well on the night pre-ceding her departure for Woodside. For one thing, she was obliged to suffer, close to her pillow, throughout the hours of darkness, a remorselessly ticking alarum clock of very inexpensive and tinny appearance, enamelled sky-blue. Actually, Miss Johnson had visited five shops before securing this treasure, price twenty-five shillings, and in spite of its pavement-toy air, and the fact that every heartbeat seemed to shake it to the core, it did not seem to resent being over-wound, knocked over, forgotten for days, and generally subjected to all the indignities consequent upon being the first timepiece owned by a young lady about to make her entrance into the world. As her alarum-clock was obviously in the last stage of pulmonary tuberculosis, and of humble origin though undaunted spirit, Miss Johnson had reverently named it "Poor Keats."

On the floor of her room, disposed after the manner of the four angels in the good child's bedside rhyme, gaped her luggage. This consisted of two pith suitcases, a black kit-bag bearing her initials and surname stencilled in white paint, and an imitation leather attaché-case, all at the moment half packed. Miss Johnson realized that her luggage was ample for a single female undertaking a cross-country journey in war-time, but there had been difficulties in the way of leaving belongings behind. Her Auntie Prue, who was a diligent reader of helpful official pamphlets, had been amongst the first to clear her attics of junk, and choose her cellar as refuge-room. She had later purchased materials for an outdoor shelter, which had become the leading feature of her back garden and was said by her brother-in-law from Cambridge to bear an interesting resemblance to Early Hittite Dwellings. Soon after Pippa had assisted her hostess to plant spring bulbs on the roof of the Hittite Dwelling, Auntie Prue had been fascinated by the possibilities of yet another type of shelter which, as it combined a spring mattress and steel-top dinner-table, really seemed to solve every problem of modern entertainment; and, moreover, since its detachable sides were of stout wire-mesh, suggested practical use in the strenuous days of post-war reconstruction as a luxury rabbit-hutch. But it was only capable of accommodating two adults and one child, or two adults and two very small children, and while she was still considering the matter, her Cousin May wrote to say that the Free French cook had what is known as a French figure.

Attics and cellar being denied her by war conditions, Pippa might have asked her hostess to store her superfluous belongings in a chest of drawers, but the experience of the don from Cambridge had decided her against this. He had left behind him, in various parts of the house, after his visit last summer vacation, a perfectly new check tie, a copy of *They Found Him Dead*, and an empty waterproof gas-mask carton cover, enlivened by a portrait of Mickey Mouse. Auntie Prue, pardonably failing to connect him with these objects, had sent them all to the F.A. Post Jumble Sale in aid of ravished Ruritania. At Christmas, exactly one hour after his departure, a telegram had startled Lawrence Avenue. It read, "Please post immediately ivory hair brushes left on dressing-table." Unless Pippa labelled everything, she could not be sure that it would be safe in any drawer liable to be visited by Auntie Prue intent upon deeds of charity or salvage, and all cupboards of the house were already overfull and locked. They contained invasion stores, maps and plans likely to be useful to enemy parachutists (including a plan of both marquees at the last Horticultural Society's Chelsea Show), and articles of purely decorative value removed from the drawing-room as a labour-saving device, after the triumphant exit of Lawrence Avenue's last surviving domestic servant.

Professor Abbadie Beadon had taken a philosophic view of his sister-in-law's servantless situation, since, to his great satisfaction, his services had by now been accepted by a Government Control installed in the requisitioned premises of St. Ebba's School for Girls, Barsetshire. In future he would only have a fortnight's annual holiday, and he took quite kindly to the kitchen being the centre of social life in the house. He had told Pippa that Anne Neville, daughter and co-heiress of Warwick the Kingmaker, and Queen-Consort of Richard III, had been discovered by her highborn suitor, after the Battle of Tewkesbury, attired in the habit of a kitchen-wench in a merchant's mansion of the City of London. Pippa, who particularly abhorred the machine, had shown Professor Beadon the mincer, well clogged after preparations for Cottage Pie, and said that she felt jolly sure Anne Neville had never had to clean out anything like that. Professor Beadon had inspected the mincer without recoil, and said that since its pattern seemed primitive, he fancied such an implement must have been early in existence. He promised to ask a colleague, formerly a constant reader in the Library of the Department of Science and Art, South Kensington, now a fellow-worker at the ignominious address in Barsetshire.

It was owing to Professor Beadon that Pippa had become a haunter of the local Public Library, and received from her best friend the nickname of Musty-Fusty. The Professor had not been really helpful. He had not gone so far as to escort his young friend to the establishment, which was truly rather awe-inspiring, being built of staring red brick, with purple trimmings and a prominent foundation stone inscribed, "This Stone was laid by Lady Jones, May 11th, 1887." The Professor had merely murmured one day at breakfast, "You could find all the information you are seeking at your local Public Library. . . . But you never will, I dare say." Whereupon Pippa had defiantly ventured within the portals of the building blessed by Lady Jones, and

after a false start into the newspaper-room, which was well
filled, apparently by unemployed charwomen and depressed
aliens in mackintoshes, and another into a downstairs department labelled "Town Clerk," and occupied by whistling boys
pushing about echoing trolleys, had found herself at last in a
well-lit gallery possessed of many desks, not more than half
a dozen of which were occupied by broken-spirited looking
figures, presided over by three haughty young ladies in cretonne
aprons, who took away your attaché-case in a manner that
suggested that it harboured bombs, and offered you a corroded
pen with which to enter your name, address and occupation,
before presenting you in exchange with a sun-burnt number
ticket, and waving you towards the card-index cabinet, which
was a very complicated game.

Naturally, on her last night in the old home, Pippa's uneasy
dreams hovered around Woodside. Dusk had been falling by
the time that one of the contemptuous, cretonne-clad ladies,
after a descent into the cellar and ostentatious use of a duster,
had staggered towards her, bearing in both arms a volume that
measured three feet by two, weighed about fourteen pounds and
was thrillingly entitled, "Georgian Homes, Period I." And Pippa
had understood for a moment why people became professors
when, after turning to the index (another habit which she owed
to a murmured suggestion of her eminent friend), her eye had
lit upon the glad words, "Woodside, Barsetshire, pp. 105-19."
There were actually fourteen pages of plates and print about
Woodside; not much compared with Moor Park, Hertfordshire,
which occupied pp. 67-114, but quite enough when you had only
nine minutes left before black-out and closing hour.

During those nine minutes Pippa had contracted severe
mental indigestion. She soon gave up the attempt to read the
text, although it contained such passages as—"In Bussan's
History of the county, published in 1780, we learn that 'Sir
Barnaby Morrison made a fair Warren to this Seat, stocked it
with a choice breed of Rabbits, all silver haired, and planted it
with great Store of excellent Walnut trees. . . .' The House, a
substantial square block, facing south (Fig. I)," read Pippa, and

turned eagerly to Fig. I, which was called "Looking down from the Heights of the Park," and displayed a breath-taking bird's-eye view of a sun-bathed facade of eight and twenty glinting windows, backed by trees and riding clouds. "Fig. II, The Smoking Room," was rather a dark photograph of an empty brocade wing chair drawn up to an unlit fire, with a marble Medusa's face over the chimney-piece, and another to match, frowning above a landscape in oils, framed into the panelling. "The Lake, lying north of the house," was an impressive but chilly picture. "An exceptionally rich and satisfying example of shell-hood," evidently described the front door. Flicking past Fig. V, "Daffodils on the mound beneath the classic temple in the park," Pippa re-entered Woodside, and found herself hesitating on the threshold of "The Segmental Corridor, or Colonnade. It contains Sir Barnaby Morrison's collection of busts, and connects the Library, in the West Pavilion, with the main block."

"His daughter," muttered Pippa, turning on her pillow, "married the third Lord Merle, successively Minister to Stuttgart and St. Petersburg. The mantelpiece of a hook-nosed gentleman with a bath-towel beautifully pleated over his arm, was in the Saloon, and the lady riding in a shell amongst breakers was in the Study. Or was the bearded river-god the Study? I can't remember. I've arrived, and my bedroom is full of silver rabbits! 'The plaster decoration of the main staircase walls represents branches of the fruiting vine, on which are perched birds and squirrels, to the annoyance of the sporting dogs seated below. . . .' I've not arrived yet, because I've got to cross London first. I've got to cross London!"

III

The alarum-clock spoke vehemently, and although she could have sworn that she had not been asleep, Pippa woke, with a start, from depths of warm ease. "Poor Keats," faithful to his habit, had gone off at ten minutes before the hour for which he was set. But she had reckoned upon this, and left herself two hours in which to dress and finish her packing and get breakfast for two. She had several problems still to settle with regard to her packing. She strongly felt, for instance, that the luggage of a full-time war-worker, aged eighteen, should, in the year 1942, contain at least one photograph of a Flight-Lieutenant. Probably all the other girls would have rows of dashing relations in H.M. Forces. This was one of the drawbacks of being an only child. She possessed a photograph of Auntie Prue's Michael. It was large, and Auntie Prue would notice, and be hurt, if she left it behind, but it was quite unmistakably an enlargement from a Poly-Foto, and of somebody still at school. Pippa did not at all want to carry to quarters which would be restricted, a life-size and speaking likeness of Michael, glaring sheepishly from behind his horn-rimmed spectacles, as if he was just about to roar, "Oh! all right!" as he always did when you asked him to do something which he was really longing to do, such as go to the cinema. But Auntie Prue would notice and be hurt if Pippa jettisoned Michael, and probably he could not help leaving all the dirt on the soap and the towels in the downstairs cloak-room, and breaking the string of the bathroom black-out, and borrowing one's new, fourteen-coupon Burberry, and forgetting it in the 'bus. His two ruling passions—wireless and destruction—might even be useful in a few years' time, if you sent him off for an enemy target with a load of bombs. Pippa packed awful Michael between her six new aprons, tripped over the swarthy kitbag, of which she was privately much enamoured, and, making her way to the window, parted three layers of curtains with a practised finger. A single peep told her that Tuesday, March 3rd, was not at all a promising day. "Snow-flakes!" exclaimed Pippa resignedly, letting the curtains fall to again over a peacock-blue world.

She was over-warm from tussling with snapping suitcase clasps, when the moment came for her to descend to the kitchen where breakfast was boiled eggs, since this was, as Auntie Prue instantly reminded her, her last meal here. Auntie Prue, evidently trying to be decent, had a parting present for her guest. "There are fifty of them," said she, pressing into Pippa's hand a packet of envelopes of varying sizes and colours, several of which were labelled O.H.M.S., and all of which had already undertaken at least one journey. "And you will find an economy label, already attached, to each. The flimsier ones I have strengthened at the weak places with stamp-edging. Your friend didn't come."

"I never thought she would," said Pippa stoutly. "She'll meet me on the platform, I expect. Anyway, she would have been rather in the way while I was packing. I got late as it was. I'm so sorry you've had to put on the kettle."

"Never mind," said Auntie Prue graciously. "I've got to be at the Post by nine, and by to-morrow morning dear old May's Mathilde will be here."

"And dear old May's whippet," thought Pippa, but banished the thought as unworthy.

From the fuss that Auntie Prue made about Pippa's departure to catch the 8.50 for London, one might have thought that she herself was embarking for the Far East. Pippa wondered anew how on earth Auntie Prue had managed—as she undoubtedly had—to join a women's unit running a canteen and first-aid post for the British Expeditionary Force in France in 1916, a subject to which she was far too apt to recur in conversation. "I expect," thought Pippa, as Auntie Prue said for the second time, "we mustn't let you forget your gas-mask," followed closely by, "Just feel and make sure that you've got your ration book and money," and "You did remember to telephone yesterday to order the taxi," "I expect," thought Pippa, "that her brain's rather gone with age, and the only sign left is the desire to make plans for other people."

Auntie Prue produced one of her worst plans while the station taxi boiled at the door, and Pippa, seated for the last time in front of the spare-room mirror, in which she frowningly regarded her reflection, pushed back under the peak of her cap a burst of flaxen curls, which certainly made one look less of a frump and feel more of a dog, but might produce a bad impression if Mrs. Hungerford turned out to be a perfect dragon about uniform, and, anyway, certainly did make one look much younger.

IV

The London train was only twenty minutes late, and Pippa, temporarily exhausted after her uneasy night, strong physical exertions during chilly packing, and strong mental exertions during hot breakfast, slept for most of her journey, although wedged bolt upright in a centre seat. She had experienced a rise of spirits from the moment that the loaded taxi, with steam rising from its radiator, had turned out of Lawrence Avenue in a perfect stage snowstorm, and, so far, everything had gone like clockwork. She had not forgotten to empty and pack her hot-water bottle; the letter from Pratt was in her pocket, and she had remembered to put her book for the journey on the top of her attaché-case, which contained also everything for the night in case she got separated from the remainder of her luggage. If she had been determined, she could have reclaimed her case from the medley on the rack, and squared her elbows for an hour with her favourite author, Rosanna Masquerier. But she decided, having kept *Polish Rose, the Love Story of Marie Walewska and Napoleon Bonaparte* so long and painfully unopened, not to spoil it by beginning under adverse circumstances. Pippa revelled in the works of Rosanna Masquerier (also authoress of *Parma Violet, the later Life of Marie-Louise*, and *Queen's Casket, the Love Story of Mary Stuart and James Bothwell*), and had been disappointed that she could not persuade Professor Beadon to share her enthusiasm. He had taken one look inside *Parma Violet*, discovered that it opened with the colour ebbing from a young girl's cheeks as a miniature fell face downwards upon a console table in a gilded saloon of the Hofburg Palace, and handed the volume back with the single word "No!" Still, he must be wrong, for he was the only man in the regiment out of step. Rosanna Masquerier's biographies always attained enormous cheap editions, and when a new book by her was announced, it was impossible for "B" subscribers to get it at the lending library for at least six months. *Polish Rose* was not absolutely new; it had been published at a topical moment in 1940, but it had only become within Pippa's reach after the arrival of book tokens for Christmas, 1941.

The train began to run into London suburbs, and Pippa noticed that the results of bomb damage fell into four classes. There was the type that reminded one of a child of six, lacking front teeth, there was the doll's house, with the face open, the one-slice-out-of-a-cake variety and the spilt box of matches. She soon got accustomed to the sight of twisted, rusting girders and mounds of honey-coloured rubble, but she could not see properly without sitting right forward and goggling, and as nobody else in the carriage took the faintest interest in the view, she deemed it most dignified to follow their example. The truth was that, as Auntie Prue was one of the few women in England who had moved her abode hastily in 1939 to a site where bombs did not presently follow, Pippa, in 1942, was in the extraordinary position of never having seen even a crater.

The train clattered to a standstill in the cold darkness of the London terminus, and the nine other occupants of Pippa's compartment, who had seemed so solid, vanished like active elves. Even the lady with the shiny red face under a green halo hat, whose appearance was indelibly printed on Pippa's memory, since she had sat exactly opposite, knitting a khaki stocking for an emaciated giant, suddenly rolled up her handiwork, flung it into a fish basket, and with the words, "Well, so long, all!" disappeared for ever.

Pippa's suitcases and kit-bag had not been spirited out of the luggage van, as Auntie Prue had thought possible. On the contrary, they were amongst the first objects to reappear, and although she had rather a long wait, she found a woman porter, who wheeled her equipment unhesitatingly to a taxi rank containing five taxis. Pippa, pattering after her more than manly woman porter, began to think that the difficulties of war-time travel had been much exaggerated.

Her drive took her through the City of London, and the taximan, though not scrupulously clean, was quite friendly looking, with a face that reminded her of Jack Hulbert, but she was too shy to explain to him that she was not in a frightful hurry, and had actually never seen a crater. Anyway, after her view from the train, she was now definitely on a level with Michael, who, since Auntie Prue thought that the children should be spared at all costs, had been obliged to take a 'bus ride fifteen miles, to perform a secret inspection of a burnt-out garage. And, within five minutes of leaving the station, she found herself in an area which bore a depressing resemblance to photographs of the Colosseum, Rome. In one very poor, blackened street, some pieces of discoloured muslin were waving from short sticks, planted amongst the debris. A second look told Pippa that they were undoubtedly, although almost faded out of recognition, national flags which slum families had bought for the Jubilee.

In the City of London, coffee-coloured snow was trodden hard, a bitter cold wind was blowing, and pedestrians were walking fast with their heads down and collars up. Pippa identified the dome of St. Paul's and the river Thames shining like slightly crumpled silver paper, and thought of Anne Neville in the merchant's kitchen, and Richard of Bordeaux, and old, old London, lying in the marshes of Westminster.

Presently the taxi began to run through more expensive-looking streets, and squares with yellow faces and gardens in their centres, which looked queer because they now had no railings. There were not many perambulators about, and she only saw one really good dogs' club, where a glossy Alsatian was introducing a learned-looking wire-haired to an elderly dachshund and a poodle.

Within half an hour she had reached her second terminus, and the bogy of crossing London was laid. She had now only to put her luggage in a cloak-room, buy her ticket for Westbury, in case there was a queue at the booking-office later, and get something solid to eat at a canteen, since the staff at Woodside, said Auntie Prue, would certainly enjoy their main meal of the day at noon.

When Pippa asked the way to the canteen, the ticket-collectress at the entrance to Platform 1 said, "Which d'ye want, dear?" "Are there many?" faltered Pippa. "Well, there's three, but you'll do best to go to the one on Number 13 Platform," said the ticket-collectress, without looking up again, and snipping tickets like mad. "Turn to the left when you get through here; keep on the left past the R.T.O.'s office, and go on as far as you can."

Pippa disentangled herself from the knot of people who were springing like hungry leopards towards a train of funereal appearance which had just drawn in, empty. It was quite a long walk to Platform 13, but there was no chance of feeling lonely, as the voice of a major prophet was booming instructions on a loud-speaker, and several children were objecting to being goaded to the run by their maddened mammas. Some shafts of light, too pale to be called sun-beams, were slanting in through the blue mist gathered in the station roof. On Platform 13, which was decidedly quieter, though far from deserted, Pippa saw a door labelled "R.T.O." and a few yards farther on, another labelled "Canteen for Travelling Forces." She pushed open the swing door of the Canteen for Travelling Forces and stepped into a new world of which she was now part.

The first thing that she discovered about it was that it had, in a marked degree, what artistic people call "atmosphere." A gust of warmth and smells, in which fortunately cookery and tobacco smoke predominated, met her on the threshold. Since the hour was now ten minutes past twelve, many Forces were demanding their main meal. Never in her life had Pippa seen so many young men eating such large mouthfuls. Some of them ate doggedly, with their caps on, but most had opened their collars and cast their headgear on the tops of their packs, which littered the floor. Pippa made her way up to a counter at the far end of the oblong room, which had girders in its high roof, and while she waited her turn, tried to take in the rules of the game. Behind the counter was a temporary wall, with shelves, on which were ranged bottles of ink and aspirin and advertisements of cigarettes. In an inner fastness behind, several pale but hot ladies in overalls were on the move, haloed by steam, their fragmentary conversation accompanied by a sound of rushing waters. There were a number of metal urns on the counter, two pieces of squashed pink sausage-meat, and a good many vivid yellow crumbs and splashes of tea. However, as the counter, like the temporary walls and the trestle-tables ranged around them, was covered by an oatmeal-coloured cardboard material, these signs of struggle could obviously be removed in an instant by anyone with a damp cloth and a moment to spare. Pippa chose sausage-meat and mashed potato, a cup of sweetened tea and a square golden bun, with a smear of lemon cheese in its central recess. The charge was 7*d*., which seemed reasonable, as the portions were large and piping hot, but you had to give up 1*s*. 3*d*. to include the hire of cutlery and crockery. That was why a grey-haired lady in a white apron, at the far end of the counter, was continually pushing collections of pennies towards customers who brought back to her loving care handfuls of necessarily disgusting-looking used knives and forks and spoons.

Pippa found a seat on a divan covered with cretonne which had once had a floral design, but now, apparently from contact with so much khaki, had become brownish nearly all over. In so lively a scene it was useless to attempt to read *Polish Rose*; besides, she wanted to see.

On the much-pitted wall opposite her hung a dart board, almost black with old age and long service, and a large, brilliant pre-war poster, called "Southport for a Winter Holiday," which depicted ladies with classic features and waved tresses, in evening dress, stepping light-heartedly along a royal blue parade towards a flood-lit entrance. At least two of them were wearing ermine capes.

The swing door behind Pippa was pushed open, and a pastry-cook's boy carrying piled trays containing several hundred meat rolls, tripped over a rifle on his way to the counter. The sailor seated next to her, who had a dog's deep, soft brown eyes, carefully spread his evening paper on the table in front of both of them, and following the lines of print with his right forefinger, continued to read while disposing of large sandwiches in two bites. Nobody noticed her, which gave her a cheering feeling of being either Ariel or a perfectly well-dressed person as described by Beau Brummel. ("If anyone turns to look at your dress, then you are not well dressed.") There were about half a dozen other girls in the room, all wearing uniforms of khaki or blue. The one nearest to her, having removed the lid from her pastry roll and looked inside, said sadly that she wished now she had had the beans. Pippa began to feel warm and comfortable for the first time since leaving Lawrence Avenue, and presently discovered that one reason for this corner of the room being particularly cosy was that two dish-cloths were drying on the radiator behind her spine. The sailor, having finished his sandwiches, transferred his attention to a hillock of rice pudding. Through a side-window some rays of silvery London winter sunlight began to slant into the smoke-blue room, finding lovely colour in sunburnt necks and ruffled hair, and yellow buns and metal badges and numerals. "It would make a marvellous war-time Academy oil-painting, 'Canteen for Travelling Forces,'" thought Pippa, half-closing her eyes. Suddenly she sat upright, shaking drowsiness from her. "NOTICE," she read. "To Troops Travelling at Night. This Canteen is for Meals only. We are sorry, but we have no space for Sleepers."

V

Auntie Prue's latest plan, which she had explained while Pippa, filled with minor apprehensions, was putting on her cap, was that as Pippa would have at least an hour to spare between her canteen meal and the departure of the Went express, she must go and call on Lady Jones. This Lady Jones had nothing to do with the one who had laid the foundation stone of Pippa's Public Library in 1887. She had been one of Auntie Prue's old Poona pals, which must mean that the acquaintance dated from round about 1920. The great points in favour of her were, apparently, that she had never quitted London throughout the blitzes, and that she lived within five minutes' walk of the station from which Pippa must catch the Went train.

Pippa, who had experience of Auntie Prue's plans, had said weakly, "Do you think that she'll want to see me?" and "She's probably never heard of me," but Auntie Prue, enslaved by the charms of a last-minute plan which had visited her active brain in the watches of the night, pooh-poohed the idea that Lady Jones might never have heard of Pippa. "I had a card from her at Christmas," and clinched the matter by saying that the call would be a kindness.

She was quite right in saying that the square which Lady Jones had resolutely refused to leave was within five minutes' walk of the station. Pippa crossed a single very busy street of small shops, and found herself in a residential terrace leading to the square. She then spent ten minutes walking round the square before she discovered the house she needed, mounted its steps and rang the bell. Lady Jones's residence, which was large but not attractive-looking, had once been painted two shades of buff, but was now almost as dark brown as the cushions in the canteen. Its lower windows were sightless, and had been filled with slate-coloured wall-board, which enhanced its forbidding air. On either hand two blackened sandbags leant against the pillars supporting the portico. Pippa, standing in a howling draught, and listening to the echoes raised by a modern tug at an old-fashioned bell-pull, pictured Lady Jones sitting upstairs all cocked up and ready to cheer on a member of the younger generation. She realized that she knew very little about Lady Jones, but she pictured her as small, shrivelled and vivacious, as Poona pals were apt to be, couched perhaps in a fleecy shawl by a brightly burning fire, with just a bunch of violets in a crystal vase on the sweet-smelling carved table by her side, and perhaps a procession of ivory elephants on the mantel-piece. You could generally tell that a house belonged to a Poona pal directly you entered the hall and saw the gong. Since Pippa was feeling temporarily satisfied after her main meal, her fancy did not linger on the possibility that open-handed Lady Jones might also possess a store cupboard simply stuffed with bar chocolate and boiled sweets.

The echoes of the old-fashioned bell died away, and Pippa invented quite another Lady Jones—accustomed to command in the East, tall, blonde and high-nosed, with a quizzical glance and lorgnettes. This picture was unnerving and dissuaded her from ringing the bell again for a decent interval. Her second effort produced results. She heard movement in a basement, followed by heavy footsteps. Perhaps poor Lady Jones, whose dining-room windows were filled in by slate-coloured wall-board, had descended to her cellar in the autumn of 1941, and never thought it wise to ascend again.

At length the door in front of Pippa trembled open, and she saw a maid. Since she was just eighteen, she did not see that the maid was just fourteen, and fresh from Dr. Columbus's Home for Orphan Boys and Girls, and perfectly terrified. Pippa saw a maid, and said, "Is Lady Jones at home?" and the maid saw a caller, her long-dreaded nightmare, and promptly forgot every word of the complicated instructions given to her on her arrival last Friday by Lady Jones's simply incredible nurse-companion-secretary. She said, after drawing a deep breath, and looking everywhere except in the direction of Pippa's scared bright blue eyes,

"I don't know."

"I mean," said Pippa, after a dramatic pause, "is Lady Jones in? She does live here still, doesn't she?"

"She's upstairs," agreed the orphan helplessly; then rallying to her duty, "But I don't think she's at home to visitors."

"My name's Miss Johnson," said Pippa as bravely, "but I don't think Lady Jones will remember it. She will remember Mrs. Beal, though."

The orphan, after another long pause for thought, turned away and toiled upstairs with a wavering gait. Pippa's picture of the brightly burning fire and bunch of violets had begun to fade before the orphan, returning with a scarlet countenance, said in a martial way, "Lady Jones is Not At Home," and then, unfortunately weakening, "Did you want to see her partickler?"

"Well, I did rather," murmured Pippa, thinking of another hour and a half in the station, with the major prophet booming overhead, and people falling over one's feet, and the utter impossibility of turning in again so soon, for another meal at the Forces canteen where there was no space for sleepers. She was just about to slip away, with the words "But it doesn't matter," when a fresh figure joined the conclave.

Down the cavernous staircase, at a pattering run, came a small and elderly female dressed in the height of the fashions sponsored by royalties at the time of Queen Victoria's second jubilee. Pippa distinctly saw a tower of auburn curls and a boned-up collar. She could almost have sworn to a jet bodice, with a watch pinned on, and pointy slippers with bronze-bead embroidery. But although she was meagre and distressingly vivacious, this character could not be Lady Jones, for she repeated in a high voice indicative of strong neurosis, that Lady Jones was not at home. "You cannot see her." Upstairs a door slammed, possibly from the draught pouring in from the open entrance: everyone jumped. The sight of two youthful uniformed figures, silhouetted in attitudes of complete indecision against a gathering snowstorm, on Lady Jones's threshold, seemed to inspire her nurse-companion-secretary with feelings of fury. Pushing forward an open palm, as if to expel the hosts of Barbary, she uttered the awful words, "You must go away. Go away! It is disgraceful that Lady Jones should be so disturbed."

Pippa believed that she said "I'm so sorry. I never meant to disturb anybody," and "I was just going anyway," but the truth was that until she regained the station, which she did in record time, she was not clearly conscious of anything except a buzzing in her ears and a dawning realization that of all Auntie Prue's plans for other people, this one had been the worst.

VI

The Went train clanked in, and Pippa, who had been obliged after all to read the opening chapters of *Polish Rose* with a bursting heart, reluctantly stuffed the volume back into her attaché-case, and stalked towards the seething equipage. Although she made no special effort, she secured a corner seat this time, and such was the magic of the pen of Rosanna Masquerier, that she quite forgot to look for craters as the train passed out of London. Her Imperial seducer was rapidly drawing towards the lonely shrine at which Polish Rose was engaged in prayer, when Pippa remembered with a start that she had not seen her porter again after recovering her luggage from the cloak-room. However, everything was labelled, and the porter had appeared neither deaf nor blind. Her watch told her that she had now been in the Went train for an hour; she had read ninety pages of her book. Rosanna Masquerier excelled in careful background work, and her setting for *Polish Rose* had included two chapters of national history. "There mayn't be a book at Woodside, and I mayn't get a day off to forage in the Smiths at Went this week," thought Pippa. The compartment was over-warm; she closed her eyes. When she opened them again, her watch told her that she should have arrived at Went junction ten minutes before. She said, gathering her belongings in a fluster, "Oh! is the train late? We haven't passed Went, have we?" and the woman opposite, who had a large brass V attached to the lapel of her mackintosh, said loftily that she was sure she couldn't say, and looked as if she suspected Pippa of being an enemy alien, but the girl with rather pretty hair and no hat, wearing a short fuzzy fur coat and bootees, who was eating rock cakes out of a bag in the farther corner, said that she was getting out at Went, and that as we had only just passed Highbridge, we were going to be at least ten minutes late. Pippa said, "I've got to change for Westbury-on-the-Green; do you know if they keep the train?" and the girl said, "It's generally waiting on the other side, but you'll have to cross by the bridge, so you'll have to look slippy. Anyway, if you're only going on to Westbury, you'll get another local train in half an hour."

Pippa did not feel like explaining to the whole company that she had heavy luggage and was being met by the Honourable J. Pratt. She looked out of the window, and saw with interest that the neighbourhood of the cathedral city of Went was undoubtedly real deep country, and picturesque even on a cold winter's day. She saw loops of a river, frozen amongst the rushes at the edges, and bare willow trees, inclining above smooth waters, which reminded her of pictures of Holland. The sky was growing the colour of horn, but snow had ceased to fall. Where small flakes had gathered, covering the surface of little ice-filled pools, the fields seemed to have as many eyes as a peacock's tail. The train began to lose speed, and she saw an elegant spire, backed by wooded heights, rising above many roofs, and chimneys with smoke coming from them, and then, with a rush, houses with verandas, and gardens with snowdrops, and cedars of Lebanon, and a blitzed warehouse, and a moment later, a station with no glass on its roof, and a long silvery platform simply packed with young men in grey-blue uniform.

Pippa performed the last stage of her journey in a compartment entirely filled by our dauntless airmen. They helped her to jump in, just as the local train began to move, and told her that Westbury was the next station but two. As the humble but heavily laden train rambled thoughtfully through increasingly romantic landscape, the young airmen seemed to grow hotter and larger, and their clouds of tobacco smoke made Pippa's eyes weep. Her companions evidently considered that the place for fresh air was out of doors. They ground fags under their big black boots, and lighted up afresh. One of them had a mouth organ, and hoped that she didn't mind music. Nearly all of them appeared to be musical, and inclined to melancholy choruses like Volga boatmen. Although they were really very helpful, pointing out Went Park through the trees, and putting her gas mask on the rack, she was not sorry when they all suddenly got out at the second station and left her quite alone in Barsetshire.

She saw a dog chasing cattle across a miry road, and a little timber and plaster cottage with diamond-shaped windows, and an orchard full of crooked trees, and a very steep hill with a lorry stationary at the top, and then the train stopped at what ought to be Westbury-on-the-Hill and probably was, as there was a tall girl in dark blue uniform on the platform, scanning the incoming train. Pippa alighted, far up the platform, which was a country one, of slippery wood, with white painted railings behind, and a garden, now planted with vegetables which did not look likely to live. To her great relief, she saw her two suitcases and kit-bag being flung out of a luggage van. The noisy little train began to continue on its journey, and the girl in dark blue uniform caught sight of Pippa, and smiled indulgently. She had long fair curls, like those of a page in the days of Richard of Bordeaux, or an angel in an Italian picture, and the largest saucer eyes that Pippa had ever seen, and she walked with a slight limp. As they drew towards one another, she called out, "Good evening. Are you Nurse Johnson? I am Johanna Pratt."

CHAPTER II

"I'M LOVING IT"
(March 10th-March 18th)

I

"AND NOW," said Mrs. Bates with relish, "tell me all about Woodside. Begin at the beginning. You'll love Mary Hungerford, of course. She was my neighbour here on the Green for years, before she made her romantic marriage. What I want to know is are the rest of them being kind to you up there? One never knows. I saw one of your trained nurses in the post office here the other day, buying shoelaces, and I thought she had rather a hard mouth. I look on you as quite my protégée, since I suggested your coming to Mary, and to your Auntie Prue, as you call her, though she's actually no blood relation. You needn't tell me how she is, for I had a letter from her this morning, all about a Free French cook. Take off your cap and coat, and here's a sofa on which you can put up your feet if you feel inclined. I always do myself after my duty at the Post, though my rheumatism has practically vanished, thanks to Hitler or Lord Woolton. I switched on the fire directly I got in, and there's a good tea, and we needn't get it ourselves, as my Mrs. Higgs has come up for the day from Lower Merle. She considers me her war work, though there's no necessity for her to work at all at her age, especially since her son Albert is making all that money at the tank factory. It's not fit for a dog outside to-day. I hope you are not afraid of hard work and stronger than you look."

"Thank you very much, I'm loving it," said Pippa, accepting a seat on the sofa in Mrs. Bates's beige parlour, which was indeed warm and might have been a pretty room if it had been quite differently furnished. Mrs. Bates was unmistakably an old Poona pal. She possessed many of the characteristics attributed by Pippa to the never-seen Lady Jones. She was tall, massive, grey-haired and evidently accustomed to command. Later on, when Pippa met the Dowager Lady Merle of Went, she recognized at once the model faithfully copied by several of the elder ladies resident in and around the cathedral city. To-day she could only note that Mrs. Bates had a searching glance, and could upon occasion assume an air of uncommon majesty. Pippa noted also, with mingled satisfaction and exasperation, the two snow-leopard skins, complete with glass eyes and pink composition mouths, snarling and sprawling upon the panels of the small light parlour. A dreamy water-colour or pastel, she could not be sure which, inscribed in flowing characters "Srinagar, 1922," hung above Mrs. Bates's writing-desk, on which lay a blotter, stamp-box and pen-tray of shiny black papier mâché with an all-over design of dark blue Eastern flowers. In the bow-window, which looked out upon a small lawn, separated from the road by white-painted posts and black-painted chains, was a brass tray table, reposing upon a wooden frame of many legs. Gritting eternally upon the brass tray, stood a bulbous copper Oriental kettle with heavy silver trimmings. Mrs. Bates was not attired in the tennis or riding kit which seemed appropriate to her surroundings. She was wearing a white overall with initials embroidered in scarlet upon a pocket, and beneath the overall a very large pair of navy-blue bell-bottomed trousers. Her grey locks were tied up in a navy-blue bandeau with a pattern of scarlet anchors.

"Are all the houses on Westbury Green, Queen Anne?" asked Pippa, disregarding her hostess's instruction to begin at the beginning. "I see yours has panelling and cupboards and shelves just like one wing at Woodside, and I noticed that several of the other houses looked as if they had too. But yours," she added politely, "has much the nicest face—just like a doll's house."

"Everyone says that this is the best house on the Green," answered Mrs. Bates, with a reminiscent chuckle. "I know poor Mary was disappointed that she couldn't get it, when she had to move. But my house is almost the most modern on the Green. It's not Queen Anne, dear. It's Regency. It was built by the mad Lord Merle for an old friend of his naval days, a retired sea captain. That's why it's called 'Flagstaff House.' They conducted mechanical experiments together on the lake at Went. Mary Morrison's

house, Willows, just across the Green, is much older. It was really
two converted seventeenth-century cottages; and the Harkers' cottage ought to be condemned, but I suppose nothing will
be done about that now. Mary had Willows painted leaf-green
throughout, which always made me feel as if I was swimming
about in an aquarium. But I seldom look in there now that she's
let it for the duration to those two depressing women."

"Why are they depressing?" asked Pippa, feeling slightly
giddy.

"Well, they are two widows—a mother and daughter,"
explained Mrs. Bates. "Not that that need make them depressing. Look at Corisande, Lady Merle, the youngest in spirit of
us all, as I said to poor Mary when she was so anxious round
about Christmas, when it really looked as if we were going to
lose the Dowager at last. (But I hear she's almost herself again
now.) Mrs. Thomas Morrison (that's the mother) is the widow
of Mary's only brother. He was killed in the Last War. He met
her staying in a house for a cricket week. She was governess to
a younger child who was mentally deficient. Her daughter calls
herself Mrs. Rosemary Morrison, since her marriage was far
from a success. She has as much right to the name as I have,
as she was Mrs. Thomas Morrison's daughter by a previous
marriage, and if I were Mary I should object. The person I am
sorry for is the poor little boy."

"Is he the one who was mentally deficient?" inquired Pippa.

"No, no; he's as sane as you or I," said Mrs. Bates, unruf-
fled. "He'll be three in June, a posthumous child; often walks in
here to talk to me. I'm very fond of poor little Ferdinand-Africa,
as Rosemary christened him, because she was acting in Shakespeare at the Cape when she made her disastrous match. She
was only twenty-three, and young for her age, and the man had
been married before, drank like a fish and was up to his eyes
in debt. I'm not sure that it's true that he beat her, but I know
that she had to write home to poor Mary for funds, almost at
once. Luckily he only lasted eight months. He had hob-nail liver.
Doesn't it seem strange that when people like our Lord Merle
really need an heir, and only get Lalage after specialists from

Vienna, Rosemary Wright—that was her maiden name—must needs have a boy straight off? In her case a girl would have been much easier, and nothing at all much for the best."

"I don't wonder she's depressed," said Pippa, sounding depressed herself.

"Well, well," said Mrs. Bates rousingly, "she's her life before her yet, as I often point out to her. What she and her mother need to do is to take up some absorbing war work and cease to irritate their neighbours by moaning about the contemptible little incendiary that happened to land in their cucumber frame."

"Tell me why Mrs. Hungerford's marriage was romantic," begged Pippa. "I've gathered that she was Mary Morrison."

"Yes, that is correct," nodded Mrs. Bates. "She was Mary Morrison, and she was born and brought up at Woodside, and Christopher Hungerford, who was a grandson of Corisande, Lady Merle, proposed to her first when she was scarcely seventeen, and she refused him. How she had the heart, I don't know, for he was quite the most fascinating young man you ever saw, but of course he was still at Oxford then, and—well, whatever her reasons, she said 'No.' And then the Last War came, and they never met, and after the war Mary's father died, and there was not enough money left to keep up Woodside, and I know she had some miserable years there struggling on alone with her mother, who was the best example I know of selfish parents making unselfish children. Lady Morrison had been a beauty."

"I should think that Mrs. Hungerford must have been very pretty when she was young," said Pippa.

"Mary's not old!" exclaimed Mrs. Bates, straightening her back. "I can give her nine years!"

"I meant when she was scarcely seventeen," explained Pippa in a hurry.

"Mary Hungerford," said Mrs. Bates judicially, "will never equal either of her parents, but she's got good regular features, a fine brow and a very sweet expression. I always used to say that if you met Mary Morrison in her little Austin in the Libyan desert, you'd have known that she was an English country gentle-woman and the President of the Women's Institute. Having fair hair and a good figure is such a help. I must say, I was delighted when I heard that Captain Hungerford, as he was then, had got safely back from Dunkirk, after being reported 'Missing,' and was marrying her by special licence the next Tuesday."

"You've left out all the exciting part," complained Pippa.

"Mary's very reserved, as you may have noticed," mused Mrs. Bates, "and with This War beginning just at the time I did not hear as much as I should have in normal times. All that I know for certain is that they met again, for the first time since 1914, at a coming-out dance, given in June, 1939, by some people called Rollo, for their daughter who's now one of the nurses at your hospital. (All the lights fused as the house-party sat down to dinner, and Albert Higgs mended the fuse with a piece of picture-wire, but there was not a fire, as there should have been.) Major Hungerford saw Mary, and fell in love with her all over again, but as it was one of your modern dances, with far too many guests and no room to dance, Mary never even knew that he was there."

"Why didn't he go up to her and say 'Hallo!'" wondered Pippa.

"He said that she looked straight through him three times," explained Mrs. Bates.

"I still don't see why he couldn't have jogged her memory," said Pippa.

"Much had happened to him during those long years," said Mrs. Bates majestically. "Corisande, Lady Merle, herself, has said that all that is past and forgotten now, so there is no need for us to think of it. It was owing to her wonderful tact and management that the marriage ever took place."

"Did he go to his grandmother and pour out his heart?" asked Pippa.

"No, he went back to his office in London and said nothing to anyone, as far as I know," admitted Mrs. Bates. "But Corisande, Lady Merle, had made up her mind that it was time he settled, and said so to Mary, and to her delight, noticed that Mary still blushed at the sound of his name. I should have told you before that Major Hungerford, after his many years of toil abroad and in London, had become decidedly affluent, while, on her mother's death, Mary had sold Woodside to a girls' school and moved to the two converted cottages just across the Green here. She had quite given up the idea of marrying, although I know that she had other chances. She was completely absorbed by her Guides and Nurses, and her godchildren, and a dozen other things, and said that she was Queen Elizabeth Tudor, only that Westbury-on-the-Green was her England."

"It sounds rather mopey," said Pippa.

"Mary never moped," said Mrs. Bates. "She went about quite a bit in the quiet way possible for a woman of limited means but good connections. She met Major Hungerford again at Royal Ascot on Gold Cup day—a lovely scene. Corisande, Lady Merle, had heard Mary say that she was going there with the Rollos, and wrote to tell her daughter, who told Major Hungerford."

"It sounds very, complicated," said Pippa. "What happened?"

He went, and proposed again," said Mrs. Bates dramatically, "and—was refused again."

"Good gracious!" ejaculated Pippa.

"And then the war clouds lowered upon us," said Mrs. Bates with gusto, "and the girls' school moved from Woodside to a safety area, and just before it was snapped up for the lunatics from Went Mental Hospital, Major Hungerford bought the house which had been the home of his first love. He had done up one wing—quite regardless—when Hitler invaded Poland. Poor Mary was called up at once, as she had volunteered mobile since Munich, and she spent the whole winter at a naval hospital on the coast, and got chilblains and laryngitis. Major Hungerford, who had rejoined his old regiment, went out to France, and they simply lost touch again. In absolute confidence, if you'll promise not to repeat it, I am pretty well sure that he was in the Secret Service before the war. Imphm! Well, as you're now a member of Mary's staff, it can't matter that you know what quite a lot of people used to guess. To return to my story. In June, 1940, Mary came on leave to stay with the Dowager, and one afternoon, while she was up here wandering round Willows, she got a telephone message from the Dowager, asking her to be so

good as to pick up Major Hungerford at Went Junction. 'Ask her
again, a third time,' advised the Dowager, 'but let her know that
this time you will take "no" for "no."' As I have said, they were
married the next Tuesday."

II

After the good tea which Mrs. Bates had promised, Pippa
was taken out into the cold blast to her hostess's bomb crater.
It was not a very interesting sight, and if Pippa had not been
told that it had been created by high explosive, she would have
guessed it to have been the work of a gang of amateur navvies
ordered to make a wild garden against time. It was, in size and
shape, very like the smaller of the two village ponds on the Green
visible from Mrs. Bates's front windows, and the resemblance
was increased by the fact that Mrs. Bates had taken to keeping ducks upon its waters. Mrs. Bates walked Pippa all round
it, and poked at its edges with her walking-stick, to show how
crumbly they were, and said that it had been much larger before
the edges fell in. She made Pippa stand in the direct line of the
twelve missiles which had been discharged from enemy aircraft
upon sleeping Westbury-on-the-Green, and told her that the
Hills' crater had been much the nearest to the house. Norah
Hill's surgeon husband, who had been out to look for incendiaries, with his pipe in his mouth, had been blown down their
front steps, and the stem of his pipe had gone through his soft
palate. The Harkers' bomb had been the noisiest, and done the
most damage, as it had landed on a paved back yard. As for the
despised Morrisons, they had received nothing at all, except a
few dud incendiaries in the moist earth of their kitchen garden.
The Morrisons were shopping in Went to-day, Mrs. Bates knew,
as she had seen Rosemary running to catch the 'bus, but she
offered to take Pippa round the Green and show her the outside
of Willows, which would interest her, as it had belonged to Mrs.
Hungerford.

In the orchard behind Willows, which they approached by
a right of way through everybody's back garden, there were
drifts of snowdrops looking, in the distance, like smudges

of Chinese white paint. The long grass in the shadows of the hedges lay bowed with silver frost, and underfoot the ground was hard as the decks of a ship. Suddenly Pippa halted, and said to Mrs. Bates, with round eyes, "Do listen a moment. Is it—could it be—lambs?"

Mrs. Bates, who felt the temperature more than her young companion, came to a standstill for a moment only, while they listened to the sound, faintly borne on the cold wind, of the first tremulous spring notes of 1942.

"Of course it's lambs," said Mrs. Bates, striding on. "Had 'em for weeks past down here. I must say, I always feel sorry for the poor little beggars, being born in such weather—so like sheep! They're attractive when they're young, and play about, dancing on their hind legs and butting at one another, like book-ends. In a moment you'll see plenty."

Mrs. Bates, as they proceeded on their journey, began to look rather like the elderly owner of a new puppy. Before they came in sight of the back windows of Willows, Pippa stopped again to pick just a few snowdrops, which, as they really belonged to Mrs. Hungerford, she hoped the depressed Mrs. Morrison would not miss. She stopped also to choose her favourite lamb, which had, she said, a face which showed her what people meant when they said that other people were perfect lambs.

Mrs. Bates fortunately forgot to ask a loyal member of Mrs. Hungerford's staff any further questions about Woodside, and even forgot to point out the plaster and timber garden-front of Willows, which was only partially visible through an interlacing of bare boughs. Her attention had wandered to the pressing problem of whether she ought to offer to the nation the metal chains which divided her front lawn from the Green. The chains were original, so perhaps sacrificing them would be rather like the people one read about in letters to the newspapers, who had sent scarce early Botany books and Tudor wills to be pulped. On the other hand, as the owner of much the nicest house on the Green, she felt the necessity of setting an example in everything, and she was loth to go scatheless when old Miss Bond at the Mill cottage had been startled by the entry of soldiers, who had, according to her own unreliable testimony, simply lifted her garden gates off their hinges, and announced that the gun would be coming for the tennis court to-morrow.

At a signpost, on which the innocent words "Footpath to the Church" had been ineffectually obliterated, the ladies parted, Mrs. Bates towards her own front door and her chains, and Pippa on an elaborately described short cut to Woodside. To cheer her guest on her three-mile tramp, Mrs. Bates told her to be sure not to slip on any patches of ice, and related with glee how young Lady Merle's Czechoslovakian cook, after getting off the 'bus at the cross-roads, on her return from her day out in the cathedral city, had slipped and fallen down on the short cut through a lonely stretch of Went Park, and there lain with a broken leg for two hours, on Christmas Eve, until discovered by a passing cowman. He, being an ardent Home Guard, and hearing a voice groaning in German in the black-out, had very naturally mistaken the poor creature for an enemy airman.

Pippa had no fears of being caught by darkness to-day, for the chilly light now lasted, she knew, until after seven-thirty, but she had considerable doubts of finding her way from Mrs. Bates's descriptions, which had included many unknown place-names and anecdotes of past owners of adjacent properties. She recognized the Hills' house, for, as Mrs. Bates had warned her, a portly dachshund, in an amber collar, emerged from the kitchen entrance, barking insanely, and saw her off the prem-ises. Between the Hills and the old Pilgrims' Way she must have gone wrong, for she found herself in a horseshoe-shaped meadow with no exit except a gate at the very bottom, which had been much used by cattle in miry weather, and could now only be approached by picking one's way between ankle-deep hoof-marks, frozen solid. She was out of breath by the time she had struggled up again on to a mossy turf ride, where a line of yews, old and velvet dark, overlooked a misty valley. The yews gave off clouds of powder as she pushed her way between them, and she would have managed better over the two stiles at the foot of the ride had she not by now encumbered herself with a resilient sheaf of spreading hazel branches with dangling catkins, and a few rods of pussy-willow, in addition to her bunch of snow-drops. She was undecided as to which of two lanes to take after crossing the Lower Merle road, but as her first choice soon led her into a yard stacked with roots, from which a cock pheasant flew away screeching, she did not waste much time there. "If I've gone right," she thought, as she climbed a high padlocked gate into parkland, "I ought to come in sight of Woodside at any moment. If I'm wrong I shall be late for supper and get cold cocoa with a wrinkled skin top." Almost immediately she came in sight of pearl-grey architecture, backed by rising tiers of grape-dark woods, but she did not at first recognize Woodside from the north. In the chilly winter daylight, fast fading, the red brick façade appeared almost colourless. The stables and outbuild-ings had somehow got round to an unexpected angle, and the ice-bound lake seemed to be right under the front windows of the house, which gave it a foreign and palatial air.

"Being frozen rather suits Early Georgian homes," thought Pippa, as she realized with gratitude that the strange building which could not be more than a mile distant, was indeed her goal. "It makes them look rather spooky, though. I wonder if Woodside has a spook. I remember I thought it looked slightly threatening and not at all like its photographs, when I first caught sight of it from the khaki utility van. Everything seemed to come in such a rush at the end. I might ask Nurse Rollo."

III

In the staff-room at Woodside, Mrs. Crispin Rollo and her sister-in-law, who was called Nurse Elizabeth, to make a distinction between them, were sitting side by side on the oyster-coloured Chesterfield in front of the fire, just as they had been when Pippa had first entered the room on her arrival at Woodside. She had then received an impression of unattainable elegance and poise which had made her feel like the poor Queen of Sheba after viewing Solomon in all his glory. Closer inspec-tion had shown her that neither of her future companions had genuine claims to great good looks. Elizabeth Rollo was tiny, and her restless black eyes and wide mouth were too large for what her sister-in-law affectionately called her monkey-face. Lalage—Mrs. Crispin Rollo—had what Mrs. Bates would call good regular features, and a lovely complexion, but for her the war-time fashion of short skirts was a minor tragedy.

But they were both over twenty-one, and had come out in the summer before the War, and been finished in Paris and been to real dances and could talk about race-meetings, and evidently knew thousands of people. Although they were wearing blue cotton uniform dresses exactly like her own, they seemed a better shape, and their hair looked as if they visited the hair-dresser every day. They looked quite different altogether. . . . Pippa had felt utter despair of ever attaining to their standard of sophistication when she had first caught sight of her future companions, seated side by side, in the becoming firelight, in the formal white and green staff-room at Woodside, which had once been the music-room and had swags of musical instruments, tied up with ribbon bows and flowers, in the plaster decoration of the panelled walls.

"Hallo, nurse," said Lalage to-night, looking up from her knitting. "Did you find Mrs. Bates successfully and give her my greetings?"

"I found her house all right, and she showed me the short cut back, but I'm sorry to say that I quite forgot your message," said Pippa. "She spoke about you both, too. How dreadful of me!"

"I hope she spoke in praise," said Elizabeth.

Pippa did not feel equal to saying that, thanks to Mrs. Bates, she now knew that Lalage had only entered this vale of tears owing to the skill of a gynaecologist summoned to Barsetshire from Vienna by a despairing peer or peeress. It made her feel a little awkward even to know that Lalage was the only child of Lord Merle, who had really needed an heir. Perhaps that was why, although everyone else must have given up grieving over her being a girl years ago, Lalage had, in repose, a wistful expression.

"Well, really she only mentioned both your names, except that she did say that all the lights had fused as the house-party rose from the dinner-table at your coming-out ball, Nurse Elizabeth," said Pippa.

"Dance, Nurse Johnson," corrected Elizabeth.

"Oh!" Pippa blushed as only silver-fair people of shrimp size, aged eighteen, can blush. "Was it lovely—your dance?" she asked presently.

"No, perfectly foul," yawned Elizabeth. "The one night of east wind in a heat-wave fortnight. I had to stand by my mother's side, for three hours, with nascent appendicitis, holding a dear little bouquet of rosebuds, with a stamped paper frill, and I was made to have a chalk-white Early Victorian picture frock, which made me look just like a black fairy doll off the top of a Christmas tree."

"She looked very nice indeed," Lalage told Pippa in her calm way.

"Oh, were you there too?" asked Pippa.

"Many people you know were there," explained Lalage. "The Gibsons, and Mary Hungerford, who was then Mary Morrison, and my cousin Kit, her husband, whom you have not met yet, and my mother, and my dear old grandmother who, by the way, wants you to come to see her one day."

"How very kind of her," faltered Pippa, almost struck dumb with apprehension.

"The Dowager always asks Mary's young nurses to meals," said Elizabeth, "and the young officers from Went aerodrome. She considers them part of her war effort."

"Good! I hope she asks me soon," said Pippa with spirit.

"You are asked to come on your next half-day, which I see on the staff notice-board will be Friday week," said Lalage, "and will you please send a telephone message to-morrow morning, early?"

Pippa, after profound thought for quite a minute, decided to risk asking outright for information which was absolutely essential. "What do I say?" she inquired faintly.

"You ask Mrs. Sydney Crippen at the telephone exchange to give you Went nine double nine, and then you say that Nurse Johnson, speaking from Woodside, thanks Lady Merle for her kind invitation to luncheon, and will be very glad to come on Friday the 20th, at one-thirty," quoted Lalage. "I'm sorry to have to ask you to call a scrap of disguised salt cod, and probably bottled gooseberry fool, luncheon, and to have to wait for it till one-thirty, but, you see, my grandmother is very nearly eighty-nine."

IV

Pippa's bedroom at Woodside was quite unlike her expectations. She had never expected to have a room to herself, and from Auntie Prue's descriptions of the last war, had pictured listening to the snores of at least four other young nurses, divided from her sight only by a Heath Robinson arrangement of curtains slung by jangling tings to wires and strings. To be sure, there would not have been space for another bed in the apartment allotted to her. She had to stand sideways if she wished to get something out of the bottom of the chest of drawers, which was also her dressing-table. But what her room lacked in width it made up in height. The flex suspending the electric bulb with a black cardboard shade from the centre of her ceiling, seemed, when she regarded it dreamily from bed, to fade into the mists of distance, and reminded her of stories of the Indian rope trick. The illumination afforded by the single bulb was unsatisfactory for reading in bed, and by the worst of luck, Awful Matron had said almost at once, "If you have nothing better to do with your off-time, nurse, than to read a book, there are plenty of the men's socks needing attention after the laundry."

Two-thirds of Pippa's bedroom had been removed to form the bathroom next door, put in during the days when Woodside was a girls' school. The bathroom pipes sighed and whined at night and, as the new wall was very thin, Pippa could hear every sound made by those brushing their teeth, and Awful Matron had warned her that she would always have to remember Night Sister, trying to sleep at the end of the passage. However, it was quite grand to be able to write to Auntie Prue that one had a room to oneself, and a bathroom next door, and nothing would have persuaded Pippa to admit that the bath-water, up here under the stars, was not always hot, and that from her window, in the depths of the living, breathing country, she had almost no view. Her window was small and square, had an ill-bred, dwarfish look, and was a worthy adversary with which to tussle. Its view was of air and four squat stone pillars which formed part of the balustrading running round the leads on the top of the mansion. She could, when she really needed, squeeze out of the window and stand on the leads and enjoy a dizzying view of wooded Barsetshire. The difficulties in the way of this form of relaxation were that she dared not gallivant on the leads in her green dressing-gown, and although the cotton frocks of Nurse Rollo and Nurse Elizabeth never looked as if they had slept in them, Pippa had already twice been rebuked for untidy uniform.

By six-thirty a.m., now that it was Wednesday, March 18th, she was woken by birds twittering, a hopeful sound, which reminded her in a flash that she had got her first wish and got to the real country. There were many yellow crocuses now in the impossibly green grass under the weeping-willow, which was the foreground of the view from Mrs. Hungerford's terrifying office (which turned out to be the room with the bearded river-god over the mantelpiece). Two days ago the weather had suddenly become mild and lovely, with pacific skies, streaked grey and silver, like the bosom of the deep. This ghastly winter was really almost over now, and everyone said that it had been a particularly trying one and we were at least three weeks behind with everything, and things would get better with a rush. Pippa's spirits rose as she remembered that to-day was Wednesday, and that Nurse Rollo, who was having her half-day, was going to take Nurse Johnson into Went, and had made an appointment for her with her own hairdresser. The hairdresser, who was called Madame Rosalthé in the telephone book, was really, said Nurse Rollo, Gladys Crippen, who had moved from Croydon to Went just before the War, with many members of her family. A brother, Sydney, who had been a photographer, was now in the Commandos, and his wife was a telephone operator at Went Exchange, and they had all come because their aunt, Mrs. Crippen, had always been postmistress at Westbury-on-the-Green.

They had behaved very well when the suburbs of Went, which they had mistakenly imagined to be a Vale of Rest, had been unhandsomely bombed, and Gladys, *alias* Madame Rosalthé, had been assistant in a Bond Street shop, and one of her girls was quite good and quick, if you warned her you had only three hours off.

Pippa's previous endeavours to explore, or even reach, Went during her daily three hours off duty, had been unfortunate. On the first occasion, she had pattered in driving rain to a cross-roads which she had never doubted to be that described by her fellow-workers as the 'bus stop. After forty minutes' wait under a blasted oak, she had gloomily retraced her steps, and devoted the rest of that morning's freedom to drying her uniform and making a tour of the walled gardens of Woodside. Three days later she had succeeded in identifying the 'bus stop, but as the hour chosen by her was nine a.m., the Went 'bus had thundered past her, already over-full of passengers taken on board at Upper Merle. Although she had run after the 'bus, halloing and waving Staff Nurse's umbrella, it had not even hesitated on its headlong course down the Went valley, and its driver had sat imperturbable, with a Buddha-like expression on his face. Nurse Rollo had said that it was nearly hopeless to try to get on a 'bus at the Royal Oak (which turned out to be quite an ugly modern public-house at a cross-roads, nothing to do with a blasted oak) on an early closing day, and she could not answer for any day at business hours. But if one tried in the middle of the morning and came back in the middle of the afternoon before the rush in the opposite direction began, one could generally manage it. She herself was going to take the seven-thirty train back and bicycle from the station, as this was her half-day, and she did not mind missing supper, as she had heard from Miss Masquerier that it was lentil cutlets to-night.

To discover that her favourite author had always been one of Mrs. Hungerford's voluntary nurses, and was now Acting Quartermaster at Woodside Auxiliary Hospital, had seemed to Pippa almost unbelievable. She had never consciously pictured Rosanna Masquerier; all the same it had been a bit of a shock to realize that the authoress of *Polish Rose*, etc., was a small and rather skinny spinster lady, in horn-rimmed spectacles, with unruly black curls under her organdi uniform veil, and what is poetically described as silver strands amongst the black. Miss Masquerier had been seated in her store, engaged in cutting out tea coupons with nail scissors, when Pippa had presented herself, as instructed by Awful Matron. Miss Masquerier, who had a fussed manner, though a very bright smile, had gratefully accepted Pippa's three ration books and identity card, and then crushingly inquired, "You're not under sixteen, I suppose?"

"No!" said Pippa, stung to self-defence. "If I were under sixteen, I could not be engaged here as a nurse."

"Ah, no!" agreed Miss Masquerier. "Still, one of the kitchenmaids who resembles Epstein's Rima, is only fourteen, and I have to hold her identity card."

"Well, if we were only living in Tudor times she would probably be a married woman," suggested Pippa.

"True," agreed Miss Masquerier, her bird-like eyes sparkling with intelligence behind her glasses.

At this moment their conversation was interrupted by the entry of Gunner Duckie, a large young Scotsman, with a solemn, hanging countenance, who disclosed in his perspiring palm a completely flattened celluloid table-tennis ball, and whispered might the fellows have a new one of these to get on with their game?

Miss Masquerier unlocked a holy of holies, from which she drew forth a cardboard carton, and with a grandmotherly air said, "I can give you just one. But you must tell the men that these balls are very scarce. I have to sign a form, undertaking that they are to be used by nobody except His Majesty's Forces. This one must last a week."

Gunner Duckie, looking shocked, thanked her kindly and withdrew, and Pippa, much encouraged, proceeded, "I was thrilled when I discovered that you were working here, Miss Masquerier, because, you see? I was reading *Polish Rose* on my journey here. In fact, I think I've read nearly every book you have ever written."

Miss Masquerier, looking much younger, said, "How very kind! Do you write yourself?"

"Oh, only things for the school magazine, so far, mostly poetry," muttered Pippa. "But my friend, Professor Beadon, says that most authors begin with poetry."

"Are you a crony of Professor Abbadie Beadon?" exclaimed Miss Masquerier. "That is indeed a privilege!"

"Well," explained Pippa, "he's practically a relation, and I shouldn't wonder if he turned up here to see me, as he's doing war work in an office the other side of Went now."

"If the Tudor is your period," said Miss Masquerier breathlessly, "you must spend a day with me at my little house in Went. I can show you some interesting nooks of our cathedral city. Are you interested in the Marian martyrs?"

Pippa, enthralled by a dream-picture in which she grappled Miss Masquerier forever to her soul by marrying her to Professor Beadon, said cautiously that she had always been rather interested in all martyrs. She did not have to go further, as one of the Norwegian sailor patients now appeared, smiling broadly. He could not speak anything except his own tongue, but dropping on to the floor a flattened table-tennis ball and lunging forward bat in hand, to plant his foot precisely upon the relic with a Norse war-cry, he left his audience in no doubt as to how this last accident had occurred.

V

Ordinary Seaman Brownell could not tell Pippa what he wanted. He had been torpedoed once too often. He lay in the big ground-floor ward at Woodside, which had been the White Ballroom, and must have been lovely when it had eight pendant cut-glass chandeliers winking rainbow colours at the frozen lake outside. Ordinary Seaman Brownell had a face as full of wrinkles as a walnut, and black hair growing like a monk's tonsure, and when he spoke his mouth twisted sideways. Pippa felt sure that he must be about a hundred. She wondered whether his hammock was down in Miss Masquerier's store and whether he would ever sling it again. Miss Masquerier found the dear sailors' hammocks most inconvenient in her store. They were black, and bigger and heavier than herself, and looked like mummy cases, and once, in the dark, she had fallen over one and under another, and torn two pairs of stockings at a single blow, as she had been wearing her civilian luxury hose under her hairy grey uniform ones, because she was going on to the Wilsons' sherry party. But she had told Pippa, with flashing eyes, that whenever she looked at the hammocks she seemed to hear the swell booming in upon Cape Trafalgar on an autumn morning, and smell seaward breezes.

Pippa said to Ordinary Seaman Brownell, holding up a forefinger and looking like a Victorian child teaching a pet tricks—"I am going into Went this morning for my off-time. Went is a lovely town with a cathedral and good shops, and the pictures. Is there anything that you would like me to get for you?" Ordinary Seaman Brownell stared at Pippa. His gaze wavered to the frieze of urns and laurel wreaths and lovers' knots, high opposite. His eyes turned to his bedside locker, and he smiled crookedly and began to talk. The dreadful thing was that Pippa could not make out a single word, and Awful Matron might appear at any moment. And only last night Matron had summoned the whole of the day staff and given them an address on discipline, and ended by saying in frenzied tones that she thought, under the circumstances, it would be best in future if they never spoke to a patient or attempted to answer a medical officer. Lalage had asked dubiously what they were to do if a patient asked a direct question, and Matron had repeated, lashing herself into a fury with her own eloquence, that the men would respect them more if they never spoke, and showed no hair under their caps. "But the poor things are painfully respectful already," objected Lalage afterwards; and old Dr. Greatbatch, faced this morning by a day staff who all looked ready for the operating theatre, and cast down their eyes and fled from his presence sighing, "I will fetch Matron, sir," had gone in a fuss to Mrs. Hungerford, asking audibly, "What's the matter with all those girls?"

Pippa handed Brownell all his treasures from his locker— his floral chintz Dorothy bag, and a tobacco tin full of things that rattled, and a writing compendium called "The Quorn." The writing compendium was packed full of letters, mostly on thin lined paper and written in faded ink and very sloping characters, and she wondered if he could write better than he spoke, and thought that it would be interesting to know. You never could tell how well a patient could write. Some of the young ones, who looked as smart as paint, went red right up to the roots of their curls if you asked them to do something quite simple, such as draw up a list of the prizes for the Whist Drive to stick up on the recreation-room floor. Some of them, after seating themselves askew to a trembling card table and pressing with all their might, produced the most laborious but perfectly clear script. Others were wizards on the secretary's portable typewriter, when she left it about unlocked.

The other night Lalage had lectured to the patients and staff on Barsetshire. She was accustomed to instructing Guides, and Mrs. Hungerford had asked her to fill in a gap, as the usual speaker from Went had failed owing to frost-bound roads. At the end, Lalage had asked for questions, and one of the pneumonia cases had asked rather a teaser, and Lalage had kindly said, while she gathered her wits—"Yes—that is quite an intelligent question. . . ." And Cadet Chaloner had looked mildly surprised, as well he might, considering that he was the second master of an Oxford College choir school, though at present most unfairly disguised in a blue serge hospital suit which showed his wrists, and a white cotton shirt with tin buttons and yellow iron-mould marks, and a scarlet turkey-twill tie.

Pippa had almost settled to get Ordinary Seaman Brownell what she would like best herself from a shopping expedition— boiled sweets—when he found what he needed. He began scrabbling over the pages of a cartridge-paper drawing book, which he had shaken out of the chintz bag. He flicked past a sketch of a spaniel with speaking eyes, and a sketch of a bathing belle drinking a crimson-lake cocktail, and pages upon pages of silver-painted ships at sea in heavy weather, which did not look to Pippa much like ships, but he ought to know. "It's quite full," agreed Pippa. "What you need is another drawing book." Ordinary Seaman Brownell nodded like anything, and pretended to put the book in his pyjama pocket and could not. He wanted a smaller book with many more pages. At least that was what Pippa hoped that he wanted. He was still talking, with words rushing out of his lips like water from a bottle, as she slipped round the door with her broom and dustpan and tin of metal polish.

In the recreation-room a loud-speaker was discoursing a march of supernaturals from *Peer Gynt*, and two aircraft mechanics, quite undeterred by the rival performance, were crouched around a gramophone. In the far end of the room, on a dais, Petty Officer Chambers, seated at the grand piano, was trying over "I don't want to walk with you, Baby," which was going to be his "turn" at Friday's concert. The post was just in, and a score of men in cornflower blue, with rose-red faces and white faces, and black and brown and shiny straw-coloured hair, were temporarily engrossed, slitting envelopes and reading letters. On a sofa, placed at an angle beneath the fine chimney-piece, which showed Endymion asleep, with hunting dogs, three sailors, seated tight together like monkeys in cold weather, were engaged in maidenly embroidery. They sewed as if they meant to get the better of this business, and the backs of their necks rivalled in hue their turkey-twill ties. The recreation-room, which had been the saloon, and had grey walls and white woodwork picked out with tarnished gold, was hazy with tobacco smoke.' Outside, spring rain was slanting down upon a parterre planted with vegetables.

Pippa had become quite accustomed to the blast of musical instruments and nicotine and large-scale cookery which distinguished Woodside during and soon after black-out hours, but still, when she returned on duty after a walk, the extraordinary atmosphere struck her anew. She hurried now to shove her cleaning implements into a redolent downstairs cupboard and mount to her room. Woodside was much larger than one realized until one came to do something by the clock, and Miss Masquerier said that you needed roller skates and a butterfly net to catch any member of the staff who had set out on a tour of the long passages with three minutes' start.

In the tall white hall, full of pillars and echoes, Pippa ran into Lalage, who was already dressed for outdoors. "Luck's in," hissed Lalage. "The post has brought furlough passes for five men going north, and Sec. is going to rush them into Went to catch their connection. She says she'll take us."

VI

Moote's was the largest store in Went. It had been built just before the war, and was a modern building, with a beauty parlour and sports department, and lifts which whisked customers non-stop to the Tudor restaurant on the top floor. Its façade was ultra modern, and, after its opening day, Alderman Craigie had written a letter to the *Went Evening Star*, which he now regretted, as he was a patriotic man, asking, "Are we in Moscow?"

Lalage and Pippa emerged from the trembling lift, and as they had arrived at twelve-thirty, had only a few minutes to wait in a shadowy queue before an attendant said "Seats for two," and led them to a table in a window with a sideways view of the cathedral spire. Moote's restaurant was always crowded on a Wednesday, and the table had already two occupants, or to be correct three, for the pallid mother ladling vegetable soup towards her bosom, had on her knee a heavily sleeping eighteen-months' child with a clean bandage round its head. Her own mother, who had a grim mouth and a black hat with a wing, had reached plums and custard.

Lalage handed Pippa the menu, which appeared at a glance to be packed as closely with printed information as the back of a current clothing card. Closer inspection showed that three columns only were worthy of attention. They were headed "Electric Grill," "To-day's Chef's Choice" and "Special Teas." Nobody but a beginner would have ploughed through the passages superscribed "Soups, Sundaes, Puffs and Pastries."

The same acute but unhistorically minded businessman who had imposed upon Silver Street, Went, a building the shape and colour of a Stilton cheese, had possibly been employed to name Moote's Special Teas. Pippa was fascinated by the thought of royalties cosily seated to "The Sandringham," which included vegetable salad, chocolate éclair and hot anchovy toast. "The County" offered baked beans, Welsh Rarebit and French pastries. On the whole, however, "The Abbot Wayne Tea," which combined mince-pie, creamed crab and waffle with syrup, made the richest suggestion to the yearning adolescent.

Abbot Wayne brooded heavily over Moote's restaurant. There were no less than four large oil-paintings of incidents in his career, framed into the panelling of the walls. In every picture he was represented with a singularly smooth and inexpressive countenance, while his limbs were performing the most dramatic gestures. "'Abbot Wayne,'" read Pippa, "'Welcomes the Child-King and Queen-Mother to his Lodgings.' Who was the Child-King?" she wondered.

"Henry VI," replied Lalage. "Went dotty afterwards."

"He looks rather dotty there," said Pippa.

"They all do," said Lalage.

Pippa decided that this comment was fair. The indefatigable artist who had decorated the walls of Moote's Tudor restaurant with no less than eighteen glossy, highly coloured paintings of famous local happenings, in which the principal characters were almost life-size, had managed somehow to convey an impression of imbecility in every case. Whether they were men-at-arms acclaiming a Standard, or mob-capped maids with lavender baskets on their arms, moved by a black-robed preacher, or wigged nobleman examining the model of a ship in an oriel window at sunset, one and all appeared mentally otherwhere. "I think it's partly because their eyes aren't looking at what they're doing," pronounced Pippa. "If it isn't rude to ask, was the Sir Peregrine Merle, who's going to be executed on a scaffold up there, one of your ancestors?"

"No, he wasn't, nor is the one dying of wounds on a refectory table," said Lalage. "I rather wish he was. He was a Cavalier. They died out, and my great-grandfather bought the house, complete with ancestors. He tried to pretend that he was a descendant, but everyone knew that his grandfather made stays. I believe they simply searched England until they found a village with a decaying family of the right name. Still, as Granny Merle says, it shows a healthy instinct to wish that one's ancestors were much nobler than they were. Granny Merle really is descended from Charles II, and I think it shows in my cousin Kit. Kit and another of my cousins, who was killed in the last war, once dressed up as ladies, and were shown over Went by the housekeeper on a visitors' day. They were both still at prep. school, but pretty tall, and they wore sweeping princess dresses and feather boas and veils, and got the housekeeper to show them my grandfather's boots as a special treat. My grandfather wopped them when it came out, and Kit's mother howled, and said her fatherless boy's spirit would be broken, but it wasn't. They both stayed very high-spirited."

"Is that your home, the house in the picture called 'Queen Bess at Went'?" asked Pippa. "It's lovely."

"Yes. It's a Maternity Home now," said Lalage, rather shortly.

"I rang up and said that I was coming to luncheon with Lady Merle on Friday," said Pippa.

"Granny Merle's house isn't lovely, I ought to warn you," said Lalage heavily. "It has stained-glass staircase windows, and fern-houses, and baths with mahogany surrounds, and an organ. However, the Victorians did know how to lay out a garden, and Granny Merle has always been a great gardener."

"I wish I knew more about plants," said Pippa uneasily. "I want to get a beginner's pocket-guide to-day and start identifying wild flowers on my walks. They'll be beginning soon."

"They have begun," said Lalage, knitting her brows. "Look here, the bill of fare says 'Roast lamb and peas with mint sauce,' and the girl hasn't brought us any mint sauce. I don't see why we shouldn't have it, even if the lamb is frozen mutton and the peas have bodies of quite a different green from their jackets."

To Pippa's admiration, in spite of the fact that Moote's orchestra struck up at this moment, the descendant of the skilful staymaker who had been a friend of leading Whig statesmen got her mint sauce.

Pippa's spirits rose as she listened to the first notes of a skating valse by a French composer with a Teutonic-sounding name, and realized that outside spring sunshine was lighting a cathedral city, and that on Friday she was going to luncheon with old Lady Merle, who gave parties for young people.

Moote's orchestra was composed of four persons—a very black-haired lady at the piano, a bald violinist, a cellist like a gorilla, and one other musician surrounded by a medley of instruments, but hidden from Pippa by a palm. All performers wore sky-blue sateen Russian blouses with a huge letter M embroidered upon them in maroon chenille.

The ladies from Woodside left the restaurant to nostalgic strains of a Viennese *Lied*, and in the lift Pippa asked Lalage to direct her first to a shop where she could get a small, fat drawing-book for Ordinary Seaman Brownell.

"That child," said Lalage, in her solemn way, as they parted, "must have been drugged."

"The one at our table?" exclaimed Pippa.

"Yes; a child of that age ought to have been pulling everything off the table and plaguing for bits."

"How awful!" said Pippa.

"Oh, I don't mean that it was a drug fiend. I mean it had probably been taken to the Out Patients at the Infirmary and the mother had a five-mile 'bus drive home and a walk, and simply had to get her dinner at Moote's. I ought to have spoken to her. I am thinking of taking up social work after the war," explained Lalage, "but am rather cowardly about people still. Good-bye."

VII

Madame Rosalthé's establishment looked quite pre-war, for outside its doors stood a well-polished large car with a handsome chauffeur in olive-green livery, dozing at the wheel. The small new shop was one of a row occupying the ground floor of a towering block of flats. The building formed the back of Moote's, hence everything about it was absolutely up to date, or at any rate 1939. Gladys Crippen did not fill her windows with pallid waxen busts of ladies in Pompadour or Edwardian coiffures, nor did she advertise *postiches* or patent hair-brushes. Her window-dressing was severely simple. Her trade name, in gold lettering and a flowing script, decorated her plate glass.

Striped red and white sun-blinds, inscribed "Arts de Coiffure," added a dashingly Continental air. Both windows were lined with only slightly faded silver-hued artificial satin. In that on the left hand, the figure of a single glass nymph aspired on tiptoe to grasp a pendant drapery of sunray pleated chiffon. In the window on the right the sole decoration was a vase of tall spring flowers—to-day pussy-willow and arum lilies. Gladys Crippen, who was a sensible girl, had early struck up a bosom friendship with Miss Cupp of Cupp & Son, Florists, Fruiterers and Fishmongers, Went Market Square.

Pippa wished that she had not forgotten to ask Lalage or Elizabeth what having one's hair done cost in Went. She was naturally awed by the appearance of an establishment, which as far as the outsider could tell might have been ready to sell her hashish. Within, although the sun was still bright in the street, electric wall-lighting illuminated an L-shaped passage, with a glittering surface of shell-pink paint, and a reception desk, on which lay a large leather-bound ledger and two battered collecting boxes. A brunette, with bare legs and arms, attired in a shell-pink overall, swept Pippa to a cubicle, and when Pippa had removed her gabardine cap, asked her how she liked her hair done. Although further daunted by her reflection many times repeated on the glass-covered walls surrounding them, Pippa answered boldly, "I want it to look right under a nurse's cap at Woodside, where I work. Mrs. Rollo and Miss Elizabeth Rollo told me that they came here, and they always look very nice."

The brunette, whose stage name was Paulette, laid a crimson-nailed finger to her ruby lips, and said, "Let me see—Miss Elizabeth Rollo. She generally has three flat curls and the back brought across sideways. I think Madam herself generally does Mrs. Rollo." She then produced a comb and proceeded to tear out Pippa's hair by the roots.

In the next cubicle, someone with a peevish voice was saying how she wished that she was in the south of France. "Oh, not now, m'lady," shuddered her attendant, who was, Pippa surmised, no less a person than Rosalthé herself. "I don't believe that things out there are half as bad as people make out," lisped the peevish voice. "They just do it to stop one going anywhere where one might possibly get a little enjoyment and gaiety." To this remark even Rosalthé failed to find reply. An electric fan began to whirr next door, and Paulette, having immobilized her victim by dressing her in a back-to-front surplice and placing a hand-towel in her fingers, begged her to sit right down in a modern chair made of steel tubing, and inclined her remorselessly towards a swirling basin of hot soapsuds. The atmosphere grew steamy. Pippa gasped and spluttered.

Fifteen minutes later, laying in Pippa's palm a sinister-looking indigo rubber ball, with switches labelled "Hot," "Warm," "Cool" and "Off," Paulette slipped from the room, and as soon as a survey of the mirrors told Pippa that she was alone, she took her feet off the elderly footstool imposed upon her by Paulette, and ducked quickly outside the monstrous machine, breathing burning air, beneath which Paulette had extinguished her to the cheekbones. Even when one knew that one could get out, the machine was reminiscent of those used by native tribes to collect souvenirs of missionary Christians. Having recovered her attaché-case and snapped it open across her knees, Pippa wriggled back under the extinguisher and resigned herself to a further twenty minutes of having her temples fanned and ear-drums assailed by an increasingly unbearable sirocco.

She was very pleased with Brownell's sketching-book, and in the old-fashioned artist's and colourman's shop in a cobbled alley behind the cathedral, to which Lalage had directed her, she had also bought something for herself. Pippa knew that collecting picture postcards was one of her weaknesses, and especially when the cards were outsized coloured ones of ancient and modern paintings, and flowers and birds. She had spent a congenial half-hour in Craik's shop. Mr. Craik himself, a silver-headed character with a walrus moustache, clad in a white apron and a bowler hat, and carrying a collapsible foot-rule, had never attempted to disturb her. During her stay several customers, or more probably acquaintances, had stuck their heads in at the door, which was of the type that rang a distant bell when touched. Their business appeared to be mostly about an alteration in the hour of choir practice, and Mr. Craik, a man of few words, generally answered them before they spoke.

Pippa spread her purchases on her knee and gloated over them. "Symphony in Blue" showed a Cornish coastline on a day of heat haze. She would stick it up in her bedroom, close to the mirror, and by Auntie Prue's birthday—August 29th—might be ready to part with it. She was not now so enamoured of "Pheasant" as she had been in the dimness of the shop. The bird whose portrait occupied a third of the card was well-fed and rather stupid-looking, sailing slowly over a tree-top of precisely his own colouring. The original of the wholly satisfying Dutch flower group was, Pippa knew, in the National Gallery. She already possessed a card which would make a pair for it, though rather more coppery in colouring, and from an original in the Wallace Collection. Her fourth card, called "Pieter de Hooch," showed a party of Charles II gentlemen and ladies caught in conversation amongst sombre hedges. Pieter had only just been quick enough. In another moment the group must have broken up, to stroll back for refreshment into the white house glimmering in the distance. Pippa, seated in Rosalthé's cubicle, could almost fancy that she heard lazy laughter on midsummer Netherlandish air, and could smell the scent of a warm shrubbery and feel the bite of a water-meadow insect. Her fifth card caused her to blush, for although she had secured a splendid likeness of "West Front, Went Cathedral, from the medieval gateway leading to the Precincts," she had not even found time to-day to walk around the exterior of the famous monument.

After examining the postcards in every light, and the yard of elastic and packet of envelopes which she had secured for Night Sister, Pippa suffered another ten minutes of growing physical discomfort. She tugged a bundle of dog-eared magazines from beneath the cushions of the tubular chair, and felt more comfortable, but found little solace in issues dated "Fall, 1940," in which all the crosswords had been half done by half-wits, and the stories, after starting in a blaze of glory and meandering down the sides of stirring illustrations for a couple of pages, died upon the reader, with curt instructions to turn to closely printed Roman-lettered advertisement sheets at the back. She was seriously but tremulously considering an expedition into the shiny passage, to search personally for the faithless Paulette, when her deliverer returned in a flutter, switched off the roaring robot, pushed him contemptuously aside, and said in fluty accents, "Nice and dry?" In the stunning silence that succeeded, the peevish voice from next door sounded again, evidently concluding a saga: "She still thought that he was fond of her, you see."

"Yes, m'lady," said her listener-in-chief sympathetically.

"People seem to say extraordinary things to hairdressers," thought Pippa. "Perhaps I ought to say more." She said, "It's getting lovely out at Woodside now."

"I expect it's always rather lively up there, with so many of the Forces?" sighed pretty Paulette.

"I actually said 'lovely'," piped Pippa, "but I think our men generally are cheerful."

"It'll be all officer patients at Woodside," hazarded Paulette.

"Oh, no," said Pippa. "All 'other ranks.' We don't get any officers. In fact, I've never heard of anyone who has, though I suppose they must be ill sometimes and get sent somewhere."

"I hope the boys appreciate Mrs. Hungerford's kindness," said Paulette, suddenly prim and possessive. "I'm waiting to be called up for the WAAFS myself," she volunteered, giving a curl on Pippa's temple a tug that suggested she mistook it for a shirker.

Pippa just caught the Westbury 'bus moving out from Went Market-place, but her enjoyment of the first part of her homeward journey, past secretive high park walls and a flying ground, was much impaired by blushful consciousness that her person was exhaling Orient odours. She was not yet sure that her visit to Madame Rosalthé could be termed anything of a success. Her last vision of her own countenance, pale and shiny, beneath a mannered erection of curls, on which her cap would not sit down or even sit straight, had filled her with shame. But in the passage she had met the late occupant of the next cubicle, and noted that she too looked like a skinned rabbit, and seemed quite complacent. Paulette had also said that it would be best not to comb out her handiwork to-night, but Pippa doubted whether Matron would share this view.

The 'bus approached a break in the long grey wall, and a large car with a chauffeur in olive-green livery, which had swept past only a moment before, turned in between lodge gates ahead. Soon the 'bus drew up at a cross-roads, and the conductor called out "Went Park," and nearly everyone got out and ran like mad to catch the Highbridge 'bus.

It was only after they were in motion again that Pippa realized that the occupant of the shiny car was probably "young" Lady Merle. Somehow, she had never expected to find Lalage's mother a golden-haired person, with baby features and a lisp, looking somehow out of place in wartime Went, pattering about on stilt heels, in a dyed ermine coat, with a bunch of orchids pinned on.

CHAPTER III
"I'M AWFUL! I'M HOPELESS!"
(March 20th)

I

"TELL MCNAUGHTON that she may send in the dog, Radish," said the Dowager.

Nobody had warned Pippa that her hostess would be the living image of Elizabeth Tudor in later life. The Dowager Lady Merle was a tall, gaunt old lady, with a nut-cracker profile, who helped herself about her pale-blue double-drawing-room on an ivory-handled ebony stick. She wore a black lace scarf over her head, and another, to match, over her stooping shoulders, and carried, together with her stick, one of the most hideous silver-mounted wool cross-stitch handbags that Pippa had ever seen. Her penetrative glance was fully as alarming as Pippa had expected, and her smile even more so. The hour was now two-fifteen, and luncheon had been accomplished without disaster. The meal had been much better than Lalage's prophecies, indeed verging on the delicious, and suggesting that the Dowager flung wide the doors of a Victorian store-cupboard when she entertained the young. But as Lady Merle was a small eater, and evidently expected intelligent answers to her unusual questions, Pippa was dreading an attack of hiccups. Fortunately the Dowager accepted complete direction of the conversation, and did not seem to have any nervous dislike of long pauses.

The Dowager was safe in a large, crackling, chintz-covered arm-chair by the side of her mantelpiece, effectively backed by curtains of emerald silk and white net, shrouding bay windows looking out on to a drive and park-land. Opposite her, but on a lower level, and at such a distance that she was obliged to speak up, sat Pippa, on the very edge of an even larger crackling chintz Chesterfield, marooned on a Persian rug amongst yards of teak flooring. The scent of many pots of freesias burdened the air, and through a side door Pippa could see one of the promised fern houses. Every object in the double drawing-room, and the objects were many, was polished to the nines. Pippa had been scarcely able to control her surprise when Lady Merle had expressed approval of Auntie Prue's action in clearing her parlour of *bibelots*, and announced that she herself had banished from this chamber, in order to save labour, no less than one hundred and fifty treasured ornaments.

"In a moment I hope to be able to show you my new dog," said the Dowager. "He belonged to a young officer from our aerodrome—used to come here quite often—a fighter pilot. He was an amiable young man with no connections, and one day told me that his sole persistent anxiety concerned the future of his dog, Radish. He always brought the faithful companion with him on his calls, and my staff had become quite accustomed to the pair. I told the young officer that, in the event of any accident, I would be prepared to take the dog. Indeed, I had for some time been thinking of getting a new personal dog, but had shrunk from making a start after the loss of my poor Flush. Have you any pets at home?"

"I hadn't any to leave, when I came away now," said Pippa. "Of course I've had rabbits and silkworms and mice, like most people."

"As soon as you have a settled home," said the Dowager grandly, "get some dogs. Never allow yourself to fall into the error of having a single pet. Always have a young one coming on to fill the sad gap. Did you find rabbits interesting?"

"I don't think I did, very," decided Pippa. "They often looked as if they were thinking, but I expect it was mostly food."

"I think their lack of physical courage is ultimately depressing," said the Dowager. "Now, to ferrets one can become quite attached. Ferrets have fire. All my grandsons used to keep ferrets here, for the holidays. It was one of the attractions of coming to stay with me. To return to Radish. When I heard that the gallant young pilot had been amongst those who had failed to return from a sweep over occupied France, I took steps immediately. I sent over a groom on a bicycle with a note, presenting my compliments to the officer in command at the aerodrome. I explained my promise, and begged that the dog be delivered to my messenger. And I must confess that it was a glad moment when I saw the cycle coming up the drive, preceded by the white dog, trotting along quite cheerfully. I had sent a lead belonging to my poor Flush, but it had proved quite unnecessary. The dog knew the road here, and as soon as his guardian turned in at the park gates, he ran ahead. There were some sad moments after he had greeted me, when he searched the cloak-room and even ran down to the garage. But a square meal and an invitation to sleep on the white fur rug in front of the fire here soon comforted him. I believe it is characteristic of the breed to sleep with a smile on the face. His name is not sensible, but when a great many young people get together in times of danger, they become very high-spirited." The Dowager broke off, to inquire of a drooping servitor, "Is Radish not to be found? Dear me, how vexing! I do hope that he has not been allowed out of the gates. Search the linen room and stoke-hole. Last week he was found in the stoke-hole after McNaughton had given him his bath. I am afraid," said the Dowager as her retainer retired, "that perhaps he does not get sufficient exercise. I used to be a good walker, especially in Scotland. My late husband was most severe about dogs hunting, and during my early married life I often stood sadly at a window at dusk straining my eyes, in hopes of seeing a familiar figure leaping a gate and slinking home to chastisement after forbidden absence. I brought five dogs to Went with me on my marriage—smooth-haired fox-terriers, great fighters; one rarely sees them nowadays. I believe it created quite a sensation, as my poor father-in-law had lived for his pheasants. But I had made it a condition of the match. My mother took many prizes with her poodles. I have a Winterhalter, very charming, showing her with a poodle, under a parasol. The Merles are not animal lovers, and there was disparity in age, but the choice was my own."

"I wish there were some dogs at Woodside," said Pippa. "It's so dull going for walks alone. But I'm getting quite keen on wild flowers. I identified coltsfoot and dog-mercury and lords and ladies on my road here to-day."

"Presently," nodded the Dowager, looking gratified, "you shall make a tour of my garden here. It was in a sad state of neglect when I arrived, fifteen years ago, but . . . Ah!" A sudden look of melancholy vanished from old Lady Merle's features as a stout white bull-terrier trotted into the room in an *affairé* manner.

"Where was he?" inquired the Dowager, offering her favourite the back of a long, knotty hand.

"He was discovered in the still-room, m'lady. He was watching the members of the Women's Institute collecting the provisions for this evening's whist drive in aid of the Russians."

Conversation flowed more easily after the entrance of Radish, who sat by his mistress's knee with closed eyes, looking deeply conscious of his honoured position as personal dog to the Dowager Lady Merle. He listened with a heavenly smile while Pippa detailed the advantages of living close to a public library, and the Dowager nodded and for a few seconds she, too, closed her eyes. But her voice was clarion-clear as she demanded, sitting upright with a jerk, "Are you a reader?"

"Oh, yes," said Pippa. "In fact, I've always rather got into trouble for wanting to read when I ought to be doing something practical."

"What do you read?" probed the Dowager. "Do you read a solid newspaper regularly?"

"No; ought I to?" asked Pippa.

The Dowager inclined her head.

"Always make a point of looking through at least one a day, when possible. If you've got brains you'll find much to interest you. If you haven't, it may save you from worse things. My late husband, during his busiest years of national service, always made a point of keeping in touch with current literature. We had many valued literary guests at Went during the summer months in the old days."

"How simply lovely!" breathed Pippa. "And did they write poems in summer-houses and things? I was absolutely thrilled when I discovered that Rosanna Masquerier was one of Mrs. Hungerford's staff."

Much to Pippa's satisfaction, the Dowager did not share Professor Beadon's ignorance. "I always buy Miss Masquerier's biographies," she announced. "I always send one to my sister-in-law in the Lakes for Christmas." As Pippa did not know Lady Merle's relations with her sister-in-law, she was obliged to wait to discover whether this act indicated admiration for her favourite biographer, or was merely a conventional move in a well-fought life-feud. "I have always approved of Miss Masquerier," continued the Dowager, coming down heavily in support of Pippa's idol. "She is an unusually agreeable learned woman. And what is more to the point in these dark days, she is showing herself a thoroughly useful member of our community."

To Pippa's disappointment, at this moment the door opened, and Mrs. Taylor was announced.

"Good afternoon, Granny," said the new arrival, pecking at the Dowager's withered cheek. "Many happy returns of the day."

The Dowager replied with a clearness of diction which many younger hostesses might have copied with advantage, "Good afternoon, Pamela, dear child. Thank you for your useful gift.

Miss Pippa Johnson from Mary's hospital is spending the after-noon with me. My grand-daughter Pamela's husband," she explained to Pippa, "is our rector at Westbury." Mrs. Taylor, who was a tweed-clad lady of middle age, as large and master-ful-looking as her grandmother, and far more unguarded in her manner, said abruptly after a close look at the new member of Mrs. Hungerford's staff, "How do you like it at Woodside? I pity you with that impossible woman as matron."

"Mary, I believe," said the Dowager, coming to Pippa's rescue, "finds her matron quite competent."

"I don't say she's not competent," declared Mrs. Taylor. "I merely say that she's a classic case of megalomania. Why Mary puts up with her, I don't know. After my quarrel with her over the men's laundry, I have simply shaken the dust of the place off my feet. I have told Mary that she need not expect to see me again until she has sacked that harridan."

"I know, dear, and I think that you are quite wrong-headed, and are depriving yourself of much pleasure as well as an oppor-tunity to do useful work," said the Dowager. "Now let me show you my birthday gifts."

Pippa privately thought the gifts sent to the Dowager Lady Merle on her eighty-ninth birthday a pretty pathetic set. They included greetings telegrams from a number of relatives in the Forces, a pea-green and black felt coal glove made by a descend-ant aged five, a book of crossword puzzles from Lalage, and a set of embroidered table-mats from Mrs. Hungerford.

"Mary's note tells me that she made these herself," said the Dowager, "but I should have known her beautiful work anywhere. I do not know how she finds the time. I wish that she had news of Christopher. You do not know whether she has heard again? I never ask."

"Mary fusses over Kit," said Mrs. Taylor impatiently. Letters from Russia are bound to take ages, and we don't even know for certain that he's gone there. Look how she fussed when he was in Greece, and he fetched up all right."

"Well, I too fuss about Christopher's dangerous and perpet-ual journeys, for he is my favourite grandchild," said the

Dowager calmly. "I know that one should not have favourites, but from a child I have always found Christopher sympathetic. He has traits of my father. Your Aunt Drant's sons are all excellent young men, I am sure, but wooden—wooden—and as for poor Lalage, she tried to show me how to turn the heel of a soldier's sock the other day. Her father's slow brain over again."

"I hope you haven't got me on your Hate List, Granny," said Mrs. Taylor, with a light in her eye.

"Not yet, dear, rather the contrary, but you display a growing tendency nowadays to allow yourself to become heated over trifles, which I am sorry to see at a time when we should all be united," said the Dowager firmly.

"And you, Granny, while we are telling home-truths," said Mrs. Taylor, regardless of the pop-eyed Pippa, "have since your illness tended to become much too meek and mild, which I am sorry to see. I always used to be able to count on you."

I I

Mrs. Taylor, at the Dowager's command, took Pippa and Radish out to see the garden. There was not, to tell the truth, much to be seen as yet in any Barsetshire garden, but two brimstone butterflies fluttered along a sunlit hedge in front of the pedestrians, and in a sheltered corner of the park Pippa found a tuft of wild violets, of a colour which reminded her painfully of the paper wrappings of a favourite brand of Swiss milk chocolate. Mrs. Taylor walked fast, and talked of anything except horticulture, and now and then her trenchant remarks were drowned by the noise made by formations of bombers based on Went aerodrome. She told Pippa that every window in the garden front of Woodside had been shattered by blast a fortnight before the hospital was due to, open, and that Mrs. Hungerford had wept. Pippa, who could not imagine Mrs. Hungerford in tears, said, "I suppose she was frightfully over-tired after getting everything ready, and just felt that this was the last straw."

"Oddly enough," reported Mrs. Taylor, "the thing that she really seemed to mind was the thought of Kit's disappointment. She said, 'Oh, my poor little Kit, and he thought he'd done the loveliest thing he possibly could for me when he gave me back my old home to have as a hospital. . . . My heart's desire. And everything has been so difficult from the very beginning.' She wept buckets."

"Is Major Hungerford little?" asked Pippa.

"No, he's six foot two," said Mrs Taylor. "Diminutives denote affection."

"Giving her back her old home as a wedding present was a very nice and romantic thing for him to do," said Pippa.

"He could well afford it," said Mrs. Taylor, "and I have heard that he had wanted to marry Mary since she was sixteen."

"Yes," said Pippa, "Mrs. Bates told me that."

"Oh, did she?" inquired Mrs. Taylor. "Well, I'm his first cousin, and I never knew for certain. But if Sally Bates says it was so, it probably was so. She's the most extraordinary women. At first sight you might be inclined to write her down as rather a menace, for she broadcasts the most incredible bulletins of local news. But in time one discovers that she's astonishingly accurate. And that's a great point in anyone's favour."

Pippa agreed, and said that Professor Abbadie Beadon was nuts on accuracy, and rolled his eyes if one said "sort of" or ended a sentence with "or something." Unfortunately at this moment the bombers from the aerodrome appeared overhead for the second time, and after two efforts to get Mrs. Taylor to believe that anyone could really be called Professor Abbadie Beadon, Pippa gave up the attempt, and asked instead, "Was Woodside blasted on the same night that they got the stick of bombs on Westbury Green? Mrs. Bates showed me her crater."

"Sally Bates," said Mrs. Taylor with fresh vigour, "is a crashing bore about her crater. When my husband and I lost our garage we determined at once to say as little as possible. By a stroke of luck there happened to be nothing in it that night, except all my cousin Rupert's civilian clothes and his unpublished manuscripts, which he had sent down from his London flat for safety when he was ordered to Gibraltar. (He used to write plays and things, but is now safe in the R.N.V.R.) I had brought in my car late, and being tired, had simply locked it and left it in front of the house, because as I came up the drive I remembered that I'd locked the garage doors after welcoming in Rupert's effects, and the key was on the hall table.

"You never saw such a mess in your life! It got a direct hit. We were in bed when it happened, but not yet asleep, as it was only about ten-thirty. It was just a solitary plane which had evidently decided not to go back to Germany with any bombs on board. Of course if there had been a siren, one or both of us would have been up, in case we were needed by any of our village people. (Though actually the only time I have ever been called put to do first aid during a blitz was when Millie Harker's baby swallowed a safety-pin, which it might just as well have done under normal circumstances.)

"We had been having a quiet time for weeks, so when I heard the sound of an engine booming steadily nearer and nearer, I said to John, 'One of our own, I suppose.' The words were scarcely out of my mouth, when they loosed the H.E. that demolished our garage, and my bed moved up and hit the wall, as our house is an old one, and my glove and handkerchief drawer leapt out of the tallboy and landed on John's legs. It was a Jacobean tallboy, which Mary Hungerford had given me as a wedding present, and its top drawers were rather a loose fit. I always think it was remarkably kind of her to give it to me, for she was still living in two converted cottages at the time, and was using it herself. I had helped her to move to Willows, when she sold Woodside to a girls' school, and she had remembered that I had admired the thing, and said that I should expect it as a wedding present. It has brass drop handles and cherubs' faces behind. I wasn't serious, because I was already at least twenty-eight, and the only people who had ever looked in my direction were the most pitiable specimens—no good at games."

"I should think Mrs. Hungerford was very unselfish," said Pippa.

"It's her bane," screamed Mrs. Taylor, as the bombers began to draw near again. "Well, to return to the raid. We both put on some clothes and went out, but the lights had fused, and we couldn't use our torches, so we didn't appreciate the full beauty of what had happened to the garage till dawn. From the noise, I had quite expected to find that the house itself had been hit. One moment I was lying in bed, and the next I found myself out in the passage, carrying my hot-water bottle, though what I imagined I was going to do with that I don't know. People do very odd things when they're taken by surprise. My husband was in the lounge of the County Hotel at Went when that got hit, and it had a glass roof, as it had once been the yard of a coaching inn, and he said that one of the funniest things he ever saw in his life was a seventeen-stone gentleman trying to get underneath a modern sofa."

"Trying to do what?" asked Pippa.

"A modern sofa. One of those that go right down to the ground," screamed Mrs. Taylor.

The bombers drew away, and she resumed in more level tones, "When dawn came, we found our house entirely undamaged, except that a lot of plaster had come down, and the blast had produced the most incredible quantity of dust. I was rather annoyed, as although I had always realized that the Rectory is practically uninhabitable, as it was designed in the days when rectors had large private incomes, fourteen children and no baths, I had hitherto hoped that I had a clean house."

"I expect you had, as far as eye could see and arm could reach," suggested Pippa soothingly.

"We didn't lose a single window," admitted Mrs. Taylor in grudging accents. "However, the garage was gone. You may think," she proceeded, looking straightly at Pippa with very fine grey eyes, "that after my saying that Sally Bates was a bore about her bomb, I'm not much better myself. But you see, when a thing has happened to oneself, it is intensely interesting to one."

"It is very interesting to me to hear about this," said Pippa, and explained how successfully Auntie Prue had managed to shelter her young from horrors.

"If you'd like to come to tea one day," said Mrs. Taylor, softening, "I could show you what's left of the garage, and I expect John would like to show you the church. I mean the tombs. Abbot Wayne's is famous, but we've had it sandbagged.

We're living under more or less civilized conditions at present, as all their mothers arrived in rages and took our evacuee infants back to London when they began to bomb Went. For the first thirteen months after the outbreak we had fifteen children under five in the house. Now we've got no children, but we've also got no maids. I don't regret them. I mean the maids. I told them I thought they ought to go and man mixed batteries while they could, and I ought to cook John's sausage, as I'm no chicken. How do you think Granny's looking?"

"I'd never seen Lady Merle until to-day," answered Pippa uncertainly, "but she said she was eighty-nine, didn't she, so I should think she's perfectly marvellous."

"She very nearly died just before Christmas," yelled Mrs. Taylor, looking skywards again in some impatience. "She got pneumonia. Mary came over every day, and so did I. There was hard frost. We were both dead tired and mingled our tears. We knew that little Greatbatch couldn't really do anything for her, and what was worse, she knew it too. She told him when I was there one evening that she had so much hoped to see the Victory procession from the stand at her son's club, and that it would be a great disappointment to her if she had to leave this war unfinished."

"Do you think," ventured Pippa, "that Lady Merle would let me come up sometimes and take Radish out for walks? I mean, I could come up quite quietly, without disturbing anyone, and just call for him. She did say to-day that she was afraid he didn't get enough exercise, and if he's accustomed to having a young master, I dare say that's true."

"Yes, certainly offer. She'll jump at it," advised Mrs. Taylor. "Ask to see her sometimes, too. Granny Merle loves seeing bright young people. I never saw Radish's master, but I dare say he was a pretty ghastly little pip-squeak. However, if somebody's got guts, Granny Merle doesn't seem to mind."

"Oh, she is like Queen Elizabeth right through, then," nodded Pippa.

"Queen Elizabeth?" cried Mrs. Taylor, inclining towards Pippa and gripping her by the arm.

"Even if Radish's master was rather ghastly," screamed Pippa, emboldened by the accompaniment from above, "I think it's rather nice, don't you, that she only saw that he was a very gallant young pilot?"

"Let's turn into the shrubbery," suggested Mrs. Taylor. "I can't hear you out here."

"I mean," pursued Pippa, very pink in the face, "that quite likely Drake and Raleigh were pretty showy at times, and I think I've heard Professor Beadon say that they probably both had broad West Country accents. But they were the goods, and those were the days."

Mrs. Taylor stared at her young companion in a bovine manner for a full moment before replying in a changed voice, and with a schoolboy's manner, "Oh! I think I see what you mean, and I think you're right and I'm wrong."

Old Lady Merle was waiting for her guests at the door of her penultimate conservatory, and the first thing she asked was whether Pamela had shown Miss Johnson the sunk garden and the peach houses.

"No, I didn't, Granny," confessed Mrs. Taylor, "because, as you know, I don't know a thing about gardens. We started off down the long border, and it had nothing in it, except sticks and labels, and some bits of green starting up out of the earth, which I suppose are hoping to be bulbs. I took her up the lane and across the park, and we're both as hoarse as crows, because there were learners out from the aerodrome, and it's a good thing you didn't attempt to come, because the wind's still in the east."

"We had a lovely walk," supplied Pippa, "and I think I did see the outer wall of the sunk garden. It had the most beautiful flowering shrub simply blazing on it—a gorgeous red, which would be hopelessly expensive in a dress material. Lots of little buds," said Pippa waving her hands, "growing all up the branches . . . and the petals were round. . . ."

"That is what I used to call my Pyrus Japonica," mourned the Dowager. "Now I am told that I have been incorrect all these years, and should say Cydonia lagenaria. I doubt if I shall make the change, disgusted as I am with the Japanese."

"When I heard what they had done," affirmed Mrs. Taylor, "I said to John, 'I shall never speak to a Jap in my life again!' He said in his mild way, 'But, my dear, you never have!' I said, 'Well, anyway, this is The End.'"

"Now," said the Dowager, gently inciting her younger guest towards the drawing-room, "I want to show you something pretty. I am only a little sorry that Pamela did not take you into the peach houses, for although peach blossom in full flower under glass on an inclement day is a lovely sight, I think I prefer my old grape-vine."

Pippa looked up, and saw that the gnarled and knotty cork-coloured branches secured to wires above her head, were decorated at every point with inch-wide miniature vine-leaves and tendrils of the palest lemon-green.

"This is my old Black Hamburgh," said the Dowager. "I say mine, but in fact it was planted by a predecessor here, and when I arrived, my head gardener, who is a relentless Scot, wished me, as I was putting in new glass elsewhere, to tear down this conservatory, which he condemned as old-fashioned and unsatisfactory. I am so glad now that I did not, for now that I do not walk so much, it is an abiding pleasure to sit in my drawing-room and watch daily to see whether the old vine has begun. I note in my diary on which day every year I see the first sign of life and on which day it begins to flower. Last year it was in bud nearly a week earlier."

"Do you think, Granny," said Mrs. Taylor, changing the subject with her customary brutality, "that Ralph and Valerie will expect us to weigh in with silver wedding presents? I have been meaning to ask you every time I came, and only remembered this afternoon when you said that one did not expect birthday presents in war-time. I mean that John and I are quite ready, and I expect Mary would join in for herself and Kit. But I can't get a straight answer out of her. I was their bridesmaid, you know. Doesn't it seem impossible that it is nearly a quarter of a century ago now, and Lalage is rising twenty-two?"

"I can give you a straight answer, dear," said the Dowager, straightening her back and moving with astonishing speed towards her drawing-room. "It would be quite unnecessary. You can dismiss the idea."

After tea, which was even more appetizing than lunch, Mrs. Taylor made the *amende honorable*, after her own manner.

"Well, I must be getting back, to cook John's dinner, so I'll say good-bye, Granny, and thank you for my good tea. I always love your seed-cakes. I'm sorry that I said you were not ruthless enough nowadays. I expect that after your illness you don't feel like battling much. Oddly enough, after mine, I felt like fighting everybody. But mine," said Mrs. Taylor, rising to her feet impatiently, "was only an episode, and will never happen again."

"I dare say that you are quite wrong, my dear," said the Dowager, looking her through and through, with the most kindly expression. Pippa had no idea of what they were talking.

"What really got me down," said Mrs. Taylor, forgetting all her good resolutions, "was your being so broad-minded the last time I was here, when that perfectly useless little woman, Hyacinth Mimms, was being so typical. She gave none of us any peace until she had shipped her two abominably spoilt brats to America—where, by the way, I hear from Muriel Gidding, that they are becoming quite decent, normal children. Now that she's got nothing in the world to do at home, she still spends her time in a jitter, saying she never knew before what loneliness meant, and if you ask her to lend a helping hand with anything, she's not on."

"I think perhaps," decided the Dowager, "that I always have been a little indulgent towards pretty little Mrs. Mimms. But she is such a very pretty little woman; and then I always think that she is just about to say something interesting, and so far she never has."

It was not until she found herself again in the staff-room at Woodside, owner of a seed-cake and two bunches of superb Parma violets, one of which she had been commanded to present to Miss Masquerier, that Pippa realized that at the Dower House she had not met any other young people.

III

Elizabeth Rollo had been up to London for a week's leave, and sat on the sofa in the staff-room looking unfamiliar, and prettier than ever, in an abbreviated black dress which seemed to be entirely composed of pleats. She twiddled in her fingers a hat made of a bunch of white violets and a ribbed black ribbon, and was telling Lalage what she had done, and whom she had met. She had stayed at the Club which Mummy and she had joined the year she came out, and the food had been foul and the service worse. Luckily she had scarcely been in for a meal. She had been to a mad party given by Buffy, and Tinker, who was still a White-hall Warrior, had been there, and both the Tonys, and she had gone to three theatres and four flicks, and had a perm., and her face cleaned, and used up all her coupons, and although London was not what it had been, it was lousy to be back.

Lalage said that in her opinion Tinker had always been rather going at the edges, and Elizabeth said, "My dear, he asked after you most tenderly, also Tony ffolliott." Whereupon Lalage set her solid legs well apart and said "Ugh!" and asked Pippa how she had enjoyed her outing with Granny Merle.

Pippa, standing by the fireside in her overcoat, still clutching the seed-cake, and the flowers delivered to her by the Dowager's reluctant head gardener, returned to Woodside with a start. She had been almost in London, as she listened to Elizabeth—not the London she knew, composed of Westminster Abbey and Waterloo, and enigmatic Lady Jones, sitting invisible in her sightless Bayswater mansion, but a place where really grown up and bright young people had mad parties, even in 1942.

She told Lalage about Radish and Mrs. Taylor, in that order, and that Lady Merle was exactly like Queen Elizabeth, and Lalage said, "I shall tell her," and Pippa said in hot alarm, "Please don't! She might think it the most awful cheek, and I hope to go again."

The supper bell might sound at any moment, so it was not worth while toiling up three flights of stairs to her slice of bedroom. Pippa slipped out of her overcoat, and took off her cap without fear, as her visit to Madame Rosalthé had been entirely successful. She sat herself down by the side of Elizabeth, and said brightly, "Where shall we go in our off-time to-morrow?"

While Elizabeth had been away, she had always had the same off-time as Lalage, and Lalage had shown her all the rights of way across the park, and field paths to Westbury and Upper Merle church, and the Pheasant Inn, and Old Mill House. She had become quite accustomed to meeting Lalage in the hall as soon as she came off duty.

"I shall be going out with Nurse Rollo to-morrow, nurse," said Elizabeth.

Pippa felt for a moment as she had done when she had tried in the black-out to walk through the double row of sandbags, piled ten feet high, which protected the entrance to Auntie Prue's F.A. Post. She looked at Elizabeth and Elizabeth stared back at her. Pippa felt her face and hands becoming hot, and all her natural instincts urged her to fly from the room, uttering loud boo-hoos, or fling herself flat on the mat in front of the fire and hammer the ground with her fists. It was horrible to be eighteen, and not wanted, and she had never meant to be pushing, and of course, if she had thought for a moment before she spoke, she would have realized that Elizabeth and Lalage, who were twenty-one and twenty-two, couldn't want to go out with her. Probably Lalage had been bored to death by all her questions about country people and things, and had been longing to shake her off, but had been too kind-hearted. Probably Elizabeth had agreed with Lalage that she would do the snubbing.

But as Pippa was eighteen, and dressed as a nurse for the Forces, she couldn't boo-hoo or bang the floor. She sat on, pressed tightly into the corner of the sofa, watching the fire-light grow misty, and wishing that she was Marine Ormerod in the Oak Room Ward, who had been run over by a Flying Fortress and had a broken pelvis, and was in plaster from his armpits to his heels. Then perhaps people would be sorry for her.

"Sister Finan says that that child in Moote's can't have been drugged, nurse," said Lalage, changing the subject of conversation placidly, and measuring her blue knitting across both knees.

Pippa managed to say "Oh!"

"She says that even a second and third dressing after mastoid is agonizing, and that probably the child had howled itself into a condition of complete exhaustion," explained Lalage.

The supper bell sounded, and Mrs. Hungerford's staff trooped into the dining-room, which was the old Adam-green drawing-room, and was shaped like an L lying on its back. The staff supped at seven-fifteen, at a single long table set in the window recess formed by the short leg of the L, and the men supped at six-forty-five at four long tables in the major portion of the room. All the tables were of the board-and-trestle variety, covered with glistening white American cloth, but they looked pretty, for Johanna Pratt, who did the flowers for the hospital, could work wonders even in a very backward March, and with vases which pretended to be nothing more than two-pound glass jam-jars. To-night the men's tables had primroses, and the staff Iris Reticulata. On the mantelpiece, above a marble Leda, hung a Venetian mirror, which reflected a twin mirror on the far opposite wall. Johanna had produced one of her most effective large-scale efforts here, with a container filled with branches of wych-elm, which had furry buds the colour of raspberries, and chestnut boughs, which had pale-yellow velvet buds with sticky tan sheaths.

Mrs. Hungerford said to Elizabeth, "Good evening, nurse; I hope you had a good time in London," and without waiting for an answer, led the way to the staff table. She looked tired, and shivered as she took her seat. The recess had windows on three sides, which must be delightful in summer, but in March was draughty, in spite of screens. Through the echoing pillared hall outside came a shattering sound, which meant that the food trolley was on the way, propelled by the junior member of the kitchen staff, who reminded Miss Masquerier of Epstein's Rima.

Awful Matron was having her half-day, so her seat of honour next to Mrs. Hungerford was taken by the staff nurse, Sister Finan, who had eyes like striped marbles, but was quite young and decent, and had a husband who was a Dental-Lieutenant in Egypt, and two children, evacuated to America.

In the village this afternoon Johanna had met somebody called Gibson, and all the talk at first was about Diana Mrs. Gibson's wedding. Diana, who had been one of the nurses here, and was coming back later, was going to be married on Tuesday week, and there was to be a sherry-party the day before, instead of a wedding reception, as they would have such a short honeymoon, and, anyway, the reception would have turned into a sherry-party, whatever one tried to do to make it appear otherwise, in these days. Mrs. Gibson wanted everyone possible from Woodside to come, and Diana was going to wear her grandmother's wedding dress, as she wanted to have white, but would obviously never wear the thing again, and the odd thing was that although one had always thought of Diana as quite a sylph, and Grandmother Gibson had eventually been the mother of seven, the dress simply wouldn't look at Diana across the shoulders.

"It's cricket and over-hand service at tennis, I think, Madam," said Sister Finan.

"I'm not sure that the whole female species isn't growing larger," said Johanna, sounding pleased at the idea.

Diana was going to be married in the Lady Chapel at Went Cathedral, provided it was not blitzed before then, and her bridegroom, who was a Lieutenant-Commander in the Navy, had got a carbuncle at the moment, and might have his leave stopped, and couldn't turn up till the night of the sherry-party, but otherwise all the preparations were going swimmingly.

Mrs. Hungerford asked Johanna in her shy, dignified way, "Where did you get the primroses, Sec.? I am so glad to see them here again, and I'm glad you gave them to the men."

"I had a job to find them," Johanna assured her employer. "I had to go right up to Dead Woman's Hill in the end. I tried Cherry-tree Copse first, because last year it was the best place, but I couldn't even see a leaf. It's not going to be a good primrose year, I'm afraid."

"Is this good country for cowslips?" asked Pippa of Miss Masquerier, in the voice of a mouse. Miss Masquerier had been touched by the Dowager's appropriate gift, and had divulged in an access of emotion that during Pippa's absence to-day, and in the intervals of waiting to check the laundry, she had sketched in the whole of Chapter V, but was dissatisfied with her opening paragraph. Naturally, Miss Masquerier could not allow that the neighbourhood of Went was not good country for anything, but on the subject of cowslips she was evidently not an authority. She believed that in Monk's Meadow, above the cathedral, one could sometimes get fine specimens.

"The best place in Barsetshire for cowslips," said Lalage, munching national bread as if it were part of her duty, "is Lower Merle Hangings. There are three fields below the mill there, each better than the last."

"How simply lovely! I shall go there the moment they begin," said Pippa. "About the middle of April, my book says."

"It happens to be private property," said Elizabeth's voice. Mrs. Hungerford looked up, screwing her eyes as if she had a headache and couldn't hear properly, and Pippa, who as youngest present, was assisting Rima to remove the soup plates, nearly dropped the lot over Mrs. Hungerford's shoulder. Elizabeth definitely didn't like her. She saw that now beyond doubt. It was ghastly to be eighteen and not liked. She saw in a flash that it was going to be impossible here, if Elizabeth was going to get after her, even in public. She wouldn't be able to stay at Woodside, which was so enthralling, although awe-inspiring. "Mrs. Hungerford, I'm awfully sorry, but I'm afraid I shall have to ask you if I may leave as soon as you can get somebody else. I'm sorry I've been a failure." Pippa blinked back tears that threatened to fall with plops into the remains of potato soup. The green drawing-room, with its cold marble faces and posed spring flowers, seemed in a moment to have become horrible. Everyone continued heartlessly to talk about Diana Gibson, who was going to marry a Lieutenant-Commander, and live happily ever after.

Only Miss Masquerier cast uneasy glances towards the pillared hall, through which the second course was now *en route* to the feasters.

The second course for supper to-night was not a popular dish. Even Mrs. Hungerford, who generally ate as if she did not notice much, winced when Rima set a steaming tureen of baked beans in tomato on the table. The staff began to consume their portion in dutiful silence. Pippa slipped back to her seat. Suddenly Elizabeth, who had sent away her soup plate half-full, said in a strangled voice, "These beans are simply disgusting," and without waiting for permission, fled from the room.

Mrs. Hungerford looked up, and this time Pippa saw a blue flash in Madam's eyes. Poor Miss Masquerier began to utter voluble apologies. She said that suppers were not easy just now, and that she knew these were not the kind of beans that the men liked, but they had been all that she could get. Sister Finan, whose marble eyes had followed Elizabeth's form with a searchlight glare, said that she would like some people to see the food that she had had to put up with when she was a probationer, and told Madam that her first Matron had allowed the young nurses twenty-five minutes in which to lay, eat and clear away their meals. "We were terrified of her, Madam. When a nurse heard that she was to go up to the office at ten o'clock next morning, she lay awake all night. I have known them to be sick outside Matron's door. Johanna Pratt, who had hitherto refused beans, said, "Nurse Johnson, I'll have some after all," and Lalage murmured, "She's over-tired after London, of course." But with the best will in the world, the atmosphere at the table until Mrs. Hungerford gave the signal to rise, was far from comfortable, and Pippa's heart, already low, sank into her flat-heeled shoes when Mrs. Hungerford said, "Nurse Johnson, I want a word with you."

Pippa was naturally scared to death of Mrs. Hungerford, who had refused the most fascinating man in the world for twenty years, and had regular features and a straight back, and blue eyes that could flash, and gave a general impression of the iron hand in the velvet glove. Pippa stood to attention, and said, "Yes, Madam."

I want you to come with the Secretary and Quartermaster and Matron and myself to Nurse Gibson's wedding-party next week," said Mrs. Hungerford unexpectedly.

I V

Lalage said that she had a vase up in her bedroom which would be just right for Granny Merle's violets, so Pippa went with her along the segmental corridor or colonnade leading to the west pavilion, and asked, looking around her, "What happened to Sir Barnaby Morrison's collection of busts?"

"They were sold," said Lalage, "when the house became a school. Rather a frost, I believe. I've heard that they didn't fetch at all what was hoped."

"How sad," said Pippa. "I'd much rather think of them stored in one of the stable lofts, just waiting to come back in all their glory with Peace."

"I don't know whether Kit is keen on busts of Roman Emperors," said Lalage. "Though, of course, he might have liked to have them because they had always belonged to the house. He has very good taste. Have you ever seen the library? It's along here. Kit had only done up one wing of the house—the one we're coming to now—when the War began."

Pippa said that she would simply love to see the library, if Lalage was sure that Mrs. Hungerford would not mind, and Lalage said that she was almost sure that Mary would not mind, because she had herself shown the whole pavilion to Matron, whose comments had been, "Oh, Madam! Creepy!" and "More like a museum than a home."

Lalage pushed open a baize-covered swing door, and the sounds and smells of the hospital—equally composed at this hour of gramophone, wireless, food-trolley and limping footsteps—died as completely as if one had turned to another station on the wireless. Pippa waited in darkness, which was at once close and chilly, while Lalage searched the walls for a switch.

"I rather wonder," said Lalage's voice, "that Mary doesn't live in this part of the house herself, since it's so completely Kit's. But perhaps that's just the reason."

"Also, I suppose," suggested Pippa, "she wouldn't be so much on the spot as she is, with her office exactly above the recreation-room. It takes ages to find someone in this house, once they get loose. The other day I lost a perfectly strange visiting Medical Officer, and Matron seemed to think that I had invented him."

"But it must be so wretched for Mary, having her only sitting-room the office, and her bedroom opening out of it," said Lalage. "I wonder she doesn't murder us all. I wish I'd brought my torch. Look here, will you take my hand and follow me down four shallow steps to the library door? I know where the key's kept. And it goes in upside down, as it's Georgian."

A moment later, Pippa heard the sound of a key turning in a lock, and a well-hung door swishing open. Lalage snapped on a number of lights, and said, loosing her hand, "This is the library."

Pippa was at once reminded of Fig. II in *Georgian Homes*, because, exactly as in that rather dim photograph, an empty brocade wing chair was drawn up to an unlit fire. A marble Medusa's face stared from the chimney-piece, and another to match frowned above a landscape in oils, framed into the panelling. She cried, pointing at it, "That picture has never left the house!"

"Hasn't it?" asked Lalage, but Pippa did not hear the question. She was silent, because she had received a false fleeting impression that the room was not empty. Someone was sitting with his back to them, in the wing chair. That the impression was false, she discovered immediately, for Lalage laid her hand on the arm of the chair as she picked her way over rolled-up rugs towards the bay windows, and no tall, dark, drowsing man leapt to his feet.

"It's good, isn't it?" said Lalage, busy with strings which swept aside heavy maroon curtains, only to disclose black-out blinds. She twitched up a single central blind, and silver-cold spring daylight mingled with the tawny artificial light which was beaming beneath the pictures and all around the walls. Although the room was aglow, Pippa could not see a single electric light bulb.

The library at Woodside was an octagon, with a gallery attained by an interior spiral staircase, and its walls were almost entirely lined by books, many of which had covers in varying shades of brown with tarnished gold letters on their spines.

"What a perfectly divine library!" sighed Pippa, standing in the centre of it, and twiddling slowly round on her heels. "I've never seen a room I liked better. Do all those books belong to Major Hungerford?"

"Um," nodded Lalage. "Before Mary married him, he explained having taken Woodside, by saying that his books were crushing him out of his London flat. Kit's a great reader."

"That's a darling grandfather clock," said Pippa, advancing to stand beneath it. "It's going, too," she added in some surprise.

Major Hungerford's library clock had a long mahogany case, and a steel face engraved with a picture of an angler. Above the shining moon face was a little piece of gaily painted stage-scenery, continually in motion. The backcloth showed a fortress, flying a scarlet standard, arising amongst tempestuous turquoise billows. With every swing of the pendulum, a courageous little frigate, also flying a scarlet standard, rocked to and fro amongst closer billows, always approaching, but never reaching the fort.

"As a matter of fact," said Lalage, "that clock has always been here. I remember it when I used to come to the Morrisons' children's parties. But it used to stand in the hollow under the staircase in the main hall. I wonder why Mary moved it. She must come down here to wind it, too." Sounding slightly disturbed, Lalage let down the blackout blind and re-drew the curtains, shutting out a view of the temple of Apollo on its mound, backed by wooded Barsetshire heights in March dusk.

"There's another room out of this, in which Kit has got his modern paintings," she said. "But I think we'd better leave it for another day, when we've got more daylight. It used to be the Orangery. I don't really understand modern paintings, do you? At least, although I can see that some of Kit's have lovely colours in them, and they are awfully like flowers and places and people, they look to me rather as if they had been done by kids."

"Is Major Hungerford an artist himself?" asked Pippa.

"He does paint," admitted Lalage, "but in the modern way. I don't understand it. The maddening thing is that he can draw perfectly beautifully, or used to be able to. I don't know if he ever has the time nowadays. When I was a hideous lump in the nursery, and he was a very gay young man about town, not at all approved of by my good aunts, he used to draw for me, for hours—all my favourite dogs and horses—and write me absurd illustrated letters. But as I grew up, I quite lost touch with him."

Lalage kept the library door open while Pippa found the passage light outside, and Pippa, waiting with her finger on a switch, had a last vision of a brown and gold room on which darkness fell swiftly and dramatically, as in a theatre. A well-hung and heavy door swung to gently, a key clicked in a lock, and a moment later they had passed through the baize door and were once more in the segmental corridor. For the first time Pippa found the sound of gramophone and wireless in competition quite cheerful and welcome.

It was as they ascended the stone back staircase to the second floor in the main block that she asked, "Is Woodside haunted?"

"All old houses are said to have spooks," said Lalage. "Why do you ask?"

"I've several times wondered," said Pippa airily.

"As a matter of fact," said Lalage, "it is supposed to be, but I think it's complete bunkum myself, and, anyway, it's no use talking about it. Only give the night staff fits."

"Quite," agreed Pippa hastily.

"This is my room," said Lalage, flinging open its door. "It's not haunted, unless by the ghost of a Morrison footman or a girls' school gym. mistress."

Nothing, indeed, could have been less ghostly than the apartment now occupied by Mrs. Crispin Rollo, and Pippa was interested to see that another bedroom existed in the world quite as unattractive as her own, though in a totally different way.

Mrs. Crispin Rollo's room had not been cut to pieces to provide an adjacent bathroom. It was the same square, unimaginative shape that it had been when it was originally planned for a Georgian domestic servant. It had a grudging view of the roof of the kitchen quarters and courtyard containing the coal sheds and game larder. A noise of washing-up penetrated to the second storey, and from a gurgling drain below arose a cloud of heated steam. The walls had been re-papered in the days of the girls' school with a design of flushed and bulbous purple roses attached to a ginger trellis. The furniture was all enamelled white.

"I've got the vase I told you about in a hat box on the top of the clothes cupboard," panted Lalage, mounting on a chair. "It's Murano glass, and rather lovely, with dolphins with silver spots and bead eyes. Mummy saw it being made."

Pippa would much have preferred to put the Dowager's superbly grown Parma violets, which were in themselves elaborate, in a vase of solemn simplicity, but it was kind of Lalage to offer her the dolphins, and after her two bites from Elizabeth, she was feeling grateful for any kindness. She was not feeling as miserable as she had done at seven-fifteen, because at seven-forty Mrs. Hungerford had invited her to accompany the staff of Woodside to a party in honour of the nuptials of a Lieutenant-Commander. While Lalage fumbled amongst the cardboard boxes on the shelf above the curtain which sheltered six wall pegs and all her outdoor clothes, Pippa's eyes strayed round the room.

She guessed that the coverlet, with its faded pattern of jolly Dutch boys and girls dancing hand in hand, was a personal possession of Mrs. Crispin Rollo, and dated from the nursery days when Major Hungerford entertained a lumpish first cousin with illustrated letters. Some women have the knack of making the most deadly rooms look homelike, others have not. Pippa saw at a glance that Lalage belonged to the second class. Two enlarged snapshots of Girl Guides in camp, framed in *passe-partout*, hung askew on the rose-infested walls. No natural flowers decorated the dressing-table. There was not a single object in the room on which the eye would choose to linger. Pippa revised her judgment, and pulled herself up sharply. On the ugly dressing-table, in a leather and talc travelling frame, stood a clear, large photograph of the handsomest young man she had ever seen—a young naval officer with flat hair and a jutting chin and smiling, steady eyes. It must be Crispin Rollo, Elizabeth's brother, though anything less like Elizabeth could scarcely be imagined. "It's not only that he's so nice-looking," decided Pippa. "He looks so nice too." Never, even amongst the heroes of magazine covers or hoardings advertising pipe tobacco, had she seen a face which conveyed such an impression of good will and vitality.

Lalage had found the object for which she had been searching, and descended from her chair heavily. "Here it is," she said. "Mummy gave it to me after her Mediterranean cruise. I've never used it yet."

The silver speckled glass bowl guarded by gnashing dolphins was all that Pippa had feared.

"Thanks awfully," she said. "I'll take great care of it." She couldn't resist asking shyly, "Is that lovely photograph your husband?"

Her fingers froze on the dolphin vase, as Lalage answered slowly, after a pause, "Yes. That's Crips. I lost him last November, you know. And Elizabeth was engaged to his captain, so she lost him too, in the same action. People say that it's worse to be left a widow, but I'm glad we were married."

V

When Pippa reached her bedroom, she snatched down the black-out and drew the curtains, and tumbling on to her bed, outdoor shoes and all, she had the good cry for which she had been longing, on and off, since seven-fifteen. She cried because she was eighteen and not wanted, and because Awful Matron had made her life a burden from the moment she arrived, and because Elizabeth had twice bitten her to the bone, and because she was an utter failure, and put her foot into everything; but principally because she had hurt the feelings of Lalage, who was a widow at twenty-two.

At Woodside people expected you to know things without being told. She had never had the least idea that Crispin Rollo had been killed in action last year, and that Lalage was a war widow. "And he looked so awfully nice. I expect he was too nice for this horrible world," sniffed Pippa. She remembered with a cold pang having said to Lalage, as they walked through that field with the lambs, "Isn't it thrilling to see another year beginning?" She remembered that Lalage, who was rather cowardly about people, as yet, was thinking of taking up social work after the War.

"I'm awful. I'm hopeless. This is what Auntie Prue calls getting up against realities, I suppose," thought Pippa, as she sniffed herself to sleep.

When she woke, with a headache, her watch said ten-thirty, so she got up and undressed, and put her wet ball of a handkerchief in the dirty basket, and took a clean one, before slipping back to bed again. Because, however miserable you are feeling, if you have got to be on your legs for nine hours in a hospital ward to-morrow, and spend the night in your outdoor shoes and stays, to-morrow you will certainly be even more miserable.

CHAPTER IV
"VALUABLE SOCIAL CONTACTS"
(March 30th, April 11th, April 19th)

I

THE MORNING of the Gibsons' sherry-party promised well. There was tinselly sunshine amongst budding trees in the park, and mist in the valley, and at breakfast-time the skies were blue, and the staff table had bowls of starry little blue flowers with white hearts, called "Glory of the Snow." While the nurses took their eleven o'clock snack, dramatic clouds and showers shadowed the landscape, and Johanna Pratt, who was reading aloud everybody's horoscope from an illustrated daily paper, told Matron that her fortune for the day was, "The strain of recent events is beginning to tell on you. Snatch a few minutes' pleasure to-day," and Pippa's was, "Valuable social contacts made this evening. Good company. Perhaps a thrill." Johanna added that as she was driving them to the party, perhaps it would be kindest not to tell them her fortune, but Lalage took the paper from her and announced, "Go slow. You have been asking for trouble for some time."

By patients' dinner-hour the view from the staircase windows was of riding boughs; and a lion of a wind was whisking doors open and slamming cupboards, and every window on the garden front was grumbling. Johanna came back in triumph, in the utility van, having picked up two wet-through patients on crutches, whom she had discovered without greatcoats, straying as far afield as Westbury Green.

By tea-time the wind had dropped, and heavy rain had set in. There never was a wetter afternoon. It seemed madness to be setting off for a party of pleasure nine miles distant. However, punctually at five-fifteen, Johanna, looking like an advertisement for waterproofs, in black oilskins, with her fair curls flying, brought round the utility van, and the company gathered in tile hall began to embark, under the shelter of a large green umbrella gallantly carried to and fro by dashing Corporal Gloucester, who had been a footman. Mrs. Hungerford, with some colour in her cheeks, and managing to look slight, even when wearing a uniform mackintosh over a uniform greatcoat, took an outside seat beside the driver. Miss Masquerier and Pippa followed Matron into the interior of the van, and after them came four patients with week-end passes, who were being taken to Went Junction, and three who were going to the Dental Centre. The most violent downpour yet, took place as they swept through the park gates, and Matron, who had stepped into a puddle outside the front door, asked Miss Masquerier if this was usual spring weather for Barsetshire. There certainly were spring signs all around. The leaves of daffodils and hyacinths were springing out of the mound of Apollo, and in front beds in cottage gardens there were brilliant edgings of crocuses and grape hyacinths. On some sun-visited walls in Lower Merle, fruit blossom was showing shielded colour, and forsythia and flowering currant were brilliant. But what was the use of spring signs, thought Pippa, when enough rain to float an ark was shuddering down from lowering skies, and along the sides of the roads, rivulets topped by foam, were hastening towards the river? The van, tightly packed, performed a first-class skid at the Royal Oak cross-roads, where the Went 'bus was discharging passengers whose one idea was to get into shelter, and even Miss Masquerier commented that Secretary was a fast driver, as they bounded up Dead Woman's Hill, and began to slither down it towards the long grey walls of Went Park. In the valley, bunches of sap-green mistletoe were hanging in crooked old apple-trees, in orchards which had once been tended by the monks of St. Mary's, and a consciously picturesque glimpse of the cathedral spire could be seen between tasselled alders, inclining above waters which were blurred as a wet mirror.

Matron said, "I shouldn't wonder if a great many people were put off by the weather," but Miss Masquerier said firmly, "Not people who live in Went. It'll be a crush."

Six o'clock was just sounding from the cathedral when the van, relieved of its seven Forces passengers, turned in at a green gate labelled "The Wilderness." The Wilderness bore the date 1907 above its front door, and had plenty of red brick gables and cheerful-looking white-painted woodwork, and was close to the golf course. Its lounge hall was already full of wet outer garments, and from a room on the left came a noise suggestive of a monkey-house. While the party from Woodside waited for their driver, Miss Masquerier told Mrs. Gibson's stately silver-haired servitor that the member of Mrs. Hungerford's staff whom he did not know was Miss Johnson, and explained to Pippa in an undertone that Glover was really one of the vergers from the cathedral. Before the war he had always come in to wait when anyone gave a dinner-party, and it was very convenient that he never had to ask anybody's name, but he was getting rather wobbly nowadays, and disliked being caught out by a strange face. Mrs. Hungerford asked Glover how his mother was, and Pippa was staggered to think that somebody so wobbly could have a mother alive, and further staggered to hear that she was getting on nicely with her new glasses, thank you, madam.

At last Glover, who had hitherto spoken in a voice suited to the south transept, took charge of the Woodside contingent, and announced in the tones of a toastmaster at a City banquet Mrs.

Hungerford, Miss Finch, Miss Rosanna Masquerier, Miss Pratt and Miss Johnson. It sounded a monstrous regiment of women, and for a second Pippa quite regretted having dropped the three patients with Dental cards.

The bride and her mother were standing together in a prominent position in the centre of the room, backed by a vista of buffet table loaded with trays of little glasses, many of which were already filled with liquid in jewel shades of golden-brown. There was a towering wedding-cake, enclosed in silver cardboard, in the centre of the table, and through the windows behind the hostesses could be seen torrents of rain, descending like a curtain upon a painstaking rock-garden and shrubbery and gravel sweep. Pippa would have recognized Mrs. Gibson anyway, because at breakfast this morning Johanna had said that Diana's mother was so like a statue of a goddess in the basement of a museum, that one always felt surprised that she hadn't a head or an arm missing. "Actually," added honest Johanna, as all knowledgeable people present laughed, "it was Madam herself said that first." Diana Gibson was the girl with pretty hair, wearing a ruffled fur jacket and bootees, and eating rock cakes, whom Pippa had met in the Went express on her journey a month ago. She recognized Pippa too, which did her great credit, considering the occasion, and said, "Hallo! I wondered afterwards if you were the one who was coming to be me at Woodside. See you later!" and turning to her other parent, "Daddy, this is my understudy."

Mr. Gibson, who had an iron-grey moustache, and was tall and soldierly, as he had every right to be, since he had retired from the Barsetshire Yeomanry in 1919 with the rank of Temporary Major, was evidently thoroughly enjoying his party. He was far from being the host of fiction, slinking about like a whipped hound while a hundred and fifty wassailers invaded his home. The Gibsons had been solicitors in Went for four generations. Indeed, Godfrey Gibson, the first, had been seated in an outer chamber of Went Park with the eccentric Lord Merle, trying to persuade his lordship that a new invention called the submarine combustible machine was not a practical proposition, when the news of Waterloo had been brought in by a still-room maid in hysterics, who had seen the London mail arrive at the County Hotel, decorated with green boughs. What Godfrey Gibson, the fourth, did not know about his guests to-day was not worth knowing. He loved people, and he loved parties, and parties, very properly, took place very seldom nowadays. He was sorry, to be sure, to be losing at a single blow, his eldest child and the last of his old brown sherry, especially as his acquaintance with his future son-in-law was limited to ten minutes in the black-out outside the Went Odeon, eighteen months ago. Had he known that the Lieutenant-Commander was going to become his Diana's teeshy little Nicky, he would have taken more trouble to notice the young man. However, he put great faith in the judgments of his wife and Diana, and as far as losing Diana went, he was sceptical. Since 1939 he had too often arrived at a country house to which he had dispatched a wedding present, it seemed only a week before, to find the daughter of the house not only re-established in her old nest, but knitting ominously shaped garments in white wool, or even keeping dragon-like guard over a contraption called the crawling-pen. Since he was devoted to Diana and a long-sighted man, he was quite resigned to losing her at twenty, and letting her, if she wished, return at twenty-one, to leave jugs of milk, covered by butter muslin weighed down by coloured beads, at odd corners on his landings. Already, the look of anxiety which pinched her features on mornings when the post didn't bring a letter, or the early news had said something about a naval action, had wrung his heart. But he was by training and profession accustomed to think dynastically; he loved seeing his acquaintance in all their oddity, and really to-day nobody in the neighbourhood seemed likely to disappoint him.

Diana's father hoped that Mrs. Hungerford had good news of his old friend Kit, for whom he cherished a deep admiration, and Mrs. Hungerford said with a fleeting smile, "Yes, good, thanks," which made Pippa remember that no news is good news. But Pippa had no time to ponder the matter further, for Miss Masquerier had introduced her to Mrs. Albany Mimms, who said plaintively that she couldn't see why they called it the Home Guard, when it took one's husband out most nights, and Colonel Mimms introduced her to Lady Wilson, who told Captain Cox that she would have a glass of sherry and a dry biscuit, and Miss Johnson wanted lemonade and wedding cake.

Captain Cox didn't look to Pippa young. He must be at least twenty-five. He had very light blue eyes, set in a sun-burnt face, and a short Roman nose, and fair hair, like lamb's wool, curling all over his head. He had been in Australia when the War broke out, and asked Pippa if the Rollos were still at Crossgrove. Pippa had never heard of Crossgrove, but she told him that Lalage and Elizabeth Rollo were nurses at Mrs. Hungerford's hospital, and he seemed satisfied. He seemed to know a good many of the people at this party, although he said he had only arrived in Barsetshire two days ago.

Pippa saw Mrs. Taylor in the distance, and old Dr. Greatbatch, whom she knew, because he came to Woodside professionally nearly every day, but nobody else whom she had ever seen in her life before, which seemed extraordinary, since the room was now filled to bursting-point, and outside more and more wet cars were momentarily discharging fresh characters. She was sipping rather sour lemonade very slowly, and trying to look as if she was enjoying herself, when the crowd disgorged the welcome figure of Mrs. Bates.

"Bless my soul," said Mrs. Bates, in high spirits, "what a menagerie! I haven't seen anything like it since poor Lalage Merle got married. That's why Mary's brought you today, instead of Lalage or Elizabeth, who really know Diana, I suppose—altogether too like, with the bridegroom in the Navy too. I hope he turns up safe and sound. I hear there's a possibility his leave may be stopped. Diana says that if he comes she's going to turn on the radiogram and have dancing, though where you're to dance I can't imagine. Was that young man I saw you talking to called Cox? Imphm! I thought so, though I haven't seen him since 1939. He used to come down and stay with the Wilsons, and at one time we all thought he was going to marry Elizabeth Rollo. But her father got him a job as an A.D.C. somewhere abroad. Imphm! There may have been nothing in it. Now tell me, whom have you met?"

Pippa told her, and said, "Please tell me something more about them, and who some of the other people here are?" and Mrs. Bates began in far from hushed accents: "Well, the Albany Mimms live at that white house right on the bad corner half-way up Dead Woman's Hill. Their handy-man was knocked over and killed in the summer before the War, just outside their front door. I know I ought to dismount from my bicycle when I reach that bend, for I've seen five people removed by ambulance from the spot, and only one drunk and incapable. They have two children, evacuated to America, and Colonel Mimms is the big noise in our Home Guard. Just one moment. You must see Lady Norah Blent. That's her, in the black satin and pierrot cap with white wool bobbles, and red hair. She used to design fabrics for a very modern house-decorator's firm in Bayswater, but now she's Salvage Queen for the Went Rural District. That's why she's arrived in a van full of bins labelled "Bones." Sir James Wilson—that's him, with the eye-glasses on a moire ribbon—and a stoop—in a grey suit—was once our Ambassador to several foreign potentates. Lady Wilson had her sable muff destroyed by a bomb meant for an Archduke. But it all happened so long ago that nobody alive can bear witness. He's nearer ninety than eighty now, and they are still living in that damp house down by the mill, with one Austrian maid. Ah! there's Norah Hill and her husband, and Rosemary Wright. They're longing to meet you, I know. I've told them all about you."

Pippa was a little taken aback to find that Norah Hill and her husband were called MacDougall, and that Rosemary Wright was Mrs. Morrison. Norah Hill's husband, who had a beard, turned out to be a Glasgow surgeon on leave from a naval hospital, and Norah, who was very plain but had a happy expression, said that she hoped Pippa hadn't been bitten by Otto the other day. "My elderly dachshund. I saw him chasing you, when you took the short cut through our garden, after having been to tea with Sally. I hope you'll come to tea with me one day, and see my small daughter, of whom Otto is shockingly jealous."

Mrs. Rosemary Morrison was entirely obsessed by her own cares. She had just received a telegram from darling old Dame Sarah Lys, announcing that she wanted to come and stay in the real English countryside, at Willows, for three weeks, until she moved into her new London flat.

"How absolutely thrilling!" exclaimed Pippa. "I've never seen Dame Sarah act, but she's simply marvellous, isn't she?"

"Then you ought to take the first opportunity," said Rosemary impatiently. "The trouble is that I know darling old Dame Sarah. She's quite likely not to have even looked at a flat in London yet. And though I'm simply delighted to have her, and it's the greatest honour (as I really don't know her well, as I was only a beginner when I retired to marry), I simply don't know what I'm to do with her for three weeks in Westbury-on-the-Green. I mean, who on earth can one ask to meet her down here? And if she gets bored, she has her heart attacks. And of course one has no petrol."

"You might ask Sir James and Lady Wilson to luncheon," suggested Pippa. "I should think Dame Sarah would get on terribly well with a retired Ambassador in a country drawing-room."

At this moment, "young" Lady Merle made her entry, closely followed by six officers in Air Force uniform, who Mrs. Bates said came from Went aerodrome. Glover stingily announced the lot as Flight-Lieutenant Young, although even Pippa could see that the leading figure was a Wing-Commander. The Wing-Commander shook hands heartily with Mrs. Gibson, and introduced his wife (whom Pippa had childishly imagined to be his mother) and his stepdaughter, Mrs. Harris, who was wearing khaki, but managed to look lovely, nevertheless, as she had a rose-leaf complexion, and like Tennyson's Maud, a little head sunning over with curls, though beneath a jaunty forage cap. Pippa, who since witnessing *Target for To-night*, had nourished the warmest feelings for all airmen (and particularly since last Tuesday, when Night Sister had read aloud from the newspaper a bit about one of our fighter-aces -whom even the Boche reverenced, as he invariably zoomed into action with, a cigarette stuck between his lips at a rakish angle) studied the officers from Went aerodrome closely. Two of them were quite old, one was middle-aged, and three were quite young. The middle-aged one terrified her, as he was of substantial figure, with scarred features, and an eye-glass, and was, said Mrs. Bates, quite famous. Of the younger three, one was rightly nicknamed "Jumbo," as he was thickset and had twinkling little eyes, another was tall and lanky, and looked as if he had only left school last term, and the third had a good-humoured, freckled face and noticeably long hands, and was, said Mrs. Bates, Flight-Lieutenant Derek Young, and a bomber pilot.

Pippa could not hear anything they were saying, but she could hear Diana, who evidently knew them well, as she called them "Jumbo" and "Tiger" and "Derek." Pippa, pressed tight between Miss Masquerier and Mrs. Bates and Mrs. Rosemary Morrison (who was still moaning about the advent of Dame Sarah Lys) could not help wishing that she could make a move, and talk to Johanna, who also evidently knew the officers from Went aerodrome quite well. She felt proprietory pride as she noticed that Johanna, even after the advent of Mrs. Harris, was quite the belle of this party. Johanna, standing with her hands deep in her overcoat pockets, with her flaxen curls and saucer eyes looking angelic, was saying slow things which made everybody laugh. She was twenty-six, Pippa knew, and the daughter of a newspaper baron, and had gone with an ambulance to Finland, quite at the beginning of the War, as she didn't get on with her people, and had a marvellous escape through Sweden, and broken her leg in the black-out outside Victoria Station a few days after her return. So she had a shortened left leg for life, but didn't care, although she had been Wimbledon class at tennis.

A shade of melancholy began to steal over Pippa as the merriment in the drawing-room at The Wilderness swelled to fever-point, and more and more shrouded cars discharged yelping passengers, and the rain continued to pour down outside. She felt that she was a person in a Russian novel, as the new arrivals increased in oddity, and the sombre rain and hectic gaiety also increased. A very untidy old gentle-man, in a sky-blue knitted tie and an amazing collar, drifted in, looking like Lob from *Dear Brutus*. He was, said Mrs. Bates, the Keeper of the Went Museum, and Diana's god-father, and he seemed awfully surprised to find a party going on. A perfectly square lady in khaki was announced as Lady Muriel Gidding, and a Mrs. Yarrow, who looked nice enough to be a best friend of Mrs. Hungerford, as she evidently was, had brought a niece with plucked eyebrows and a very supercilious nephew, who was a staff officer, and said "No! Really! Really!" in a high head voice.

Pippa saw "young" Lady Merle button-holing Mrs. Hungerford, and thought again what a very unexpected mother for Lalage "young" Lady Merle was. . . .

The group around Pippa melted away, and Flight-Lieutenant Young suddenly stood in front of her, and was offering her a cocktail, which she was just going to refuse, when a disturbance occurred and everybody's attention was arrested. The two fleetest station taxis—indeed the only two fleet station taxis—had swept hissing into a drive considerably encumbered by parked cars. The first taxi contained the bridegroom, the Lieutenant-Commander and all his wedding presents, and many personal effects, which, as he was an orphan, he was trusting to leave under his father-in-law's hospitable roof for the duration. The second taxi contained his best man, who was not the best man everyone had expected, but Nicholas's own younger brother, who was in the Fleet Air Arm, but could not possibly get here for the wedding. The brothers met on the doorstep, and exchanged cryptic though brief explanations. Pippa watched like a spectator at the play, as Diana skimmed to the hall, and reappeared after a short interval, much enhanced in beauty, heralding her Nicky, whose true name appeared to be plain John. The Lieutenant-Commander was even older than Captain Cox. Pippa charitably guessed his age as thirty-two, and was glad to think that he was going to settle happily. He had quite black hair still, and though very pale and tired-looking about the eyes, showed no signs of the promised carbuncle. And he was clearly a dauntless fellow, for he displayed not the slightest alarm at being introduced into a heated assembly of one hundred and fifty strangers gathered to celebrate his nuptials.

His younger brother, who was much taller, and had even darker hair, as shiny as patent leather, was Pippa's first partner in the dancing that followed almost immediately. She fell over his feet and couldn't hear the music, and when she had explained that she had never really met Diana until to-day, and had only been in Barsetshire a little over a month, so didn't know many people here, she couldn't think of anything to say. She wished wistfully that she was Johanna Pratt, who, in spite of being twenty-six and having a permanently shortened left leg, was dancing like a leaf with Flight-Lieutenant Derek Young.

II

The sage who had forecast that persons born under the sign of Neptune would make valuable social contacts on the evening of March 30th, was correct so far as Pippa was concerned. Lady Wilson, whose husband owned the three fields below Lower Merle Mill, said by Lalage to be the best in Barsetshire for cowslips, had told Pippa to telephone and invite herself to morning service at Lower Merle Church, followed by lunch, any Sunday. As Pippa's off-duty hours were invariably ten a.m. to one, one-thirty to four-thirty or five to eight, and her half-days began after the midday meal, she could not see how she was ever to combine church and lunch. However, she accepted gratefully, by letter for church only, for Sunday, April 19th, explaining her situation, and asking if she might pick some cowslips on her way to the house. She would have liked to take Radish cowslipping, but Lalage had instructed her that one of the first unwritten rules of country life was never to take a pack of your own dogs to a strange house, where the hostess may possess jealous bloodhounds or be a dog-loather; and after several expeditions in his company, Pippa realized that the Dowager Lady Merle's personal dog was rather an overpowering character.

Dr. Hovenden, of the Went Museum, who had been told by Miss Masquerier (not quite correctly) that Miss Johnson was a niece of Professor Abbadie Beadon, had been delighted to learn from Pippa at the sherry-party that the Professor was now employed at a Government Control somewhere in Barsetshire.

He had desired her to write to her uncle and ask him if he could possibly see his way to addressing the Went Historical and Architectural Society, on any Friday evening in May or June at six p.m., choosing his own subject. Pippa, who did not know the name of Professor Beadon's new habitation, sent him a letter care of Auntie Prue, and Auntie Prue replied that Abbadie had rather typically gone off without leaving her any address. She had forwarded Pippa's letter to his college at Cambridge.

The remainder of Auntie Prue's news concerned the vagaries of Cousin May's Free French cook. Mathilde, it seemed, was all that the most exacting employer could wish for, so far as the culinary art was concerned, and unbelievably economical. She enjoyed taking her basket to the shops and doing her own marketing. As she would in any case have been obliged to do this, it was highly satisfactory. The trouble was that she possessed marked artistic temperament, and when suffering from what Auntie Prue unimaginatively described as the dumps, she immured herself in her own bedroom and refused to cook, or even appear. This did not matter greatly when one could foresee an attack of the dumps, but the other night Cousin May and Auntie Prue had returned to Lawrence Avenue after witnessing *Blood and Sand* at the cinema, to find themselves locked out of their own house. The casting of gravel from the drive at Mathilde's bedroom window had evoked a dishevelled head, which had announced in dramatic French that it was tired of life and was not coming down. Auntie Prue had eventually effected a burglarious entry by means of the scullery window, a feat which had entailed stepping into the sink, which Mathilde, in an access of Gallic despair, had left half-full of hot, greasy water, cutlery and tea-leaves.

Professor Abbadie Beadon's Cambridge college forwarded his correspondence to the zone where he was doing full-time war work, with the utmost dispatch. Within three days of Auntie Prue's taking action, Pippa received a beautifully written note from her learned friend, so neat as to margins that one felt he must use a ruler. The Professor replied guardedly that he would be writing to Hovenden. He had been glad to hear that Philippa-Dawn was still at Woodside, as he would much like to come over to see the plaster-work of the main staircase. Would twelve o'clock next Saturday suit her commanding officer?

This short and slightly cold-hearted communication threw Philippa-Dawn into a fever of apprehension. It meant, in the first place, that she must go at ten a.m. to Mrs. Hungerford's office, where Mrs. Hungerford sat, with tortoiseshell-rimmed spectacles on the tip of her short nose, adding names in block capitals to the columns of an immensely wide-sheeted volume, reminiscent of that kept by the recording angel at the gates of Paradise. At the typewriter, in the bay window, sat the invaluable Pratt, looking incredibly efficient. It must be marvellous, thought Pippa, to be Mrs. Hungerford, and simply sit in an office and issue orders to a perfectly organized staff, and never be in a hurry, or hot and bothered, or in the least doubt as to what to do next.

Pippa explained breathlessly that an old friend, who was not exactly a relation, but was doing full-time war work somewhere in Barsetshire at a place called Nettlerash Court, much wanted to see the main staircase at Woodside. Mrs. Hungerford said, rather shortly, that Nettlerash was the other side of the county, and asked the name of Pippa's friend. On hearing this, her manner quite changed. Major Hungerford, it appeared, particularly wanted Professor Abbadie Beadon's opinion as to the authorship of the plaster-work of his main staircase walls, and had actually been in touch with him on the subject when Hitler had invaded Poland. Mrs. Hungerford asked when the Professor could come, and Pippa answered, "He says about twelve on Saturday. He must mean twelve noon, I suppose." Knowing the Professor's habits, she sounded doubtful. Mrs. Hungerford then thanked Pippa, asked the invaluable Pratt to send a line to Professor Beadon at Nettlerash Court, asking him to luncheon on Saturday next, and the interview ended with Pippa's exit and the miserable entry of Privates Howard and Kennet, summoned to explain their arrival at Woodside three hours after lights-out last night.

On Saturday Pippa was on duty from ten to one, and nine new patients were admitted at midday. She managed, nevertheless, to obtain a good bird's-eye view of the arrival of Professor Beadon. She had written to him, telling him that she was no longer known as Philippa-Dawn, and only hoped that he would note this. She also hoped that he would not lower their joint prestige at Woodside Auxiliary Hospital by appearing more than usually unshaven, but did not see how she could even drop a hint to this effect. To her impotent rage, she perceived at once that all her worst fears were to be realized. At five minutes to twelve the front door bell rang violently, and a familiar deep voice was heard inquiring if this was Mrs. Hungerford's house. A small figure, perilously inclining over balustrading composed of S-shaped bar iron with crinkled leaf ornaments, saw a tall figure wavering on the threshold. Professor Abbadie Beadon had arrived by bicycle. As she dressed that morning, Pippa had congratulated herself that, at any rate, Auntie Prue had sent that kid's gas-mask carrier and check tie to the jumble sale. Professor Beadon was looking quite his worst, hatless, with his wild dark locks in great disorder, clad in a roomy and well-worn waterproof. His tie was a peculiar salmon pink, made of stuff, and far from fresh, and he had managed, by some sinister means, to obtain another kid's gas-mask carrier, exactly like the last, except that it was adorned with a humiliating likeness of the Giant Pandar. To crown all, on a Saturday, when the head cook was never very approachable, and nine new patients had been decanted at noon, he had brought a friend. Pippa heard him introducing to Awful Matron "My colleague at the Ministry," name inaudible.

The guests were escorted upstairs, and as they viewed walls decorated with fine plaster-work representing branches of fruiting grape-vine, inhabited by birds and squirrels and admired by seated hounds, Pippa heard "My Colleague" say in very throaty tones, "Definitely Artari," to which the Professor replied chillingly, "Or Bagutti."

Pippa slipped back to her seat on the first-floor landing, and returned to her task of rolling bandages, with a bursting heart.

Mrs. Hungerford did not appear for staff dinner at twelve-forty-five, but since Fate was not utterly unkind, Miss Masquerier, who usually went home on Saturday mornings and did not return until Monday, had been detained by the entry of the nine new patients, and she told the assembled company at the staff table that Nurse Johnson's uncle had a European reputation, which surprised nobody more than Pippa.

At one-thirty Awful Matron told Nurse Johnson to go to the office, and Pippa entered the dreaded apartment, to find Mrs. Hungerford seated at ease in a wing chair, drinking in the words of Professor Abbadie Beadon, who was draped against the river-god mantelpiece, quite at home, or at any rate, as much at home as someone so loose-limbed and utterly unhomely could ever be. "My Colleague" was engaged on his knees in the window-bow, with Johanna Pratt, who was busily dusting the frames of several large modern oil-paintings, and saying in clarion tones, "Give me Landseer."

Professor Beadon greeted his young friend quite genially, saying, "Ha! Pippa!" which showed that he had digested her letter, but he immediately returned without apology to the subject of Major Hungerford's Chinese-Chippendale style ceilings, and regretted, with literal tearings of his locks, that he had not his lantern slides of the plaster work at Royal Fort down here. "I wish I could have compared them. . . . I wish that I could have seen Major Hungerford."

Mrs. Hungerford said with feeling, and without the least trace of huffiness, that she too wished so, and "My Colleague," who was much better covered than the Professor, and decidedly London-y in attire, looked deeply interested when his hostess suggested a move towards the dining-room. The Professor, after evidently repeating a statement that he had enjoyed some sandwiches provided by his landlady on his road here, was delivered to Pippa for a tour of the gardens, with special reference to the Temple of Apollo.

Pippa led him instantly to the Quartermaster's store, and as she pattered by his side, reminded him urgently that Miss Masquerier was the author of *Polish Rose* and other masterpieces. She added with conscious guile that Miss Masquerier had told them all at dinner—even Matron—that he had a European reputation. Professor Beadon, wrapped in his own dark thoughts, or proof against female flattery, merely uttered another characteristic "Ha!" But in the interview which followed, he certainly showed himself to advantage.

Miss Masquerier was discovered engaged in the pleasantly womanly task of delivering red, white and blue hospital uniforms to the new patients, after their inspection by Dr. Greatbatch. Pippa thought that her idol looked decidedly like a medieval saint or princess clothing the poor, and hoped that her learned friend was receiving the same impression. As soon as the patients had shambled away, the Professor inquired in the most jocund manner how Miss Masquerier was getting on nowadays, with all her original authorities full fathom five, and whether one might hope for a sequel to her biography of Marie-Louise as Empress, in these days. Miss Masquerier, who had written this in 1938, took no umbrage, and divulged with a sprightly air that all she had on the stocks at the moment was a treatise on local Went Marian martyrs. It was sweet music to Pippa's ears to hear her authors discoursing so comradely in the jargon of their craft, and she almost wished that she could leave them to inspect the romantic Temple of Apollo without her disturbing presence. But she was afraid that this might look too marked, and, to her chagrin, just as they were preparing to leave the store, one of the new patients reappeared, explaining in dumb-show, as he was Polish, that he needed a longer pair of trousers.

Professor Beadon was so pleased with the Temple of Apollo that he did not appear to notice when Miss Masquerier rejoined them, but Pippa saw to it that the authoress stayed with them until the moment came for his departure. This took place, in the end, in rather a rush, as the Professor glanced at his watch, said in horrified tones, "Four o'clock already!" and started in the wrong direction with giant strides to reclaim "My Colleague" from the Orangery. He said that "our good landlady," evidently a strong character, got quite upset if they failed to be punctual for their supper, or forgot to say that they would be out for the meal, when she happened to have prepared their weekly joint. It was very inconvenient, said the Professor wistfully, but one understood that catering difficulties must be considered, in these days.

As they waited for "My Colleague" in the hall, the Professor mentioned, "I did not catch the name of the young lady who kindly fetched Major Hungerford's Renoir from the basement to show to my colleague."

"What was she like? What was she wearing?" asked Pippa.

"A Botticelli, attired in blue serge," said "My Colleague," making his appearance at this moment.

"Oh, that's the secretary, Johanna Pratt," said Pippa. Anxious to give the best possible impression of the social amenities of Woodside, she added, "Her father's Lord Billingsgate."

This information produced the most disappointing results, for Professor Beadon groaned aloud, and "My Colleague" said silkily, "Poor young lady! What a fate!"

"But she doesn't get on with her people, and went to Finland with an ambulance, and has a permanently shortened left leg for life," said Pippa, telescoping Johanna's career in hot haste, as "My Colleague" mounted his velocipede unhandily.

She watched the experts until they were safely past the lorry which was collecting the sweepings from the ditches in the lane outside the lodge. There was plenty of debris, as the hedges had been cut and laid last week.

III

Mrs. Hungerford had heard from Major Hungerford, and he was in Stockholm, and had been in Moscow, and was probably going back to Moscow. Diana Gibson had returned to her duties at Woodside, with her new surname, by which nobody could ever remember to address her, and two two-pound boxes of chocolates and the remains of her wedding-cake. For several days past, the weather had been balmy. The wistaria on the garden-front was showing colour, and the long border was bright with polyanthus and forget-me-nots. The staff table had poet's narcissus, and the men's tables daffodils, from the mount of Apollo. Outside Mrs. Hungerford's office, a bowl of hyacinths scented the whole landing. Decidedly things were looking up.

On Sunday, April 19th, Pippa went cowslipping in Lower Merle hangings, taking Radish. By a stroke of luck, Lady Wilson had replied that she and her husband must be absent from home that week-end—their first absence for eighteen months. They were going to stay with Sir James's brother, in the Cotswolds. He had been rather ill throughout the winter, and needed cheering up. She hoped that Miss Johnson would come to lunch the next Sunday, and meanwhile advised her that the meadow nearest the Mill House promised to provide the best cowslips this year.

Pippa, whose off-time had been altered, and was now one-thirty to four-thirty, borrowed Sister Finan's bicycle, picked up Radish at the Dower House at two-fifteen, and by two-forty-five was pedalling rapidly in the direction of the hangings. The morning had been lovely, but the afternoon was turning out most peculiar. The sun had disappeared, and a pea-green haze enveloped the landscape, making it look like country in a dream. She thought the mysterious effect suited the neighbourhood of the Mill House, which was rich in lush grass and olive-green waters, and approached by two steep lanes and a notice saying, "Deep Ford." A fine tithe barn somewhat dominated the low-browed house. Pippa hoped that the Wilsons were not going to bring Sir James's brother there for a return visit yet awhile, for she thought that the picturesque dwelling breathed the word rheumatics. There was not a soul to be seen as she parked her bicycle by a stile and, scrambling over, found herself in a field with a path leading to a plantation around which hidden waters tinkled.

There were primroses and violets in the banks, under hedges snowy with blackthorn, and already she saw signs of cowslips, and as she stepped into the wood she heard the cuckoo. Lalage had said that she would not hear him down here before April 14th. His call was far away, and not on so high and thrilling a note as Pippa had expected, but she stopped to listen, and called up Radish and told him to listen too. The wood was lovely, though decidedly unkempt and very wet underfoot. She found a few exaggeratedly tall cowslips amongst long grass, in shade, and delicate pale-mauve lady's smocks abounded, but she judged them too fragile to survive a journey in a bicycle basket. The path through the wood ended in an invitation to cross a swelling stream by means of a decaying fallen tree-trunk with a hole in the middle, supplied with a broken handrail. This gave access to the hangings, and through the trees could be seen daubs of yellow, shining like patches of sunlight.

Pippa pulled herself together, and began to work her way slowly across the fallen tree-trunk, eschewing the handrail, which had collapsed to knee height, and Radish, quite abominably, dashed past her, and then, to give her confidence, back again. The drop into the stream below was not more than three feet, and its banks were beautifully decorated with tufts of primroses, but she did not want to arrive at the Dower House making squelching noises, wet to the waist, and clothed to the knees in Barsetshire mud. As soon as possible she caught hold of the boughs of a friendly osier, and a moment later she was across, and in the first cowslip meadow.

Radish celebrated their safe arrival by going berserk, and rushing away from her. He ran away as a mad dog and returned as a Derby winner, in figures of eight, barking foolishly, with his ears laid back. She stopped for a moment before she began to pick and, shading her eyes with her hand, took a careful note of the scene—the three undulating fields alight with sweet-smelling spring flowers, sloping towards the distant white house; the tithe barn, with a cherry in full flower effectively posed against its grey walls, and the happy white dog scampering aimlessly with the spring in his blood.

She enjoyed the next half-hour as much as any since she had left Lawrence Avenue in a snowstorm, and had a feeling that she would remember it all her life. She soon had so many cowslips that she had to return to the fallen tree-trunk and leave a bunch there before setting to work again. It was still pick-and-choose work, for there were more buds than flowers as yet, and her back began to give out before her spirit, but this was all for the best, as retracing her steps towards her bicycle was bound to be a tedious business. She was triumphant, but limb-weary, as she gathered her spoil. Her only regret was that she had not brought some wool, with which to secure her bunches. Several fine specimens plopped into the brook as she essayed the fallen tree-trunk again. They floated downstream looking like poor Ophelia, but the tree-trunk was less deadly to return by, as it sloped uphill into the wood.

The cowslips looked radiant, even in the unromantic wicker basket on her handlebars, and Radish behaved much better on the homeward journey, and only once nearly over-set her by galloping ahead at a corner. It was when she was almost home again, on the road alongside the park wall of the Dower House, that he disgraced himself. For no apparent reason, and without a sound, he suddenly deserted. He plunged over a gate, bucketed down a lane leading to some farm buildings, and was no more to be seen. Pippa dismounted and whistled, and said, "Drat the animal!" He had played this trick on her before, but never when she had been encumbered with the bicycle, and generally in answer to leers from a cottage cat. "Now he's going to make me late," muttered Pippa. She did not at all fancy turning up at the Dower House to tell the Dowager's very up-stage Scottish lady's maid that she had mislaid the Dowager's personal dog; but her watch told her that this looked like being her fate if she was to report on duty at four-thirty.

She called out, "I can see you, you silly animal!" which was an incantation that sometimes produced a conscience-stricken white form. Presently there was nothing for it but to prop the bicycle against the gate, and follow on foot. The gate was high, padlocked and wreathed with rusty barbed wire, and as she let herself down on the farther side, she heard the sound of rending cotton. In spite of all her care, she had caught her skirt, and right in the middle of the back, where a darn would show even when she was wearing an apron. Moreover, the gate had been mossy, and her palms were now bright green. When her renewed whistling brought to her side an innocently simpering bull-terrier, she fell upon him and spanked him with all her might and main. She was not a good dog-beater, as she had explained to the

Dowager's disapproving maid, who never delivered the personal dog to her care without mentioning that he was not allowed to hunt, and that Lady Merle would never forgive her if anything happened to him. Besides, Radish was tightly packed with good fare. Pippa suspected that her efforts indeed hurt her more than they hurt him. However, she was exasperated, and for everyone's sake this escaping must be stopped.

Her palms were stinging, her ears were singing, and her face was already hot, when a strange voice very close to her said hesitantly, "Do you want to beat my dog?" and looking up, she saw a surprised-looking young man in Air Force uniform.

IV

Derek Young was the Flight-Lieutenant from Went aerodrome who had offered her a cocktail called a Bullet at the Gibsons' party. A brother officer, who was going to Highbridge, had set him down at the Westbury cross-roads, and he was on his way to pay a Sunday afternoon call upon the Dowager Lady Merle. Very naturally, he had brought with him, to visit his litter-brother Radish, his own bull-terrier, Beetroot, who had also once belonged to a fighter pilot, and whose record, he said darkly, was "fourteen confirmed."

Pippa had never felt such a fool in her life, and what was worse, as she explained in remorseful pants, such a beastly fool. "I don't really go about the country banging dogs," she explained, almost in tears. "But you see, I'm allowed to take Radish out on the condition that I don't let him hunt, and he's getting better and better at escaping."

Her companion said handsomely that an extra bang would do Beetroot no harm, and when the fawning Radish presently reappeared, he addressed "You miserable hound!" so loudly and so severely, that Radish became an aspen leaf, and an obsequious Eastern slave, and the Serpent of Eden—"Upon thy belly shalt thou go, and dust shalt thou eat all the days of thy life." Radish closed his eyes and shrank upon the mire, trembling in every limb, waiting for the quietus.

"Since I had my go at your dog, I suppose it's only fair to offer you a go at mine," said Pippa. "But I warn you, I shall have to stick my fingers in my ears and turn my back, if you're going to make a job of it."

Derek Young suggested that they should call it a day, whistled the dogs to heel, and after he had shown her the way over quite a simple stile within fifteen yards of the high gate, took charge of her bicycle and began to push it uphill. He said, "Those are good," looking at the contents of the wicker basket.

"I'd had such a lovely off-time until the brute escaped," mourned Pippa. "Have you noticed what an extraordinary day it's turned out—everything the colour of gooseberry fool?"

She felt futile again, directly she had said this, for naturally he must notice weather a good deal. "Did I understand you to say that that dog flies?" she continued in a hurry.

He murmured with a smile, looking first at Beetroot and then at her, "Well, I dare say he's got a few hours logged up."

Pippa saw that she was not going to hear any more about that, and obediently changed the subject. "Diana's back at Woodside," she said, wondering if he remembered the Bullet; but she could not tell, for in return he merely asked whether it was true that Elizabeth Rollo was also working at Mrs. Hungerford's hospital.

"Everyone down here seems to have gone to Elizabeth's coming-out dance!" exclaimed Pippa.

"Yes," nodded her companion. "I did, too. Mrs. Hungerford took me in her party, and I spent the night at Willows. I was at Oxford at the same time as Elizabeth's elder brother," he explained.

Pippa heard this with interest, for Elizabeth's elder brother, Tony, was the subject of dark surmise at Woodside. He wasn't in the Forces, and when he had come down last winter to see Mrs. Hungerford, who was his godmother, Nurse Lluelyn, who had left now, had heard noises like arguing coming from the office, and Mr. Rollo had gone off, slamming the door and stumbling downstairs, without any supper, and Mrs. Hungerford had come down looking very tired. But as he wore those magnifying glasses, and appeared as blind as a bat, perhaps it was his eyes.

"I've never been to a real dance," said Pippa. "Was it lovely?"

"It was rather a good show," admitted Derek. "The Rollos had just moved into Crossgrove, so everything was very spick and span. And Crossgrove is a dream of a house, even for Barsetshire."

"Do you know the country down here well?" asked Pippa.

"Not as well as I should like. I was a Londoner."

"Perhaps you'll settle down here in a dream of a Barsetshire house, after the War," suggested Pippa brightly. "Shouldn't you like to?" she inquired, looking up at his face, as he did not immediately answer.

Up at the Dower House, Lady Merle's Black Hamburgh had myriads of bunches of green seed pearls, which would be luscious purple grapes in September. The double drawing-room smelt sweetly of flowering currant. Twenty-four hours in a warm room had transformed the large crackle bowl of budding boughs which the gardener had sent in yesterday.

The old lady stood at a spacious window of her empty double drawing-room, looking out at the uncanny green haze clouding her park. Corisande, Lady Merle, who had been accustomed to entertain appreciative Cabinet Ministers at week-ends, foresaw another silent Sunday afternoon. Her expression brightened as she perceived guests approaching—two striding, laughing young people, making a pretty picture in their blue uniforms, and followed by two well-behaved white dogs.

The Dowager was sorry when she heard that Miss Pippa Johnson must be on duty at four-thirty, so could not stay to tea at the Dower House, and she thought that the young officer looked sorry too, as he returned from seeing the little creature off down the drive on her bicycle.

He was a pleasant-looking young man, decided the critical Dowager, as he took tea with her. Although his features were plain, they were frank, and he had good, even teeth, and the hands of an artist, and a quiet, agreeable voice, which was unusual amongst young people nowadays. She understood from him that before the War, his plans had been to go into trade—

the manufacture of paint. He had been interested in flying ever since he could remember, and had been a member of the Auxiliary Air Force while still at Oxford. He had a slight look of eye-strain, and she noticed that, unlike most young people of fair complexion, when he was embarrassed, he lost colour. A direct question, not unkindly meant, had elicited from him the information that he had a mother, with whom he had made his home before the War, and a father alive, who had remarried. The Dowager accepted with a stately bend of the head, an unhappy situation, rarer in her youth.

At Woodside, later that night, as she listened to the sound of friendly aircraft pouring eastwards into black darkness, Miss Pippa Johnson noted in her diary, under date April 19th, *"Picked cowslips. Met Flight-Lieutenant Derek Young."*

PART II
MRS. HUNGERFORD'S POINT OF VIEW

CHAPTER V
ALL RATHER TYPICAL
(February 12-13th, April 23rd, May 2nd)

I

THE NEWS that "young" Lady Merle was divorcing Lord Merle burst like a bombshell upon the neighbourhood of the cathedral city. Indeed, it is fair to say that in Went, news of the assassination of the Führer would have aroused far less interest. The repercussions penetrated even to Mrs. Hungerford's office, where Mrs. Hungerford sat, feeling far from calm and much in need of her husband's support. For Mrs. Hungerford had been born in 1897, the daughter of an English country house, and when she had attended her first home nursing lectures in Went Town Hall, in August 1914, an ex-nurserymaid had accompanied her in the dog-cart on this dark and dangerous expedition. She had been brought up distinctly on what used to be called "pre-war" lines.

As her husband was a first cousin of Lord Merle, and Lord Merle's only child was amongst her staff, Mrs. Hungerford might reasonably be expected to know all that there was to be known about this latest nine days' wonder, and it says much for the manners of her Barsetshire neighbours that, during that period of feverish interest, no acquaintance directly mentioned the subject in her presence. Mrs. Bates, it is true, pinned on a face suitable for a funeral when she met Mrs. Hungerford in Westbury Green post office, and her voice as she inquired after Mary's health, was equally lugubrious. On hearing that everybody at Woodside was going on as well as could be expected, and enjoying this lovely weather, Mrs. Bates merely said, "You are always so brave!" accompanied by a warm handshake, before taking a self-controlled departure. But then, reflected Mary, Sally Bates, who was never wrong, had probably long foreseen this domestic tragedy. The family were always the last to hear a thing.

Mary's chief troubles came from inside her own family circle. She had a dreadful tea with Valerie Merle, who, having invited herself to see, for the first time, the hospital where her daughter had now worked for seven months, showed upon arrival not the slightest inclination to enter a ward. She arrived at five-forty-five on a wet February evening, saying that she was tired out and starving, after a hectic day in London, choosing a flat. Mary, who had had her tea more than an hour before, with her staff, rang the bell and asked for a tray to be sent up to the office. The tray was brought by Miss Reeny Dudman, aged seventeen, Tuesday and Thursday pantry helper, and in public life daughter of the Art Needlework Shop on Went Market-place; and while Reeny performed her voluntary duties, Lady Merle of Went continued a particularly unbridled monologue.

She said that, as no doubt Mary had always guessed, her marriage to Reginald had been a failure from the first. "I was far too young. It ought never to have been allowed."

"You were twenty-one and Reginald was twenty-nine," said Mary, feeling the solid ground failing beneath her feet, as she wondered fatuously whether she had got to call Rex "Reginald" for the rest of her life now, and whether she would ever remember. Kit had always been very fond of poor old Rex.

"I felt 'This is all wrong,' as I walked out of the church on his arm," said Valerie, shuddering out of a fur cape, and beginning to use it as a muff. "Something seemed to warn me," she explained, searching Mary's face with wide eyes.

"Oh, well, I expect if you felt that, it wasn't likely to go well," said Mary, miserably groping.

"I have always said that I would give Reginald his Freedom," said Valerie, "and now that the time has come, I think that it would be best if you told Lalage."

Mary, who had checked upon her lips the question whether Reginald wanted his freedom, was by nature mild. But she had not been in command of an auxiliary hospital for eighteen months for nothing. She said, "I think it would be best if you told Lalage. Let me see. She comes on duty to-day at five. It's Nurse Lluelyn's half-day."

"Dear Mary," said Valerie in far from affectionate accents, "do you never think of anything nowadays except your little hospital?"

"I do, of course," said Mary, knitting her fair brows, "and I'm very sorry to hear what you are telling me. Have you considered it seriously from every point of view?" she asked, staring at her cousin by marriage, who was looking far from serious, attired in a youthfully short London black coat and skirt, a white blouse of many frills, and an impossibly small witch's hat, set at an acute angle on metallic gold curls. "I mean," said Mary, blushing hotly, "you did promise for life, you know."

Reeny Dudman reappeared at this moment, breathing heavily and bearing a tray, which, after rolling her eyes around the room, she temporarily parked upon a table just inside the door.

As she approached her commanding officer, she mentioned in a bedside voice, "Quartermaster had given out the chocolate biscuits for to-morrow's tea, Madam, but we thought you might like some now." Her awed glance at the decorative figure seated beside the fire said, "As it's for Lady Merle," and it seemed possible that Keeny, who adored wearing her becoming and spotless uniform on Tuesdays and Thursdays, even nourished hopes that "young" Lady Merle might recognize her. After all, when "old" Duly Merle had paid her first visit to Woodside Auxiliary Hospital, she had made a progress distinctly regal, from ward to ward, had spoken to nearly every patient, said "Good afternoon" in the most stately manner to every member of the staff on duty, and where she recognized a face, paused to make inquiries after the war work, or health, of the member's family.

"My dear, from every point of view," said Valerie. "And at last, I've chosen my flat, and I take possession on March 25th, so it's no use going over all that. Do you know that it's almost impossible to get a decent flat nowadays? Later, of course, I shall get something small in the country too, within easy reach of London. Everyone tells me I'm too brave to be going back to London yet, when it may be blitzed again at any moment. However, I just feel that I must have a few months of London first, after the dreadful time I've been through since 1939. I never touch chocolate biscuits," she added, waving an impatient hand as Reeny set the tray in front of the guest, on a coffin stool, from which she had carefully removed a used ash-tray and a packet of outsize envelopes.

"Thank you, nurse," said Mary. "You may take away the biscuits." When the door closed behind the abashed Reeny, "Why have you had a more dreadful time than anyone else since 1939?" she inquired.

"Now, Mary, dear," said Valerie, with justice, "you know I didn't say that. And if you don't consider it a perfect nightmare to have your house taken over for an unending procession of depressing women, every one of whom is expecting a baby, I'm sure few people would agree with you. I simply couldn't stand it for six weeks. As you know, I moved into that cottage in the park as soon as possible. But I'm not really comfortable there, and I still have to see that Matron person. Do you know, when I went up to lunch at my own house the other day, and asked for some more butter, the woman had the impudence to tell me that two ounces per head, or something, was enough for a week?"

"But it is," said Mary. "I mean, it is an adult's weekly ration."

"Is butter rationed?" asked Valerie. "How squalid! I'm sure my people will find no difficulty in London. I'm just taking Lloyd, my maid, and a married couple and one chauffeur. I've taken the flat furnished. It was really the furniture that attracted me. It's all Empire. Kit will appreciate it."

"Kit was very fond of Rex—of Reginald," said Mary unhappily. "I'm afraid he will be terribly disappointed when he hears that you have parted."

"Kit, my dear Mary," said Valerie, "is a man of the world. He won't be at all surprised, you'll find."

"Won't he?" wondered Mary, reflecting dismally that although no woman liked to think that she has married a simpleton, she does not like anyone else to describe him as a man of the world.

"I'm not going to say a word against Reginald," continued Valerie, "but, as you know, since 1939 he has virtually deserted me."

"But he's on active service," exclaimed Mary.

"He's sitting at a barracks only fifteen miles the other side of Highbridge," said Valerie, "and you, who know him so well, can guess what that means."

"I don't think you can be right," said Mary delicately, "or else he would have come unstuck long ago. And every time I've seen him, I have thought he looked better and younger. He likes being back in the Army, I think. It suits him."

"Every time I've seen him, we've had the most ghastly scenes, and he's never ceased complaining from the moment he crossed the threshold," said Valerie. "However, that's all done with now, and I shall be leaving next month, and all I need is for you to explain to Granny Merle and Pamela, and anyone else you can think of who'll be more than usually unpleasant if they see it first in the newspapers.'

"I think you ought to tell Granny Merle yourself," said Mary weakly, "and Reginald. . . ."

"He doesn't seem to fancy it. He says he's going to write her a letter, but I doubt if he does. Actually he's just been ordered somewhere, but I don't expect it's abroad," said Valerie.

"Oh, well, then," said Mary, "I will tell Granny Merle, for after her illness, I don't think she ought to be allowed to see it first in a newspaper."

"If you'll send for Lalage then, I'll get that over,' said Valerie rising and smoothing her frock. "After all, I am her mother."

While Mary used the house telephone at her desk, she looked at Valerie, who had moved to a window, and was smiling quite cheerfully at some thought of her own. The light in the window was not so kind as that from the fire, and her face, in spite of careful make-up and a smile, suddenly looked definitely middle-aged. A pang of remorse flooded Mary's bosom. She told herself that Valerie had perhaps been very young, at twenty-one, and had undoubtedly married a stupid man, and lived a very sheltered life and been much spoilt. She might be going to burn her fingers painfully. Her heart told Mary to say, "Don't do it!"

She spoke to the staff-room, asking Nurse Rollo to come to the office to see Lady Merle, and when she had replaced the receiver she rose, and taking her courage in both hands, approached her guest, saying, "Valerie! Don't do it!"

I I

Mary lay awake a considerable time on the night following Valerie's visit, and having made an appointment with the Dowager for twelve-fifteen, but not luncheon, next morning, she spent a disagreeable forenoon. When she arrived at the Dower House, she was shown into the conservatory, where she was obliged to admire several pots of cyprepediums, for which she had no heart. She said, "Yes, I do think they are quite lovely, and dreams of elegance in their all-green outfits. It's such a clever green too—the real fairies' colour. They're the only orchids I appreciate. I believe it's because they are the only unworldly looking orchids."

"Ah, no! Some odontoglossums are ethereal," said the Dowager.

Fortunately the Dowager had a quick eye, and was not the woman to beat about the bush. She was soon seated in her outsize arm-chair opposite her favourite grandson's wife, and said briskly, "Well, Mary, dear, I don't expect that you have taken the morning off from your work for no reason. I only hope that you are going to tell me something pleasant."

Mary said, "I'm not, I'm afraid," and gulped, and then plunged. "Valerie came to see me last night, to tell me that Rex and she have decided to part."

Lying awake last night, Mary had almost persuaded herself that the Dowager, who had a quick eye, would not be surprised by her news. She realized, as soon as she had spoken her opening sentence, that hers had been wishful thinking. What she was saying was evidently an utter surprise to the Dowager.

Mary heard her own voice talking and, in the pauses, the ticking of a Louis XVI clock on the mantelpiece. From the cool and distant staff quarters came the leisurely sound of elderly feet on stone flags. Outside, in the tops of the trees half-way up the drive, the rooks were building. Mary had noticed as she ascended that the ugly indigo asphalt was littered with twigs. The Dowager's drive was not a thing of beauty. It had been the work of "my predecessor," and was so like a public gardens that one always expected to see notices saying, "Please keep to the path," stuck under the shrubs. "I always used to think the rooks building was such a cheerful noise. I suppose I shall some day come to associate it with something else than this morning," thought Mary.

"Valerie wanted me to tell you before Rex wrote," she continued, "in case a letter should be a shock. He's been ordered somewhere, she says, but not abroad. She was very sorry, but she seems quite adamant."

Behind the Dowager, on the top of a buhl cupboard, stood alabaster models of the Leaning Tower and Baptistry at Pisa.

Mary had known all her life that the Dowager and the late Lord Merle had chosen these models on their honeymoon, and after she herself had visited Italy and seen the originals, she had been surprised to discover that the Baptistry was in fact not nearly as tall as the Leaning Tower. The honeymoon couple had evidently ordered a much more expensive baptistry than tower. Both models were enclosed in glass shades, furnished with worm-like, crimson chenille guards, and stood on black pedestals. What struck Mary at the moment was the resemblance between the pose of the Dowager and the Leaning Tower. Her news seemed to have had the effect of a physical blow.

"I didn't ask many questions, or hear anything more, really," she faltered. "I tried to persuade her not to act rashly, but I had no success."

The Dowager stirred, and uttering for the first time, spoke her son's name under her breath.

"She said she had always promised to give him his freedom, and that now the time had come," said Mary, thinking it best to keep on talking. "She told Lalage before she left, and I've just a word with Lalage, and she sent her love, and would like to come to see you presently."

The Dowager asked, still tonelessly, "What are her plans?" and Mary did not make the mistake of thinking that the question alluded to Lalage.

"A furnished flat in London at once, and something smaller as well in the country, close to London, later on," she quoted. "She says that as Went is an assize town, the case will be heard early in July, and she'll get the decree absolute with the New Year."

The Dowager asked nothing more, but sat for several long minutes, thinking profoundly. Obviously her thoughts were covering years. Outside, the garden was dressed in sober greys and browns, and die view of the village in the distance, far below the drive and calling rooks, reminded Mary of "St. Agnes Eve. Ah! bitter cold it was." There were dove-coloured heights beyond the valley, and in the park, frost had pinched all colour from the grass. A robin, hopping on thin legs, came to the window and looked in curiously at the old lady, sitting sideways drawing a rusty black lace shawl round her shoulders. She had quick, dark, eyes, as bright as his own, but she did not notice him.

Mary thought, "I wonder whether the first great disappointment of Granny Merle's life was when she realized that after six spirited daughters, all renowned for their looks, she had produced an entirely undistinguished son." The Dowager never pretended that she had anything but a stupid son. Indeed, her allusions to the undoubted fact were embarrassingly frequent. Nevertheless, Mary knew that her son had always been the Dowager's favourite. "And it must have been a second disappointment when he brought home as bride, a young woman with a pretty face and not much heart, with whom he had not one taste in common," thought Mary.

She was startled from her reverie to hear her hostess say, without altering her pose, but in vigorous tones:

"Let her go!"

III

Pamela Taylor was distressingly talkative on the subject. She arrived in high dudgeon on a windy mid-April day, to say that Granny Merle had told her that Rex and Valerie were parting, but had then shut up like an oyster.

"So I thought I had better come straight to see you. What on earth has happened? I can as soon imagine Went without the cathedral. I mean, no such thing has ever happened to a Merle."

Mary repeated the little that she knew, and Pamela, who had been one of the last people in the landscape to hear anything, was clearly disappointed.

"Granny seemed to be taking it fairly flatly, too," she commented. "She reminded me quite snappishly that Rex was descended from Charles II. When I said that it was just countenancing Sin on her part not to nip such an idea in the bud, she told me not to talk nonsense. Nothing will persuade me that Rex wants it. I mean, having stuck Valerie for nearly twenty-five years, no man in his senses could want to put his head in that noose again. And I'm reasonably sure that he's not been drawing other coverts. And it can't be anything else, because he's been practically Pussyfoot since he rejoined his regiment. He's been much better in every way, if you ask me, since he's been away from Valerie."

"Perhaps that's what he thought himself," suggested Mary.

"No," said Pamela decisively, "Rex hasn't the brain to realize that, or the guts to put it through. Granny has had him over, and slated him, I hear. She got him on the telephone the evening before he left Highbridge, and he spent the night at the Dower House. John met him next morning, just leaving, with his luggage being put on the car at the front door. John says that Rex came downstairs from saying good-bye to Granny in her bedroom, holding himself very straight and blowing his nose in a trumpetty way. I'm glad to hear that he seemed ashamed to meet John's eye. But John has such high ideals, he may easily have imagined that Rex was ashamed, when he was merely burying his face in his handkerchief because he had a roaring cold. In Rex's position, as I said to Granny, he ought to set an example, and especially in war-time. Now, as a family, we shall be no better off than those awful people who took Nettlerash two years before the war, and she put her head in the gas-oven, and turned out to have had fourteen lovers."

"Oh, no, dear, surely we shall be a little better off than that," sighed Mary.

"It's some idea of Valerie's," said Pamela darkly. "Well, I suppose we shall just have to wait and see. Meanwhile, it's going to be very unpleasant for John and me. I never had such a shock in my life. Aren't you surprised, too, at Granny? I mean, if you had sprung this on her last winter, I should have said that it would have killed her. Now, on the contrary, she seems rather the better. She's having her chinchilla cape done up for the spring. And yet, I shouldn't say that she's really just too old to care much about anything any longer, should you?"

"No, I shouldn't," agreed Mary. "And I'm sure it has been a blow to her. But I'm sure she's right, and setting us the best example in saying as little as possible and hoping for the best."

"I didn't say hoping for the best. I said, 'Wait and See'," said Pamela vengefully.

Mary got another surprise when she found it necessary to mention the matter to her secretary, Johanna Pratt.

"If you notice Lalage looking a bit down-in-the-mouth," she said one morning, trying to sound casual, "I'm afraid it's been rather a blow to her that her parents have decided to part."

"No! Have they?" asked the invaluable Pratt, looking up from her typewriter with the light of envy in her saucer eyes. "I wish to Heaven mine would!"

At last, a pantechnicon, after long waits in the driving rain outside the house itself and Valerie's cottage in Went Park, took the London road. It contained, according to rumour, no less than two hundred diaphanous ball-dresses which her ladyship had kept in a room specially built for them, and many pieces of furniture which ought never to have left the house. Rumour exaggerated, but it was a fact that by the following November three of Lord Merle's married sisters still felt so strongly on the subject of a missing Chippendale bird-cage, which had been brought to their old home by a regency ancestress, that they made a solemn pact to take no notice of their erring brother's birthday this year.

The news filtered from Westbury-on-the-Green to West-bury-on-the-Hill, and down the valley to Hydden Hall and the Old Mill House, where it was heard with much regret. It reached Captain David Cox in his mess at Highbridge, and Professor Abbadie Beadon, quite the other side of the county, and Major Hungerford, in the Grand Hotel, Stockholm. Nine days after the announcement had appeared in the London morning newspapers and the *Went Evening Star*, Mrs. Hungerford told herself that she supposed that in time people would find something else to interest them.

At Willows, Mrs. Rosemary Morrison, who might be trusted to get hold of the wrong end of a stick, said to her honorary aunt, with brimming eyes, "Poor, poor Valerie!"

"Yes, I think it's sad for her," said Mary, to which Rosemary replied infuriatingly, "Ah! But you see, I know. She confided in me all along."

In spite of her insistence that Mary must break the news to her nearest relatives, Valerie had, it soon appeared, confided in a large and sycophantic audience of outsiders.

On the ninth day, Mary's prayers for a new local topic were answered, and all interest in Lord Merle's divorce waned, never to be fully revived, but at undesirable cost.

For on the nights of May 2nd and 3rd, Went was blitzed again.

IV

On the morning of May 2nd, Mrs. Hungerford took the eight-ten 'bus into Highbridge. She was going to visit the families of two, patients, but she felt that as she was also going on a personal shopping expedition and to lunch with her sister-in-law, she could not honourably use the khaki van. She further nourished hopes that her arrival on foot at Willows might check her sister-in-law's customary monologue on the subject of petrol for civilians.

She felt a little guilty at deserting Pratt, as Professor Beadon had sent a note, dated a week ago, which had arrived yesterday, saying that he had managed to obtain the photographs of plaster-work resembling that at Woodside, and would like to call to show them to Mrs. Hungerford, if she happened to be disengaged on the afternoon of the 2nd. However, Pratt had promised with great cheerfulness to explain all to the Professor, and see that the poor thing got a meal this time.

The Highbridge 'bus appeared five minutes before it was due, but with only one other passenger on board. Amy Squirl, who was a Wednesday and Sunday pantry helper at Woodside, was also going to Highbridge to shop. Amy's younger brother, Ted, had been garden boy at Woodside, and afterwards an under-gardener at Went Park, and Mary had attended his wedding to Florrie Potts at Westbury-on-the-Hill Church on Whit Saturday, 1939, so she had naturally been sorry when Ted had been reported "missing" after Dunkirk. Florrie had given birth to a daughter in the summer of 1940, and Mrs. Potts, who had wanted her son-in-law to resign from the Territorials as a

condition of the match, had taken gloomy pleasure in pointing out that now his child was what she called "posythumious."
But after a sad interval, Amy Squirl had arrived in the office at
Woodside one evening, clutching an official envelope in large
hands on which the knuckles stood out. Florrie had got the letter
by the eight o'clock that morning, and after summoning her
sister-in-law to solemn conclave, had decided that Mrs. Hungerford would know what they ought to do for the best. As Amy had
walked from Westbury-on-the-Hill to Lower Merle, and back to
the hill to get her father's dinner and settle her mother for the
day, and change her clothes, and then on to Woodside, she must
have covered nearly fifteen miles in August heat by the time that
she stumbled into Mrs. Hungerford's office with dusty shoes.

"We thought you'd like to know, ma'am," said Amy in a gasp-
ing manner, "Ted's alive, ma'am. He's been wounded, but he's
out of the hospital now. They've written to tell his next of kin.
He's at a place called Stalag."

Mary asked after Ted this morning, and Amy, who was a
heavy, pale girl of eight-and-twenty, with the same fishy eye and
furtive look which had distinguished her brother, said that Ted
had got a parcel in his last letter, he said, and the leg was giving
no trouble, he said, and he'd got the snap of Baby Joan on her
Anty's knee which Mrs. Crippen's nephew had kindly taken, and
he wanted to know was the glass at the Park all O.K.

Mary said that she would like to write to Ted herself some
day soon, and tell him about Amy working in her hospital, and
about all the gardens he knew growing splendid vegetables, but
Amy, although pleased at the general idea, said depressingly
that Ted had never been the one for vegetables. The stove plants
and chrysanths had always been his ideal.

At the north lodge gates of Went Park the 'bus made its
customary halt, and a small figure with neat grey curls and a
Roman nose, who had been standing in a vigilant attitude holding up an imperious umbrella, stepped on board briskly. Lady
Wilson, who was going to change her library books and get the
fish, greeted Mrs. Hungerford affectionately. As her husband,
the ex-Ambassador, was decidedly hard of hearing, she was not

in the least dismayed at: the prospect of carrying on a conversation in a country omnibus. She wore a well-worn, full-length coat and a skirt of two startlingly different shades of grey, a navy-blue blouse with a stand-up net collar, an amethyst and seed-pearl necklace, a ruby brooch and a brown felt hat. She carried on her arm, in addition to the umbrella, a green mackintosh and a raffia basket on which the word "Menton" was embroidered in scarlet wool. Lady Wilson, who was seventy-nine and the size of a pea, managed nevertheless to convey an instant impression of distant Court and Camp.

The 'bus began to run alongside Went Park, and Lady Wilson pointed out that the lime avenue was in bud, and said that those first small leaves standing out like green dots on bare boughs reminded her of nothing nowadays but camouflage nets. She asked if Mary would like some lilies of the valley from the Old Mill House, as she thought that she remembered the girls' school had let the Woodside lily of the valley beds run to ruin. She was delighted that nice young Captain Cox had been ordered to Highbridge. He had been in to supper the other night, bringing two friends, and some of Mary's staff had kindly helped her to entertain them. The evening had been a great success. "Diana and little Nurse Johnson," she added, slightly to Mary's surprise.

The 'bus continued its questing course on the Went avoiding road, and presently collected from outside the Cottage Hospital, Mawton post office and Giddy's Gate, a full load of passengers. A steady hum of desultory talk was in progress when a loud roar of aircraft suddenly predominated. Everyone in the 'bus gave up the struggle, and craned their necks to catch a glimpse of the new Bomber Station. It looked very impressive in the pale spring sunlight, thought Mary—rather like a battlefield strewn with sleeping whales. Everything about the new station seemed to be on the largest scale—blocks of buildings, painted in colours which blended into the contours of the surrounding country, a network of roads, and wherever the eye rested, the shadowy shapes of outsize aircraft. Enormous shadows from the clouds overhead dappled the air-field, and miles of barbed wire stretched as far as eye could see. As the 'bus passed, close to the perimeter track, a string of laden figures in horizon-blue uniform emerged from a long shed, and trod purposefully towards a waiting monster. Somebody said, "Ow! Look! They're just going out," and somebody else, "They're larfing their 'eads off. Crikey!" A pallid little girl with fair plaits wanted to know what that man was carrying, and her mother said, "Don't you ask questions. Airmen has to carry all sorts of equipment."

"They always has to take something called Mae West, I know," piped the sharp little girl, and her mother said, "The Idea!"

"Oh, dear!" said Mary, as the 'bus began to drop downhill. "I know one of those young men—Derek Young. Did you happen to notice him—the one walking in front?"

"With carrotty hair and a good figure?" asked Lady Wilson, whose long sight was excellent.

"Well, yes, I suppose so," agreed Mary. "But your example makes me feel so guilty, for I knew him before the War. He has stayed at Willows. And I've known since Diana's wedding-party that he is stationed down here, and I've never asked him to a bite or a sup."

"You have very little opportunity. But you could send him a line to-night," suggested Lady Wilson, as a deafening roar swelled on the air, and somebody murmured, "There they go!"

"Yes, I think I had better write to-night," thought Mary, as the bomber which might, or might not, contain her prospective guest, thundered over her head.

The 'bus rumbled past the fringes of a wood where there were drifts of bluebells the colour of the blue in medieval stained glass. It turned abruptly off the avoiding road on to a lesser high-way, of a different colour, and bounced happily between bright green fields, and past gardens where daisies and dandelions were flourishing in once neat front lawns, and double crimson and pink may-trees were in bud.

"You can hear the cuckoo now whenever you choose to listen," screamed Lady Wilson in Mary's ear. Mary, who could hear all sorts of other things at the moment, nodded and told herself that her neighbour must mean at home, amongst the sap-green waters and smooth turves of the Old Mill House, where tumbler pigeons cooed soothingly, and life always seemed to move at a gentler pace than in the outer world.

Although she always enjoyed the road to Highbridge, she was not altogether sorry when her equipage snorted to a standstill outside The Three Horseshoes, in the Old Cattle Market, where all the country 'buses came in, and passengers began to reclaim from behind the stairs, parcels which ranged from a sack of potatoes to a doll's perambulator. She noticed that although the year was still young, every package bore a fine coating of dust.

V

Potts, the tailor in East Street, Highbridge, had successfully altered Mary's old skirt and overcoat, so that they were now fifteen inches off the ground, and the change in her appearance raised her spirits. Potts, too, was in good spirits this fine morning. He said, "May's the queen of the months, ma'am," as he ran round on the floor beneath Mary, using a stiffened measuring tape and a murderous-looking razor-blade, with which he ripped open seams contemptuously. How on earth he could tell, even with the help of the tape, that her skirts were the same length all round Mary could not imagine, for his establishment had floors crazy with age, and stood on the very steepest part of the hill. From its bow windows could be seen shop-starers, all of whom had one leg higher than the other, and those on the move were either pounding up or mincing down the pavement. Indeed, as Mary stood to attention in Potts' shop, on unsteady boards, seeing through a slit in faded green serge curtains a view of small-paned windows and crooked horizons, bathed in strong sunlight, she received distinctly the impression that she was on a ship at sea.

Potts, whose true name was Myles, was a great-nephew of the founder of the firm. He was a small, thick-set man of five and forty, with pale protuberant eyes and a bronzed complexion. If we all had to be fish, flesh or fowl, Mr. Myles would have been a toad, but a nice toad, for his expression was amiable. Since experiences on Lancashire Landing Beach, Gallipoli, he had been stone deaf in one ear, which he much regretted. "It makes me feel such a duffer sometimes, Madam." The brains of the family he admitted as frankly, had been his cousin, Sergeant-Major Charles Potts, who had succumbed to influenza in Cologne in the winter of 1918. The loss of his smart son and the return of a nephew who could only hear half he said, had broken the heart of Potts the second. His nose had grown a shinier and shinier red, and his hand shakier and shakier. There was an awful story that once, when summoned to fit the Dowager for a side-saddle riding habit, he had appeared amidst an avalanche of bales of check suiting, in so hopelessly exuberant a condition that the august lady had swept out of his life and into her waiting landaulette, attired in a feather boa, a finger-length, tight-waisted habit coat, rich in chalk marks and tacking threads, and petunia moiré petticoat. Mary could not answer for the truth of this tale, but it had been a relief to all in the neighbourhood when Potts the second had sunk into the grave, and his nephew had begun a creditable attempt to pull together a once-flourishing business.

After bidding Myles a grateful farewell, Mary began to pound up East Street. She got the knitting-needles of a pattern kept only by a small, melancholy shop behind the churchyard, and retrieved her travelling clock, which had re-posed for three months in the care of Messrs. Myllar, Goldsmiths and Silversmiths. Boy dolls and bedroom slippers appeared unobtainable in Highbridge. This was a blow, as Mary had wrenched the heel off her last pair of mules a week ago, and she knew that her godchild at Hydden Hall was confidently mentioning in her nightly prayers that she was hoping for a boy doll for her sixth birthday on Tuesday.

"I might get both at Moote's, if I could only get there," Mary told herself, as she shook her head at the selection of dolls offered to her at her last port of call—the Big Bazaar. "The little girl specially wants a boy," she explained. "I'm afraid a celluloid baby, or a negress or an all-felt fish-wife would only be a disappointment."

In the parking-place by the 'bus stop, Colonel Albany Mimms was engaged in packing the back seats of his car roof-high with bundles of battle-dress. Mary poked her head in at a window and said, "Good morning. You are not, by any chance, going on to Went, are you?" Colonel Mimms was delighted to say that he was, and by letting down the luggage carrier and using straps and a mackintosh sheet, he would soon be able to clear enough space to accommodate Mrs. Hungerford. He seemed slightly shocked to find Mrs. Hungerford stranded in Highbridge, and Mary was haunted by remorse when she saw how much trouble she was giving, for Colonel Mimms was rather old-fashioned, and would not let her help at all, and he was also very neat, and did not mount the driver's seat until he had fastened the straps exactly opposite one another, and rolled up their spare ends into twin Swiss rolls. He had faded hazel eyes, and many lines in his countenance, and was a decidedly enervating driver, as he murmured as they approached their first traffic lights, "Green. That means stop. No! I'm wrong."

He was not in the least deaf, but Mary always found conversation with him a little difficult, because he failed to collect what she had said. This was because he had already made up his mind as to what would be the response of a happily married woman, aged forty-five.

As they flew along the heavily cambered Went main road, he told Mary that Lower Merle platoon had three Home Guards needing outsize uniform, but they were not, as you might expect, the blacksmith, the ploughman and the porter. They were a schoolmaster from London, a dentist and the Dowager's pantry boy. He was particularly pleased to have met Mrs. Hungerford, as he had been meaning to telephone to tell her that Westbury-on-the-Hill platoon were playing the Went Fire Services at Westbury-on-the-Green on Saturday fortnight, and he much hoped that any of her staff and patients who cared for cricket would come to watch. He had been up all night on an Exercise, and was going home to get some sleep now, so trusted his poor wife had not asked anyone to lunch, as he feared he would be stupid company. He had given his poor wife's nerves a sad shock yesterday evening, as he had marched into the drawing-room to say good-bye to her before setting out, and he had smeared his face and hands with mud, in preparation for the Exercise, and his wife had been entertaining Dame Sarah Lys.

Mary exclaimed, "Has Dame Sarah Lys arrived? What an excitement! I am going to lunch with Marcelle and Rosemary to-day, so perhaps I shall meet her. Tell, me, what's she like?"

Colonel Albany Mimms said that for her age and size, the celebrity seemed to him to have marvellous nerves. While his wife had been recovering from the shock, Dame Sarah herself had accompanied him back to the garden, and had advised him that it was quite childish to try to scrape up mud from the bed under the boot-room window, where the soil had been trodden to a paste by his dogs jumping in and out. She had led him to the forget-me-not and tulip bed, where the earth was friable, and had egged him on until he was as black as my hat. And then she had led him back in triumph to the drawing-room, and chanted in a marvellous voice—

> "'Mislike me not for my complexion—
> 'The shadow'd livery of the burnish'd sun,
> To whom I am a neighbour and near bred.'"

"She sounds rather a sport," said Mary. "I hope Hyacinth was not really upset. I remember my grandmother-in-law old Lady Merle, was once much upset when she led a party of ladies into the study at Went Park, saying, 'And this is my husband's study', and they all were just in time to see old Lord Merle, who loathed strange women, dropping out of the study window into the knot-garden."

Colonel Mimms said, without a change of countenance, that he could well understand that must have been very embarrassing for everyone, and Mary remembered too late that he did not see the funny side of things much, and wondered anew why he always alluded to Hyacinth as "my wife," as if she were a chronic complaint, like "my rheumatism" or "my game leg." Not that he ever complained of Hyacinth. On the contrary, as Mary knew, for he had told her more than once, he was the kind of fellow who had always set women on a pedestal. Colonel Mimms had sent in his papers when he had become engaged to the beautiful girl, who had been a child in the nursery when he had been A.D.C. to her father. It distressed Colonel Mimms most dreadfully to see old Sally Bates in her slacks, on her bike, off to scrub bins and trestle-tables at the Westbury F.A. Post, which, as it had been a Victorian Infants' School, was profoundly gloomy. He went about Barsetshire nowadays, groaning over the things delicate women were doing, regardless of the fact that fourteen stone of Sally Bates, coasting down Dead Woman's Hill twice a day on her bike, was a far more present menace to the community than a stray and unlikely German bomber.

"And then there is that poor little Diana Gibson," he sighed. "I remember we met at that truly pathetic sherry-party. As I said to my wife afterwards, 'In Godfrey Gibson's place, I should have felt it my duty to refuse my consent'."

"Oh! Why?" asked Mary, who had found the party rather over-cheerful, and would hardly have recognized from Colonel Mimms's description, the largest and sturdiest member of her staff.

"The awful risk for a young girl, barely out of her teens," said Colonel Mimms impressively.

"You mean her marrying a man on active service?" said Mary. "But I don't think Diana would have given Godfrey any peace until he consented. And although it is a risk, of course, I have two members of my staff—Lalage and Elizabeth Rollo—who were engaged to naval officers, and the one who married and was widowed appears the less miserable. However, I dare say she's the stronger character. Diana's back at work again, you know."

"I know. I heard," said Colonel Mimms. "I could hardly believe my ears. I had naturally expected that she would have flown back after her sadly brief honeymoon to the shelter of her father's roof. As I said to my wife after that party, 'I cannot be sufficiently thankful that I married late, and my daughters are still too young to want to marry anyone'."

"How are your children getting on in California?" asked Mary, who had scarcely dared ask this before.

"They quite astonish the kind friends with whom they are living by their sensitiveness," said Colonel Mimms, turning right round to look his alarmed passenger full in the face. "Do you know that every time they hear there has been a raid on Great Britain they sob themselves sick, worrying for their parents' safety? Mrs. Jackson says that she has never known such fascinating and highly strung children."

To Mary's relief, she was able to change the subject by saying, "Could you stop? Isn't that Dolly Yarrow we've just passed?"

It was, and Mrs. Rolfe Yarrow explained, as soon as greetings had been exchanged, that she had not taken her bicycle this morning, on the chance of getting a lift, and had just begun to give up hope. She had been unable to obtain a seat on the ten-thirty o'clock 'bus from the Old Cattle Market, and unlike the majority of other would-be passengers, nothing would induce her to stand on her flat feet, twenty minutes, waiting in case the next one came in empty. She had much regretted taking her bicycle on her last visit to Highbridge, as the Hills had overtaken her and offered her a lift, and their car was too small to take the bicycle on behind. So she had propped her bicycle against a gate and padlocked it. "Rather like the days of King Alfred, wasn't it?" she asked, "when public morality was so high that the old boy hung up a pair of gold bracelets on an oak for three months, and nobody ever thought of pinching them. The only drawback was that little Owens rang up from the police station while I was having lunch with Muriel Gidding, to say that my bicycle had been found deserted against a gate on the Went road, and I had to tell him that I was coming this moment to mount it, and I would skin him if he dared to move it. I now shove it into people's drives if I see a chance of a lift, whether I know them or not."

Colonel Mimms, whose social sense was strongly developed, was deeply grieved to find the widow of the late M.P. for the Went Division, a mother of five, on foot upon the King's Highway. He began to make preparations for removing yet more bundles of battle-dress from the back seats of his car, and undoing the collection in the luggage carrier, and it needed violent persuasion from his passengers before he was reconciled to the scheme of Dorothy, who was *petite*, sitting upon Mary's knee for the three-mile journey.

As soon as they were on the move, Mrs. Yarrow cheerfully asked how were Colonel Mimms's children.

"My wife and I feel that we can never adequately express our gratitude to the gracious lady who has given them a home from home—and such a home," said poor Colonel Mimms, looking miserable indeed. "After our decision was made—in such a hurry—and the children had sailed, we suffered literally agonies of doubt as to whether Mrs. Jackson would appreciate the necessity for adhering strictly to the Richter-Flügel Diet."

Mrs. Yarrow, to her school-friend's disgust, was now fool enough to ask what was the Richter-Flügel Diet, and Colonel Mimms, with the light of a fanatic in his faded hazel eyes, explained at great length, and with precision, that it was the result of researches into what he called Child Metabolism, by two learned foreigners—refugees from Nazi persecution. His wife had sent with their children to their new home, five pamphlets on the subject, a clock-face lightning calculator by which you could in a moment discover how many milligrams of the twenty essential nutrients were included in every proposed component of a meal, and a volume providing six thousand specimen menus and recipes for children on ordinary and special Richter-Flügel Diets throughout a calendar year. To their unbounded delight, Mrs. Jackson had not only taken the greatest interest in the publications, she had actually engaged a talented lady to come every day to superintend the feeding of all the English children under her roof on Richter-Flügel lines, and lecture in the afternoons to a circle of her friends on the result, Could a perfect stranger have done more?

"Well, Violet Jackson is Muriel Gidding's mother, so I suppose she is naturally interested in the children from here," said Mary in muffled tones. "I know she has an awfully kind heart."

Mrs. Yarrow, who was known in sporting circles in Barsetshire as a good woman across country, could not, however, let well alone. "What happens when your girls become eighteen and twenty-one, and want to dance till four a.m. in hot, smoky London cellars dressed in chiffon; and sit in draughts and stuff themselves with stale lobster and sweet champagne and ice-cream?" she asked.

"They will not," explained Colonel Mimms almost happily. "Any child reared on strict Richter-Flügel lines loses the taste for unwholesome sweets, and snacks between main meals."

"My eldest son," said Mrs. Yarrow unrepentantly, "the last time I went down to see him at Prep. school, ate the whole of a five-bob chocolate rabbit (which I had madly given him on my arrival) directly before a heavy lunch. He then made seventy-five not out in the Fathers' match."

The lure of a subject which was of older standing in his affections than the Richter-Flügel Diet, attracted Colonel Mimms's attention, and he generously pressed Mrs. Yarrow and any of her friends to witness Westbury Hill platoon play the Went Fire Services on Saturday fortnight.

As they entered the suburbs of the cathedral city, Mary's thoughts strayed to Stockholm.

VII

"Poor old Mimms," said Mrs. Yarrow to Mary, as the Good Samaritan who had brought them safely to Silver Street departed at dreadful speed towards the market-place traffic lights. "It's awful to think what he must have endured while Hyacinth was what he calls in a hushed voice, 'expecting the coming' of those two skinny little spoilt brats. Thank goodness they did not then inhabit this neighbourhood."

"Violet Jackson is right that they are fascinating children, though," said Mrs. Hungerford mildly. "I remember they once came to tea at Willows, and I thought I had never seen such lovely heart-shaped little faces, and enormous eyes."

"I remember when they came to my last Christmas party before the outbreak," said Mrs. Yarrow, who was a mother herself, "I registered a vow never to have them again. The little pests picked all the currants out of my buns, and told other children that they were not good for little children. And whenever anything was offered to them, they demanded, 'Has it Protective Value?'"

Mary changed the subject by recounting her unsuccessful search for boy dolls in Highbridge, and Dorothy said that as lately as last Tuesday, Mrs. Dudman had been exhibiting in her windows a boy doll dressed in woollies knitted by herself. It was, indeed, seeing him that had put the idea of a boy doll into Jemima's head. The ladies accordingly made straight for Mrs. Dudman's Art Needlework Shop, where they found Reeny in charge, and purchased the boy doll, to the great satisfaction of all present, and one not yet present. Reeny was much flattered that Mrs. Hungerford had bought her mother's handiwork for Mrs. Yarrow's eldest daughter; and as she stood beaming, holding open the door of the shop, with strong sunlight finding golden lights in her tawny eyes and curly hair, Mary thought what a very pretty girl she was. Her look of youth and health was additionally noticeable in these surroundings, for Mrs. Dudman, if truth must be told, had never deigned to move with the times, and was well supplied with tea and egg cosies, and duchess sets, and needlework pictures of ladies in lavender crinolines, walking in old-world gardens. Mrs. Yarrow, since this was a tale of true life, was not entirely enchanted by the prospect of having to carry the boy doll back to Hydden Hall on the top of the fish, but, as she admitted, she had known worse things. Last Sunday she had been obliged to take the Wilsons' fish to church at Lower Merle, before lunching at the Old Mill House; Lady Wilson having telephoned urgently to ask her to collect it on Saturday morning.

"I wish we met more often, Dorothy, dear," said Mary, as they prepared to part on the market-place. "Couldn't you come to tea at Woodside one day soon?"

"I could, of course," agreed Mrs. Yarrow. "But you know what it will mean. Last time, just as we had got down to a good gossip, Nurse Pop-Eyes came tapping at the door, to ask could Sergeant Blinkers have his khaki for week-end leave, as Miss Masquerier had gone home and locked up the kit-store. And in the middle of my story about the Russian princess, a medical officer from the base rang up to ask what was your Bed State?"

"I know," admitted Mary. "Can I come to you, then?"

"Delighted," said Dorothy warmly. "If you don't mind my twins all over the place, and the Occupational Expert in charge of the toddlers bursting in to ask which is the best shop in the landscape for harmless coloured beads and raffia. Sometimes," said Mrs. Yarrow, who was nobly inhabiting her ex-chauffeur's cottage, and doing the catering for the fifty children under five, and attendant staff, housed in Hydden Hall, "sometimes I think I shall murder Matron."

"But so do I!" said Mrs. Hungerford, staring at her friend. "I'm thankful to say," said Mrs. Yarrow, "that it's not quite so bad now that the spring vegetables are coming in, but, believe it or not, when the kitchen gardens were eight inches under snow in January, the Gorgon came to ask me why I could not provide any fresh greens."

"Mine seems to be getting rather worse with the spring in her veins," said Mrs. Hungerford, biting her lip. "However, I'm having a fortnight's respite, as she's on her annual leave now."

"Look here," said Mrs. Yarrow, with a sudden light of wild enthusiasm in her bright blue eyes, "I don't see why on earth we shouldn't use up the last of my May basic and go for a picnic, and be just girls together, for one afternoon. I say 'go,' because, although we couldn't find better places for picnics than there are in the park at Woodside, or down my way, as sure as death, even if we sneak out like spies, when the telephone rings, someone helpful will have noticed, and be able to fetch us. We'll take my car, and I'll pick you up at three, and we'll go right up on to the Downs, or up the river—whichever you like. What about May 20th? It's a Wednesday. I happen to know, because it's my beastly little birthday."

"I think it's a splendid idea," said Mrs. Hungerford, quickly consulting a small and worn black diary, which she produced from her pocket. "Excuse my muttering over this sordid little book. Wednesday the 20th. Yes, I'm almost sure I could do that. As far as I can see, it's perfectly good for me. 'Wednesday, 20th,

3 p.m. Picnic with Dolly.' That'll be lovely. I shall write and tell Kit, and he'll be delighted to hear about it, and it will be a nice change for him to hear about something else than Woodside Auxiliary Hospital." She checked herself, and made a business of returning the diary to her pocket, for no sooner had she mentioned writing to Kit, than she had remembered that poor Dorothy couldn't write to her husband.

"That's settled, then," said Mrs. Yarrow. "Now I must rush off and see my aunts. I suppose you wouldn't like to come with me? They are absolutely priceless—two sisters, aged seventy-six and seventy-eight. Unless you get them together, you never can tell which is which. Their poor mother can't have had one new idea on the subject of babies between producing them. Their names are Lily and Louie, and Lily is the widow of a judge, and Louie never married, but, as I said before, they're now identical. They've been sticking it in London, come what may, and now they've boldly come to Went for a little change, as Louie has had pleurisy. They are staying at the Victoria Hotel amongst endless cats and antimacassars and knitting-bags, because for two ladies travelling alone, to stay at The County would be 'fast'. They have many pleasant acquaintances in the Cathedral Close and district, and hire a taxi to take them out to see famous gardens and views. They attend every possible service at the cathedral, and going to tea at the Deanery is absolutely the high light of the jaunt."

"They sound sweet," said Mary, "but I know I can't make it. Would they care to come out to tea at Woodside? Ask them, and send me a message. Good-bye, Dolly dearest, and I was so glad to hear about Rolfe's prowess in the Fathers' match. It sounds as if he might be going to be his father over again; and I was so fond of his father."

"I think he has got a pretty useful pair of hands," said Mrs. Yarrow, forgetting her hurry and aunts, "and he's fortunately inherited his father's perfectly unaffected, kindly interest in other people, and general *bonhomie*. He's not in the least shy—never has been—and there's no doubt he's an original boy. The headmaster was very nice about him last time I saw him. Rolfe's got my quick temper, though. The other day he drew a picture, very modern, intended to represent himself. He had to explain, for it looked to me like a surrealist still-life. He said he had put in a cricket bat and a pony and a tent, to show his tastes, and a tree and axe for his carpentry, and a slate with a sum done wrong, to show he loathes mathematics. And on the carpet there was a broken vase, and he ruefully said, 'And that's my beastly temper!'"

VII

Miss Masquerier's old Florence, known before the War as "my invaluable and devoted old retainer," and more recently simply as "my old retainer," had an extraordinary way of knowing if Mrs. Hungerford had been in Went.

After parting from Dolly, Mary bent her steps directly to Miss Masquerier's house in French Row. She did not need or want a cup of coffee, but if she failed to report herself, Florence would somehow learn that she had been seen in the market-place at eleven-fifteen, and next time Mary met Miss Masquerier, the authoress would tell her pathetically of Florence's disappointment, and hint that the *ménage* of French Row was slighted. Mary had more than a suspicion that nowadays Miss Masquerier, who could be so sarcastic on paper about the Bourbons, went in fear of her once devoted and invaluable retainer. Florence, like many of her type, had not taken at all kindly to the idea of a Second German War. Indeed, Miss Masquerier herself had recounted in serio-comic vein that, the other day, after an unusually trying experience of ordering meals for the odd hours entailed by her hospital duties, she had said, "But surely, Florence, you can't imagine that Mrs. Hungerford and I invented this War for our own enjoyment?" to which Florence in the most lofty and knowing manner, had replied, "Well, as to that, Madam, this is a free country still, and everyone is at liberty to form their own opinions."

Miss Masquerier's house, which had quite a good eighteenth-century knocker, in the shape of a mermaid (which Florence kept brilliantly burnished, and unhooked and took indoors every night), stood on the sunless side of French Row. It was called "Fleur-de-Lys," which looked well on notepaper, and in *Who's Who*, but was hard on new postmen. Miss Masquerier had discovered, in the course of local researches, that the building, originally the residence of a sub-cellarer to the cathedral, had been the house at which captive French nobles had been entertained after Agincourt. She had not invented the name. The Fleur-de-Lys posting-house had been so called until the last Highbridge coach was discontinued, on the opening of the railway to that place. It possessed an underground stable, capable of accommodating a dozen horses, and tradition said that a subterranean passage led from this cellar to the cathedral. Outside, it was not particularly attractive—a long, rambling structure, with a gable at either end, built in the local grey stone, and much weather-beaten. Further, in 1858, a gentleman who either had advanced ideas on the subjects of light and air, or else knew someone ready to purchase diamond-paned windows and old oak, had torn out all its casements and doors. The result was that its face now had the perpetually surprised and yet characterless expression noticeable in elderly ladies with plucked eyebrows. Inside, as Mary knew, Miss Masquerier had been clever with promising material. However often she arrived at this house, Mary never failed to experience a thrill of pleasant anticipation as she waited for the front door to be opened.

She gave a delicate tap with the mermaid's tail, and soon Florence stood before her, backed by a vista of long, stone passage, painted in the shiniest wasp yellow, which reflected green lights from waving leaves, in the open air somewhere beyond. The yellow enamel managed to convey an impression of sunlight, even on the dullest day, and to-day the weather was far from dull. From Florence's expression, had Mary not been well acquainted with her, the guest might have imagined that her arrival was most untimely. Florence admitted that the morning was fine, said she was expecting Miss Masquerier at any moment, and suggested that Mrs. Hungerford might like to take her coffee in the garden. The garden was really the cobbled courtyard of the once-famous coaching inn, but Miss Masquerier had cultivated every possible inch of soil, so the description was not so absurd as it sounded. To-day, as she gazed on a brilliant display of polyanthus, forget-me-nots and cascading purple aubrietia, backed by grey stone and urban greenery, Mary was honestly able to say that she had never seen the garden look lovelier, to which Florence grudgingly replied that May was its month, but that Miss Masquerier wore herself out with that weeding after her hospital work. Florence really was a frightfully disobliging-looking old soul nowadays, thought Mary compassionately, as her companion, after shaking up its cushions with jealous care, presented her with a wicker chair placed beside a metal table, with an orange umbrella starting from its centre. Florence's mouth turned down naturally, in repose, her iron-grey hair was scraped back un-compromisingly from a narrow brow, and her spare figure, attired in rusty black, was the embodiment of permanent dis-approval of this life. It must be dull for her, cooped up all alone in a house in a street in Went throughout the week, thought Mary—so unlike peace-time, when Miss Masquerier was always having interesting ladies in to call, and Fleet Street gentlemen down from London for very good Sunday suppers in the courtyard, on warm nights, Continental style.

Florence withdrew in search of the promised coffee, and Mary took off her overcoat and hat, and sank back gratefully into the clutching embrace of the creaky wicker arm-chair. Overhead a tall and very old laburnum was meriting the nickname of Golden Rain, and opposite, over an oak staircase of silvery hue, with balustrading, designed to lead to a vanished gallery, sentimental trusses of wistaria were swaying gently in the breeze. The "Fleur-de-Lys" had been almost entirely rebuilt about the time that Marian martyrs were suffering in Went, but in a certain wall, which Mary could see by turning her head to the right, a treasured cusped window-head, below which Crown Imperials were flowering, spoke of the days of Agincourt.

A pattering sound aroused Mary's attention, and she realized the presence of Miss Masquerier's King Charles spaniels, a purchase made by the authoress in 1935, after the outstanding success of her *Stuart Reverie.* Mary, who like many English country ladies, was fond of animals, and anything to do with

King Charles, asked the gentlemen how they were, but they, after snuffing her skirts and overcoat, told one another that she was no good, and departed unanimously for the kitchen quarters which, judging by their figures, they frequented too often. Eventually the coffee, Miss Masquerier and the spaniels again, entered the courtyard simultaneously.

"Please tell me about the French prisoners who were lodged here on their way to London," asked Mary, who knew that Miss Masquerier liked this kind of opening. "What time of year did they arrive here? I've been thinking about them as I sat here."

"Well," said Miss Masquerier, her black eyes twinkling with intelligence behind her glasses, "Agincourt was fought on the morning of October 25th, 1415, after a night of heavy rain. The mud helped us. On paper, we ought not to have won. The enemy outnumbered us by four to one. I don't know the exact day on which the noble prisoners arrived here, but Henry V landed at Dover on November 16th, and entered London in triumph on the 22nd. He wore what the men at Woodside would call 'his civvies' when he rode to give thanks for his victory at St. Paul's and Westminster, and wouldn't let the battered helm which he had worn at Agincourt be exhibited to the people. Very odd. I have never quite been able to make him out. Do you like milk and sugar? We have no sugar shortage here, as I never take it."

"Milk, but not sugar, thank you," said Mary. "Was he a deep dog, then? I'm afraid I've always thought of him simply as the Shakespeare hero—not a bit deep. So the French got here in the middle of November. They can't have formed a very happy impression of Barsetshire. I wish it could have been in May, for their sake," she continued, looking beyond the wistaria-hung balustrading and the backs of houses in Fishgate and Northgate, to the cathedral tower, which looked startlingly close and venerable against cloudless heavens. In a garden, somewhere between Fleur-de-Lys and the tower, a fine beech-tree with young leaves, shiny as if they had been lacquered, reflected blue skies.

"They were extremely lucky to be alive," said Miss Masquerier sharply. "We got a message that we were being attacked in the rear while the third French division was still unbroken.

It was really only a small band of peasantry plundering the baggage, but as he couldn't spare sufficient men to guard them, Henry ordered all the prisoners to be slain. Only a few of the most important escaped the massacre before the mistake was discovered. The French losses were very heavy—five thousand of noble birth killed, including the Constable, three dukes, five counts and ninety barons. One thousand more taken prisoner."

"Did they all come here—to Went?" asked Mary, looking around the small courtyard amazedly.

"No, only a few of the most illustrious came here," said Miss Masquerier proudly. "And they may have come much later than November. They may have been lodged here on their way to one of their many later places of captivity. The Poet-Duke of Orleans, who was our unwilling guest for nearly a quarter of a century, lived at Pomfret, Ampthill and Wingfield (Suffolk), as well as the Tower and Windsor."

"More than a quarter of a century!" echoed Mary. "What did he do when he got free?"

"Remarried, first of all," said Miss Masquerier, her eyes twinkling more than ever. "He was twenty-four when he got here—a most interesting young fellow. His rondels on Spring and the Harbingers of Summer are charming. He was the son of the beautiful Valentina Visconti, and grandson of Gian Galeazzo, Duke of Milan. Of the ones we got here, he is the prisoner who attracts me most," proceeded the authoress, getting well under weigh. "But I know a romantic story about another of them—the young Comte de Richemont."

"How old was he?" asked Mary.

"Twenty-two," said Miss Masquerier. "He was the third son by her first marriage of Joan of Navarre, who at the date of Agincourt was the widowed Queen of England, stepmother to Henry V. Comte Arthur knew England already, because he had been over to visit his mother when he was eleven. He had been a soldier since he had entered his teens. Nicolas's story is that when the young man arrived in London, wounded and a prisoner, and presented himself to call upon his mother, she made one of her ladies-in-waiting occupy her high seat, and Comte

Arthur duly made his reverence and compliments to the strange English lady, and did not recognize his true mother until she betrayed herself."

"Oh, yes! It is a charming story," agreed Mary. "Poor Queen! I wonder what was her motive? I suppose she wanted to take a good look at him first, without his knowing. I hope he turned out well?"

"Not particularly," said Miss Masquerier unbendingly.

When her guest had finished her coffee, Miss Masquerier led her upstairs to the sitting-room on the first floor, which was dark, as it faced the street, but gratefully cool on a hot day. It had walls painted sea-green, a stone-hooded fireplace, too large for the present room, bearing initials cut by Cromwellian soldiery, and in one corner, a strip of much earlier and very crabbed Latin script, protected by a glass plate. While Miss Masquerier, who was a trusting lender of books, searched in her adjacent bedroom for her *édition de luxe* of *Ballades de Charles d'Orléans*, Mary listened, to the sounds made by the traffic in the cobbled street outside, and thought how odd it was that it had needed a second German War to bring back to English county towns at noon the sound of horses' hoofs as a predominant note. *Ballades de Charles d'Orléans* proved to be a tall though not very fat volume, printed on paper which Mary would have been glad to use out sketching. It was beautifully bound in yellow Niger, and had an impressive gilt coat of arms on both back and front of the cover. Judging by the thumping noises which had issued from the bedroom, it had been difficult to find, which was hard to believe, and Miss Masquerier seemed conscience-stricken when she realized its proportions. She nobly volunteered to bring it to Woodside by train, but Mary, who had provided herself with a gardening trug in preparation for her various purchases, insisted on being her own porter. Her only fear was lest the book was too beautiful to be lent. Miss Masquerier then said with even greater nobility that beautiful books were meant to be read, and, with a distinct look of strain visible on her features for the first time to-day, asked her guest to stay to lunch.

"I can't, thank you very much," explained Mary. "I want to buy a pair of slippers, and visit the belongings of two of our patients, before catching the 'bus to Westbury-on-the-Green, where I am due to lunch with my sister-in-law at one-thirty. I must say I rather dread visiting Pocock's family. Do you remember him? The one with a bunch of auburn curls and a leg in plaster, who helps with the potatoes? He told me quite dispassionately when he came to ask for another Went pass, that last week-end his wife had howled most of the time, and she is expecting her ninth baby at the end of the month, and the eldest girl is not fourteen, and they have no help. Norah Blent, who does soldiers' wives, says she will do what she can for them, but I feel I ought to go too. Thank you so much for my welcome refreshment. I always love coming to your house and seeing your garden, and as Charlie Myles said this morning, 'May's the queen of the months.'"

It was, perhaps also, the best month for an old and picturesque cathedral city, she reflected, as she made her way down the narrow medieval street, overhung by irregular gables, and under a stone arch labelled "Wax House Gate," guarded by headless saints, which led up an echoing passage—the shortest route from the market-place to the cathedral.

CHAPTER VI
A LOVELY DAY
(May 2nd)

I

DAME SARAH was out in the garden.

On her arrival at one-thirty, both Mrs. Thomas and Mrs. Rosemary Morrison told their guest this piece of news with bated breath, glancing nervously out of the window, rather as if a royal Bengal tiger was loose. As they were evidently disinclined to do anything more, Mary, who had hurried from the 'bus stop in order to be punctual, and had never been a big game hunter, was conscious of faint annoyance. She was reminded of the people who had taken Nettlerash Court in 1935 (Nettlerash had always been an unlucky house), and announced that they hoped nobody would call, and had left Nettlerash in 1937, saying that Barsetshire was an unfriendly county. However, as she was naturally of a peaceable nature, she asked how Dame Sarah was liking Willows, and Marcelle and Rosemary replied simultaneously that she was simply loving it. So she should, thought Mary, when she heard further that Marcelle had given up her bedroom so that the celebrity should have a south aspect and a view, and that so far they had been able to provide an entertainment for her every day. Dame Sarah never appeared until lunch-time, and had not, as yet, suffered a heart attack.

The cuckoo clock, imported by Marcelle, cooed from the hall, and in spite of Florence's coffee, Mary began to feel empty. She asked after Rosemary's offspring, Ferdinand-Africa, and heard with regret that he had gone round to Mrs. Bates.

"I can't see why the child wants to go to that house," said Marcelle fretfully.

"Old Sally is jolly," said Mary.

"But so materialistic," sighed Marcelle.

"Oh! I don't know about that," said Mary. "She's robust."

Marcelle shuddered, and Rosemary said that the broad beans had got black blight—such a disappointment. She had been watching them with pride since November.

Marcelle and her daughter Rosemary were a most untidy-looking couple. They both had what Mary classed as "bird's nesty" curly dark hair, and evinced not so much a disregard of prevalent fashions, as a perfect genius for discovering the most unattractive possibilities of modern dress. To-day Marcelle was attired in a blue blouse, of the type worn by French artists in fiction and by French porters in fact. Around her neck was a heavy silver necklace of barbaric design. Her back locks were enclosed in a coral chenille bag; a green Harris tweed skirt, bare legs and gamboge Morocco slippers, completed her toilette. Rosemary, who had dark shadows under her eyes, and was thin and childish-looking for her twenty-six years, wore a tumbled cotton dress originally designed for an Austrian peasant, embellished with a light-hearted pattern of children dancing round a maypole. Considering that both she and her mother had now lived in the depths of the country for many months, they were astonishingly pallid.

Millie Harker, of a family well known to Mary as the most unsatisfactory in Westbury-on-the-Green, now appeared looking, to tell the truth, much neater than either of her employers, and said that lunch was ready. Marcelle and Rosemary looked at one another.

"You might take the little cow-bell from the hall, Millie," suggested Marcelle finally, "and sound a gentle ring out in the garden. It's so tiresome," explained Marcelle, when Millie had departed. "Somebody on the Green (I suspect the Hills' old aunt) must have complained of our ringing our dear Swiss bell for meals. After all, with everyone working like negresses amongst the fruit and vegetables, hours were apt to slip away unnoticed, and we needed a clear summons. But on a pouring wet day in February an enormous red-faced policeman arrived in the hall, with the rain streaming off his mackintosh cape, and a notebook in his hand, to ask us if we could tell him if anyone in our household had heard a bell ringing loudly on the Green, and if anyone had been alarmed. Apparently it's the sign for a gas-attack in this dreadful war-time."

"No, Mummy," said Rosemary. "Gas is rattles. Church bells is parachutists, and hand-bells is 'gas-clear'."

To the general relief, a figure now came in sight through the French windows, and Rosemary was able to announce in rapturous accents, "Here's darling Dame Sarah! She's coming in."

"Run and tell Millie, dear," said Marcelle, sounding more nervous than ever.

Dame Sarah was walking slowly towards the house, pausing now and then in her progress to collect a Darwin tulip from the border. She was strikingly clad in a billowing taffetas cloak of the rich colour and material appropriated by cardinals, and the sheaf of tall tulips which she had gathered were rose-pink, lilac, saffron and purple, so they made an effective contrast. Mary, who had last seen Dame Sarah behind the footlights, in a Pompadour costume, and had cherished memories of an exquisitely tiny face under towering white curls, was astonished to see that in private life Dame Sarah had quite a large and somewhat heavy countenance, heavy black hair, and a figure far from fragile.

"Let me take your cloak, dear Dame Sarah," said Marcelle, fussing forward.

"Let me take your tulips first," said Rosemary.

"These flowers must be put in water or they will die," announced Dame Sarah, seating herself without a backward glance to see if a seat was there; and Mary remembered at once the story of an audience gathered in a darkish drawing-room to hear Mrs. Siddons recite, and the fact that the poor *tragédienne* had been obliged to exclaim "I must have candles!" three times before the audience had realized that this remark was not part of the play.

"You may fetch me a vase, but I will do the flowers myself," murmured Dame Sarah, sounding benevolent.

Rosemary fled, and Marcelle draped the cardinal cloak over the arm of the sofa on which her guest had enthroned herself, and Dame Sarah was revealed wearing black velvet and looking the image of a French *bourgeois*—the kind of mother-in-law of whom a neurotic young French husband might walk in terror. She wore no make-up, and did not look the kind of person ever to wear make-up. Indeed, sitting there smiling on the sofa, with lids drooped over her sleepy black eyes, she looked, thought Mary, just like a nice old tortoise in black velvet.

"Dear Dame Sarah," began Marcelle, with a glance at Mary, who was still hovering in the background. But at this moment Rosemary reappeared with a solid glass vase well filled with water. Before Mary could scream "Look out!" Dame Sarah had seized the tulips and stuffed them into the vase in a single gesture, after which, waving off Marcelle and Rosemary, she arose amongst cascades of water and, making her way unhesitatingly to the best place in this room for a floral display, dumped the trophy on the top of a high black lacquer writing-desk. Nobody seemed to mind that the carpet was deluged with water, and Mary afterwards noticed on her return to the parlour half an hour later, that never had she seen a more tasteful arrangement of tulips.

"Dear Dame Sarah," began Marcelle again, "I want to ask you to know my sister-in-law, Mrs. Christopher Hungerford."

"How do you do?" said Dame Sarah, uttering resonantly, and stretching out an unexpectedly fine hand in a peremptory manner. She retained Mary's fingers, and, drawing her companion to sit on the sofa beside her, murmured, "But—Hungerford? Marcelle never told me that the sister-in-law with the beautiful home which she has given for a hospital was Mrs. Hungerford. Is it possible"—her eyes searched Mary's face—"that you are a relative of . . ."

"Kit," suggested Mary. "Yes, I am his wife." For the life of her she could not afterwards imagine what had possessed her to add, "We've not been married long. But I was the girl in his own village whom he'd known all his life, and he asked me to marry him first when I was sixteen."

Dame Sarah enjoyed this, and said, "He, too, was very young then. And so dark! He must have French blood."

"Oh, yes—but not very recent—Henri Quatre," smiled Mary.

"I remember that he once brought a young friend to see me— years ago—a friend who wanted to write a play for me," mused Dame Sarah. "It was to be about Marie Stuart in later life. All five acts must take place within prison walls!"

She looked quickly behind her, and Mary, following the look, almost expected to see Tudor damp streaming down Norman stone.

"Did the young woman write it?" she inquired.

"Oh, yes, poor little creature. She wrote it," said Dame Sarah sadly.

"But I suppose it was no good," said Mary, sounding not so sad.

"It would have been much better if your husband had written it; as I told him afterwards," said Dame Sarah, with a great recovery of spirits and patting Mary's hand.

"Kit loved the theatre," said Mary.

"Yes," agreed Dame Sarah, looking ineffably sad again, as if the theatre were a dear friend who had died. "Your husband—he is well?"

"Quite well, thank you," said Mary. At least, I expect he's back again in Moscow now."

"Moscow!" echoed Dame Sarah lingeringly, and at this point, in fairness to the celebrity and her public, it had better be stated once for all, that from the moment that Dame Sarah began to talk to her directly, Mary no longer thought of her as a French *bourgeois* or a tortoise, and, indeed, never in after life did these similes recur to her brain. Afterwards, she only remembered of what Dame Sarah had talked, and realized why the critics for fifty years had been maudlin about a golden voice.

A move to the dining-room was now made, and Dame Sarah, sweeping to the sideboard, and rolling up her sleeves, began to create the salad. Marcelle, fussing inordinately, pointed out that she had now managed to obtain all the ingredients demanded by the guest.

When they were seated around the table, to cold salmon and a truly delicious salad, Dame Sarah returned to the subject of Moscow.

"I was there first in the year of the coronation," she said in boding tones, "the coronation of the unfortunate Nicholas. Two thousand poor people were crushed to death on the Khodinskoe Polye that day."

"I should simply love to see Russia!" breathed Rosemary.

"Oh, yes, but you would like it best in the winter—all English do," said Dame Sarah resignedly. "In the winter there are very few hours of daylight, but there are many little shrines, painted dark blue and full of stars, and above, nearly all the time that one is awake, there are also dark blue skies and little stars. And at our supper-parties—I never shall forget our supper-parties, where they served us caviare or the Volga out of tureens with ladles—when we entered the room, there stretched, as far as eye could see, waiters in white coats, with shaven heads, each bearing a whole salmon on a silver-gilt salver on his forearm—so! Do not attempt their champagne of the Crimea. . . . But—it is all so long ago—all I remember. None of you in this room were born then."

"I was born in the year of the murdered Tsar's coronation," said Mary honestly.

"Ah!" Dame Sarah looked at her with kindly attention. "One sees that you have had a happy life, madame, and have happier times yet to come."

"Well, I never want to make out that I am younger than I really am," explained Mary, with heightened colour, "because then, you see, I should have missed the Last War."

"It is reasonable—and full of courage—and very English," commented Dame Sarah softly to the chandelier.

"Thank you," said Mary gruffly.

"I have no maid now!" exclaimed Dame Sarah, as if the idea had just struck her. "My maid Natalie was a Russian. She had been with me fifteen years, and had often promised me that she should die in my arms. But she came in to me on that Sunday morning, and said to me, 'Madame! My country is invaded. Although I was born in exile and have been an exile all my life, I am a Russian. I think that I must go to a factory now to learn to make a tank.' I replied, 'Yes, my child, I too think that you should learn to make a tank.'"

"How very fine of you, darling Dame Sarah!" said Rosemary, her eyes burning with adoration.

"Have you ever found anyone," asked Dame Sarah, becoming very normal, "any thinking man or woman of your circle who was not surprised on that Sunday morning?"

"Well, no, I don't know that I have," agreed Mary.

"I was simply flabbergasted," said Rosemary.

"I always thought that this War would spread," said Marcelle, perversely gloomy.

"But you did not think that the Boche would attack Russia that morning, Marcelle," said Dame Sarah sharply.

"I didn't expect it, because I thought it would be madness from their point of view," said Mary hastily. "I mean, I thought of 1812."

"Ah, yes," said Dame Sarah, "and the Boche too, I think, had thought of 1812, and last winter he thought again, much, of 1812, and next winter he will, perhaps, think of very little else. That is what I hope. Oh, how he exasperates me, this bull in our shop of fine porcelain—my Europe . . . !

With the fruit tart, Millie Harker brought in Rosemary's child. Ferdinand-Africa was a stolid little boy, with straight flaxen hair and grey eyes, solemn, even for three. He must, Mary realized, take after his unknown and unregretted father, which perhaps explained why Rosemary showed no particular interest in him.

Ferdinand-Africa made straight for Dame Sarah and, laying a paw on her sleeve, demanded something which Mary could not catch.

"He wishes that you were wearing what he calls your red coat," translated Rosemary. "People don't wear coats in-doors, Ferdinand. Let me see your hands. Well, they're not so bad. Oh, Mrs. Bates washed them before she left for her Post. Well then, you can go and say 'how do you do' to your Auntie Mary."

"I will wear it this evening when we go together to the little orchard to feed the ducks and hens,' whispered Dame Sarah, suddenly all the country wife and grandmother.

"Ferdinand loves dressing up," said Marcelle. "I found him powdering his face in front of my mirror yesterday, I am sorry to say."

"The first year in life," said Dame Sarah, taking Ferdinand's paw, "is the year of Dependancy. The child looks to his mother, who nourishes him and thinks of him only. She is his world—for one year. . . . Remember, mothers—no longer . . . ! In the second year he becomes aggressive. Do not punish him too much. He needs outlet. After three years, he begins to like companions—good company. From the fourth year, he enters the world of Fantasy—you cannot see his friends. . . . Ferdinand is not yet four. He is, perhaps, to be an actor."

"I should simply love my son to be an actor," gasped Rosemary. "He's rather neat-fingered, we think. We had hoped that perhaps he might be going to be a surgeon."

"Anything that does not take life," explained Marcelle.

"Oh, dear, and I can see Sandhurst written all over him," thought Mary.

"But I'm afraid he's hardly got the face or the figure for an actor," said Marcelle.

"That does not matter," said Dame Sarah, impatiently waving aside all the handsome men in the world. "Indeed, for a good actor to have great good looks is sometimes a misfortune. I have known it to be the christening gift of the Bad Fairy. The best Romeo I ever knew could not walk and had not the legs for tights. But he never knew it."

"What really matters?" asked Mary, much interested.

"For myself, I should say," smiled Dame Sarah, looking down, "hands—and a Voice."

II

Mary's last view of Dame Sarah, with Ferdinand-Africa seated beside her on the piano stool, was a charming one. For several moments Marcelle had been fretting because the taxi would be here at four to take her guest to the Old Mill House, and Dame Sarah must go upstairs and get her rest. Mary left obediently, and Rosemary escorted her to the garden-gate. Half-way down the garden path, Rosemary said, looking back furtively, "If you're not in a frightful hurry, Auntie Button, I rather want to ask your advice about something."

"Ask on," said Mary. "If it's anything I know anything about I shall be only too glad."

She remembered that people seldom ask for your advice except when they have already made up their minds.

"I've practically made up my mind that I ought to go and drive an ambulance in Wapping," said Rosemary.

"Why Wapping?" asked Mary.

"Well, it needn't be Wapping or an ambulance, but I mean something somewhere right away from all this," said Rosemary, waving a hand at the village pond. "I think I ought to be mobile. After all, I'm only twenty-six."

"What about Ferdinand-Africa?" asked Mary.

"I can't see that the child needs five women to look after him," said Rosemary.

"Five!" echoed Mary.

"Well, there's Mummy and myself, and Millie Harker, full-time," said Rosemary, "and Mrs. Harker comes in every morning, and anyway he's over at Mrs. Bates's house most days."

"What would happen when your mother wanted to go out for the day, or away?" asked Mary.

"The Harkers are awfully fond of children and good with them," said Rosemary, "especially Mrs."

Since Mrs. Harker had uncomplainingly added to her family of eleven the three infants of her two unmarried daughters, and had certainly never lost a child, Mary supposed that this was true. She continued to look doubtful as Rosemary proceeded, "I've had the idea simmering in my brain for some time, and hearing Dame Sarah talking so wonderfully about what women are doing in Russia has sort of brought it to the boil. Mummy and I don't hit it off. We never did, even in London in peace-time, and down here, cheek by jowl, day in and day out, it's just not possible to continue. She'd be much better without me. And considering our ages it's obviously her duty to stay at home and look after Ferdinand while I drive an ambulance."

"I quite see that you feel you ought to be doing something," said Mary. "Have you considered trying to get some part-time work down here? If you worked in Highbridge, even all day, you could probably arrange to come home for weekends. Would you like me to speak to Lady Muriel Gidding?"

"No, thank you," said Rosemary, tossing her gipsy locks, "I want to go right away from here. My sacrifice must be absolute."

"Have you discussed it with your mother?" asked Mary.

"No," said Rosemary. "But I wanted you to know, in case you heard suddenly one day that I was gone."

Mary prepared to walk back to Woodside by the Pilgrims' Way. She would much rather not have walked again, as she had already covered a considerable distance on pavements since she had caught the eight-ten 'bus. She was also now feeling the deflation consequent upon having been to a lunch-party at which one person had made great demands upon her attention, and two had been infectively nervous. However, she told herself that the afternoon was a lovely one for a quiet stroll across country, and she set off, moving with the measured, unhurried stride of the country bred.

In the Hills' garden, a somewhat tasteless and glaring display of yellow daisies, scarlet tulips and tawny wallflowers, assailed the eye, but the lovely scent of the wallflowers in strong sun was a compensation. Norah's dachshund, Otto, appeared, barking less madly than usual, and attended by a sober and majestic Great Dane. "Hallo, Hengist!" said Mary to the Great Dane. I didn't know that you were down here. Your mistress is on leave, I suppose. I must telephone."

Ike gooseberries were forming in the Hills' cage, and in a pear-tree on the wall Mary noticed a nest. Although it was the Hill's pear-tree and nest she couldn't resist stepping on to the mint-bed and looking inside. The nest was neatly mud-lined and held as yet only three greenish-white eggs, blotched reddish-brown and lilac. She told Hengist and Otto "Missel-thrush" before they turned back into the house. She then climbed the stile into the horseshoe meadow beyond, and found herself regarded of many disapproving sheep. The lambs were growing up into quite unattractive young men and women, she noticed, and their mothers tended to shift away, looking prim when their offspring came running and bleating towards them. The green lane leading to the Lower Merle road was already overgrown with tall grasses and wild flowers. "Campion, speedwell and garlic," thought Mary. "Hooray for the Red, White and Blue! All the same, you could make rather a nice wet water-colour of them. And of course, they're not scarlet, navy and Chinese white. They're ruby-velvet, deep-sea and wax-candle."

The country was needing rain. Up on the Pilgrims' Way the turf was showing cracks. All the may-trees were exhibiting their best snowstorm effect, and under one of great antiquity, backed by skies of lavender-blue, a white cow was bending the gaze of a full brown eye upon a sleeping white calf as if she thought it the most beautiful thing anyone had ever seen. "That subject would call for oils and a Dutchman of the seventeenth century," thought Mary. The horses in the last meadow before she entered the park looked as if they had been ordered by the half-dozen. Every one was in exactly the same attitude—nose to the grass, while a light breeze played amongst the tail.

The Woodside orchards were what Ted Squirl would have called "a sight," and Mary paused a moment, after breasting the hill, to look down upon them. "It's humiliating, the way one keeps on thinking of food these days," she thought. "They remind me of nothing but the big famille-rose bowls of mushed-up strawberries and cream which we used to have at Woodside pre-last war, on trestle-tables and flapping clean tablecloths, for the Dockland mothers' outing. I can almost smell urn tea and see out of the corner of my eye the hovering curate and the sixty bunches of country flowers, sitting in buckets of water, waiting to be handed into the char-à-bancs.

She forgot to take a closer look at the orchard, for directly she passed through the swing gate into the park, she descried coming towards her, across the right of way from the house, two figures in blue uniform, followed by two white dogs. When they got within hailing distance, she recognized little Johnson and Derek Young. She stopped, and said, "Good evening, nurse. Are you taking Radish home?" and to Derek, "This is a case of talking of angels! Do you know that I believe I saw you this morning as I passed your station in the Highbridge 'bus, and I believe that you flew over my head? I was going to send you a line to-night to ask you to call upon us. "

Derek Young said that it might well have been him, and Mary wondered if he could possibly have been for what was called a sweep over occupied France between nine a.m. and now. He went on at once to say that he had been so sorry to miss Mrs. Hungerford at the hospital, because he had come over to ask if any of her staff would care to come to a dance at the aerodrome next Tuesday. "It's called a dance," he explained frankly, "but, as a matter of fact, I'm afraid there is bound to be a sing-song too, and the dancing will be in one of the hangars, where you can hardly hear the music for the sound of shuffling feet. Linoleum on concrete. . . . But we've got quite a good band and should be awfully glad if anyone cared to come."

Mary, thanking her stars that she had an engagement for Tuesday evening, thanked her would-be host politely on behalf of her staff, and said that she would look at the off-duty list for next week, and get her secretary to send him a line. She said, looking down, "Have you got a bull-terrier too?" and Derek Young said yes, that this was Flying-Officer Beetroot—fourteen confirmed and the gift of a friend. Feeling completely out of her depth, Mary bade the young couple farewell, and they passed on briskly, attended by their smirking escort, and she entered languidly on the last lap of her journey.

Outside the house, on the oval central lawn, a jocular party in hospital blue, some of which showed signs of having been to the laundry often, were engaged with two recalcitrant hand-mowers. Another group were rolling the drive, and round the corner, where yew-hedges cast angular shadows, a third party were playing bowls on Sir Barnaby Morrison's bowling-green. In spite of the whirring noise made by the mowers and the grinding and spitting sounds produced by the team in charge of the roller (who sometimes let the instrument escape), a number of plaster-cases, in wheel and deck chairs, continued to sleep profoundly under the Orangery walls. They slept with their bodies tumbled in all directions, like the bodies of drowsy babies strapped into push-carts, and most of them looked mere infants, thought Mary, as her glance swept the line of roughened heads and shiny faces glistening in the sun, with mouths hanging open. Only here and there she saw a head touched with silver and a wrinkled brow. "Petty Officer Robins. I'm glad he's getting a nap," she thought. But Petty Officer Robins was the one who lifted an eyelid and an arm, and in a moment was wide awake, as the lady of the strange house to which the fortune of war so strangely had sent him, passed close by, with her shopping basket on her arm, on her way into the cool hall.

A soporific calm brooded over the interior of Woodside, and the typically country scent of new-mown grass, and sound of bowls clicking, floated in through open staircase windows, as

Mary proceeded to her office. "It's going to be a perfect night," she thought. "It does seem a pity on a lovely day like this, that one has to grope one's way up the second flight." But permanent boarding-up had been the only means of complying with black-out regulations, as far as the top of the main staircase windows of Woodside were concerned.

"I wonder how Professor Beadon got on with Johanna, she thought, looking at fine but dimly seen plaster decoration in the Chinese Chippendale style.

Her office looked pleasant, with golden evening sunshine slanting in, and the morning's post, neatly sorted into "Personal" and "Hospital," by Johanna Pratt, waiting on her desk and on the mantelpiece.

Mary looked at the pile on her desk first, taking off her hat as she did so, and running her fingers through her flattened front hair. On the top of the pile, a sheet in Miss Masquerier's artistic hand, stated *Lance-Corporal Stovin's boots have been condemned*. On the mantelpiece, propped against the clock above the unsmiling face of the river-god, were four receipts, a letter from Rolfe Yarrow at preparatory school (who admitted in the body of the letter that he was getting rather short of boiled sweets, and on the back or the envelope, "I urgently need some boiled sweets"), and two Indian mail letters. One of them was from a Hungerford cousin, now a colonel in New Delhi, and the other from Catha Rollo, an old school friend and neighbour, and the mother of Nurse Elizabeth. Mary tore them open, and from between the thin sheets of the colonel's letter fell a snapshot of a small boy in a bathing-suit, holding the collars of a curly-coated retriever and a spaniel. Lady Rollo, who covered six rather opulent sheets, seemed worried about everything. Her husband, General Sir Daubeney Rollo, who, Mary remembered, had rather tended since the War to fight with everyone, regretted being in India. Elizabeth had written to tell her mother that she was still losing weight. "And she tells me, Button dear, which I cannot believe, that there is a question of her being sent on night duty." Mary sighed and flicked over the page. "Tony's letters too, or rather the lack of them, worry me, Button. Have you seen him?

We have heard nothing since he wrote to tell his father that he would soon have to decide whether or not to continue as a medical student, as he was now practically a convinced conscientious objector. We feel that as his godmother, and being on the spot, you will be using your influence. . . ."

"Is Elizabeth getting any gaiety? Her last letter said that she was going to London on leave. My poor little Monkey-Face! It is too pathetic that she is getting nothing that a girl of her age should have. I am so afraid, Button, that it is going to be the same story over again, and that all the little débutantes will meet no one, and marry all the wrong people, as our generation did."

Mrs. Hungerford was quite glad to see Johanna Pratt entering. Johanna, who brought a further pile of letters for Mrs. Hungerford's signature, asked if her employer had had tea.

"I haven't, but I don't need it, as I've been to a lunch-party," explained Mary. "We've a couple of hours' work here, I reckon." Johanna used the house telephone, and told the pantry to send up China tea for one, on a tray. Before she seated herself, with notebook open and pencil poised, she mentioned:

"Three things! A lady whose name I could not catch is coming at seven. I am sorry, but she would not repeat her name, or spell it, and she would come. It sounded like angry German, but of course it can't be. She said that she was speaking from Lady Muriel Gidding's office, and that you would know. She said it was very important."

"Oh, yes, I do know. It's Aggie Sherman. We were at school together," said Mary, thinking that surely she had been at school with rather trying people. Even her nearest and dearest could only stand Aggie Sherman in very small doses. "What were the other things?"

"A young Air Force officer, appropriately named Young," reported Johanna, "arrived at tea-time, to ask if Nurse Rollo was on duty. We brought forth Lalage, who had just got up after night duty, and they looked upon one another blankly. It turned out that he meant Nurse Elizabeth; he said he had been at Oxford with her brother. Sister Finan asked him to staff tea, and Elizabeth turned up and scarcely seemed to remember him, and rather bit his head off. He was naturally of a blushful complexion, and wanted us all to go to a dance."

"I know him too," said Mary, "and I met him on my way home. Remind me to ask the staff at supper about the dance. What was the third thing?"

"Professor Beadon," said Johanna, rising to sharpen her pencil by the fireplace. "He brought a bundle of super photographs which looked to me uncannily like the staircase here, and he was leaving them for you to see, but seems to have gone off with them in his pocket. Anyway, he wants to come again on Tuesday evening."

"There seems to be a fate against my meeting the poor man," said Mary. "Tuesday at seven is the meeting of the Local Defence Committee at Westbury-on-the-Hill, isn't it?" Miss Agatha Sherman arrived in a taxi at six-forty-five. Her step, even upon the shadowed second landing, was unhesitating, and before her friend entered the office, Mary remembered with a start, that Aggie's voice had stayed that of a child. Perhaps it was because she had met Dame Sarah to-day that she noticed Aggie's shrill high tones particularly.

"Don't trouble to come any farther," said Aggie's voice. "Yes, Mrs. Hungerford is expecting me. I have an appointment. I can see the way perfectly. Just up those four dark little steps, and the first door on the left. Thank you. Hallo, Mary!"

"Good evening, Aggie," said Mary, rising.

"I was so surprised not to find you working when I telephoned in the middle of the morning," said Aggie. "I mean, I thought that you were always hard at work. Is this a very busy hour at your hospital? I only ask because I had to ring three times before anyone came."

"Quarter to seven is patients' supper," said Mary. "I hope that you will sup with us at seven-fifteen."

"No, thank you, though I should like to meet your staff," said Aggie. "I've got a taxi waiting, and I'm dining with Norah Blent, so I can't stay. I'm going to move this chair by the typewriter, so that I can see you properly. Now, I shall only keep you ten minutes."

She produced from her pocket a collapsible pocket time-piece, snapped its face open and set it on the table in front of her. In spite of her friend's business-like air, or perhaps because of it, Mary's spirits sank. Aggie Sherman was very large, and her costume, like her voice, was young for her age. She had fair curls of an unconvincing shade, tied up with a scarlet ribbon, and a countenance which looked permanently heated and curiously out of sympathy with her hair. She was wearing a summer or tennis dress of a washable striped silk, which suggested that it had been designed for gentlemen's pyjamas. Like Alice in Wonderland, she wore round-toed black leather slippers with a strap, and white socks. On the floor beside her she had set down a very full leather bag, with two handles, and a zip fastener, which was not fastened owing to overcrowding difficulties.

"First of all, I want to tell you confidentially," said Aggie, fixing eager gooseberry eyes on Mary's face, "that I'm definitely leaving my present job at the end of the month."

"Oh, Aggie," said Mary regretfully, "and you got me to write to Muriel Gidding on your behalf."

"I know you did," said Aggie triumphantly, "but did you know that the poor woman is ga-ga? I'm sure I didn't, or I would never have applied to enter her office."

"I should never have thought that Lady Muriel was ga-ga," said Mary a trifle stiffly. "A little dictatorial, perhaps—I warned you. . . ."

"No, she's absolutely ga-ga," explained Aggie. "Waves her hands when you come in and says, 'I shan't sign anything more to-day. I'm going now. Good-bye! Good-bye!'"

"But surely you don't have to come in," said Mary. "You told me you were working in Mrs. Tytler's department?"

"It isn't worth while wasting time talking about the place now, as I'm definitely leaving," said Agatha, "but I think you ought to know that the real reason why they can never keep anyone, and get such an appalling type of woman, is that they simply have no idea of organization."

"What do you think of doing next?" asked Mary meekly.

"That's what I came to talk to you about," said Agatha, with increasing eagerness. "Now, look here. I'm thirty-nine and sound in wind and limb."

"Aggie!" exclaimed Mary.

"Oh, I changed my age to thirty-six on the outbreak of war, for patriotic reasons," said Aggie loftily. "That makes me thirty-nine now. And I'm ready to go anywhere and do anything."

"That sounds good," said Mary, brightening.

"And I don't want to join anything where I have to wear uniform," proceeded Aggie, "and I need something where I can use my previous experience. My present job is beneath me. Considering all the appeals that one sees in the papers, simply shrieking for capable women over calling-up age, I should think I ought to get something very good as soon as I'm free."

"You've been nearly a year in your present job," calculated Mary.

"Fourteen months," corrected Aggie.

"And before that . . . ?"

"I did Refugees, which was a job that simply died on me," said Aggie. "But the point is, not what I have done, but what I'm going to do."

"I expect people will want to know what you have done, though," mused Mary. "I know you were at that Ambulance Depot."

"I left that simply because the men bagged all the work," said Aggie indignantly. "I don't see the sense, in war-time, when one's country is engaged in a death grapple, in sitting with one's hands in one's lap."

"No, of course not. Well, I don't know anything about what the arrangements were there," agreed Mary.

"Anyone who knows anything about the Went Fire Services congratulates me on having left that," said Aggie, dismissing that subject. "I joined up as a full-time nurse a week before the outbreak, and went straight to the Went Infirmary, as you know. I only stayed there a fortnight, it is true, but because I had been accustomed to work in the operating theatre throughout the last war, and I absolutely refused to be set to scrub lockers."

"I should have thought that one could have scrubbed lockers to the confounding of one's enemies," murmured Mary.

"I wasn't allowed to use my experience," said Aggie, looking very fierce indeed. "But anyway, I've quite given up the idea of spending another war in a hospital ward. I ought to be Administrative this time. I thought if I came here I could help you in your office."

"Were you thinking of coming here?" asked Mary faintly.

"My dear Mary," said Aggie affectionately, "if you had been running your own hospital two years ago, when I left that incredibly badly run market garden, I should never have thought of going anywhere else. But you see I never heard that this place was going to be opened until after I had got fixed up."

"The trouble is," said Mary helplessly, "that I'm rather fixed up here now. I've got a secretary. . . ."

"You would have to sack her," admitted Aggie, "but in these days she would easily get something else, and as she sounded quite young, on the telephone, I dare say it would be more suitable that she should do something more active."

"She's got a permanently shortened left leg," mentioned Mary.

"If you wanted to keep her on, to work under me, then," suggested Aggie. "I can type a bit but I can't do accounts at all. Perhaps she could stay on and do them. Though that, of course, would be entirely for you to decide."

"I was going to say that I've got a secretary who took a First in History at Oxford," said Mary, "though that possibly is not to the point. But she is also a first-class shorthand typist, and, although this sounds unlikely, a chartered accountant."

"I know, Mary, dear," said Aggie indulgently, "they all are."

"Indeed they're not!" said Mary, startled.

"I mean, I know exactly the kind of little person," said Aggie. "What you need, for your own comfort, is someone like ourselves. I mean someone who can speak the King's English."

"But Johanna Pratt," said Mary, beginning to blush. "You see—her father is Lord Billingsgate."

After a nerve-racking pause Aggie rose, and said, "I am very sorry, Mary, to see that what I have heard about places like this is true. But what most disappoints me is to find you giving way to being a snob."

No one cares for such an accusation, especially on a warm evening, after they have caught the eight-ten a.m. 'bus, and walked eight miles and lunched with a *tragédienne* and dictated for two hours.

"I'm sorry too, Aggie," said Mary, "but I'm afraid I really have no vacancy here and no prospect of one." In her mind's eye she saw prison bars receding.

"I had thought, you see," said Aggie, who never bore malice long, "that it would be so lovely for both of us if I came to work here. And it would be such a score for me to be able to tell Lady Muriel, when I resign to-morrow morning, that I'm leaving because you've asked me to come to you."

"However," said Aggie, reclaiming the bursting bag, "if you've got no vacancy, that's that, and I shall just have to go on to Norah Blent, who I hear is making a frightful muddle of her salvage."

"I believe you've heard wrong," said Mary coldly. But her heart smote her as she looked down and saw the Alice in Wonderland slippers preparing for another dauntless journey, and she ended the interview by saying, "As you're ready to go anywhere and do anything, Aggie, I'm sure it won't be long before you hear of something worth doing and worth sticking. . . . I realize I'm lucky, being able to stay on in my own home. I wish I could have helped. Good-bye, and good luck."

Not until after Aggie's taxi had carried her away did Mary discover on the typewriter table a business woman's open pocket timepiece.

III

"I realize I'm lucky being able to stay on in my own home," thought Mary, as she looked out of her bedroom window at eleven p.m., "but I do wish that Kit was here. It's almost two years since Dunkirk, and his return, and our wedding. . . . I know what it is that's making me think of him so much to-day. It's because the pinks are just coming out. Smells are notorious for arousing vivid memories. It's almost exactly a year since that night when I thought he was in Lisbon, so didn't take any notice when I heard a taxi drive up in the middle of the night. . . . And the next thing I heard was his voice calling 'Mary! Come down. It's lovely down here.' And when I opened this window and stuck my head out he was standing below in the paved garden, looking ten feet high in his long great-coat, with the moonlight white on his face. . . . I wish it could happen again, to-night. But nothing will happen to-night."

At staff supper she had announced Derek Young's invitation, and it had turned out that on Tuesday the nurses off duty would be Nurse Elizabeth and Nurse Johnson. Elizabeth had said promptly that she did not intend to go and shuffle in a hangar off the Went avoiding road, and little Johnson had said nothing, but twisted her hands in her lap and looked like the hunted hare. However, Diana, *née* Gibson, who was always ready for what she called a "do," said that she would gladly swop her Thursday for Tuesday, if Madam would allow. Nicky had told her to keep going, and would certainly approve when she wrote to tell him that she had been shuffling in a hangar. Her Lieutenant-Commander took the view that the next best thing, when one could not accept an invitation to a dance oneself, was to get a letter from one's wife who could, and had. Diana said further that she believed Air Force bands were pretty hot stuff, whereupon "shrimp-size" Johnson divulged in a gasp that she had never been to a real grown-up dance. She had filled out, on country fare, Mary noticed, or was growing up. She had decidedly come on since her arrival at Woodside.

They had, in the end, quite a cheerful supper, for Diana, who did not lack courage, had asked Madam outright was Woodside haunted? and over the eternally popular subject of ghosts the whole staff had relaxed and become what Diana called "matey." Diana said that her father had once told her that there was a ghost here, and he knew things about most Barsetshire houses. Lalage had given Mary the opportunity to close the subject if she wished, but Mary had not in the least minded giving them a judiciously expurgated version of the fatal duel fought by Sir Crosbie Morrison in the garden behind the yew hedges.

"Then it's not in the house at all," said Diana, sounding disappointed.

"Well, they brought the Vicomte into the morning-room, and he died on the table there," smiled Mary.

"The place I always think is eerie, Madam," said Sister Finan, "is the long gallery leading down to that baize door."

"Pippa thought she saw a man in the library," acknowledged Lalage.

"What sort of a man?" asked Mary quickly.

"Well, I didn't really see him properly, Madam, and as soon as Nurse Rollo laid her hand on the back of the chair in which I thought he was sitting, I saw, of course, that I was wrong. It was just as we came in"—little Johnson puckered her brows—"and I was still standing by the door. But I thought I saw a tall, very dark man sitting in the big chair by the fire. I thought he was asleep and would jump up and be surprised. At least, I don't exactly know that I thought he was asleep. He just seemed to be sitting in the chair, doing nothing, with one hand across his forehead and the other drooping over the arm of the chair— rather as if he was a tired fire-watcher," ended little Johnson, raising a laugh.

"There isn't any story of a man in the library, as far as I know," said Mary. She did not add, "But that is the chair in which my husband always sits, and you could hardly have described him better if you had seen him."

Little Johnson had not ever seen Kit, but she might, of course, have heard descriptions of the absent master of the house or even seen a photograph somewhere. And very likely her thoughts had been running on him, as she was shown the wing which had been his.

"I shall write and tell Kit that it's high time he looked in upon us, as my probationers are beginning to see him," thought Mary. "Oh, dear, if it wasn't that the amenities of civilization are now suspended I might easily be hearing his voice to-night, even though he is in Stockholm or Moscow. Granny Merle has told me that he'd put through personal calls to her on the telephone from Berlin and Bucharest. And on her eightieth birthday it was from Adelaide. Very showy!"

She was undressing slowly, setting her lace-up shoes neatly side by side and regarding the collar of her cotton dress critically. Downstairs she heard the telephone bell. "If that's Kit," she told herself whimsically, "he'll get on to Night Sister, and then she'll switch him through and he'll say 'Hallo, Mary! Is it Mary'?"

"Hallo, Kit, dearest!"

"How's all at your end, Mary?"

"Pretty fair, thanks. That is to say, we are all blooming like the rose, but as cross as two sticks."

"What? Not at your end, too?"

"I've been awfully worried about Valerie and Rex, Kit."

"I don't see why you should worry, my sweet. Leave that to me. I'm Valerie's trustee."

"Are you everyone's trustee, Kit?"

"Pretty nearly, I sometimes think. It's my kind face."

"Actually you've got rather a wicked face—sinister features and colouring, at any rate."

"But a nice kind expression, don't you think?"

"Not at the moment—teasing monkey, verging upon hairy gorilla."

"Poor old Rex! I only hope he doesn't make it an annual event."

("No, that's cheating," thought Mary. "He said that in his last letter.")

"Are you upstairs in your room, Mary?"

"Yes, with the scent of the pinks blowing in. You remember—the white pinks that look so miffy by day and come into their own with moonlight. Where are you, Kit?"

"In the Grand Hotel, Stockholm, Madam, where it isn't really dark, although a later hour than in Barsetshire. Some day we'll come here together, Mary, and eat asparagus on an island after midnight. Or perhaps it would be better for you to make your first trip in the Krafter season. Oh! they're sort of baby lobsters.

The natives eat anything up to three dozen at a sitting and feel new men next morning. Or would you prefer to come in the ski-ing season and walk in a fur coat, leading a Borzoi, to see the statue of Jenny Lind? The flats here are more than comfortable. We might take one. What's that? No, I have not, during my misspent youth, been the owner of a more than comfortable flat in every European capital. The best one I ever had was in New York. Yes, I'm in Stockholm, Mrs. Hungerford, and I can see the Old Town across the black water opposite and lights shining in the windows of the Palace, and the spire of the Knights' church in the square, where Axel Fersen was beaten to death with umbrellas."

"You're making that up, Kit!"

"Well, there were umbrellas used. That shows one how a fellow could see the death of one regime and another in full blast without having to live very long at that date. Odd to have driven Marie Antoinette on the road to Varennes and end amongst umbrellas in a Stockholm street riot."

The telephone by Mary's bedside really rang and she laid down her dressing-gown and unhooked the receiver.

"This is Night Sister speaking, Madam," barked a distant voice.

"Oh, yes, Sister," said Mary, her heart racing absurdly. "The Head Warden A.R.P. has just given us the 'Air Raid Warning Red,' Madam. Secretary said she had left you only a few minutes ago so I thought you might like to know."

"Oh, thank you, Sister," said Mary. "I'll come down."

IV

"Come in," called Mary, in answer to a tap at her door. "A Red Warning," announced the deep voice of Johanna Pratt. "I haven't heard the siren, but on this side of the house one doesn't always, so I thought I'd let you know."

"Thank you," said Mary. "Rather uncalled-for, after so many months of peace, isn't it? I'll be in the office in three minutes."

In the office, Johanna Pratt, martially attired in gum-boots, a tin hat and an overcoat, was enjoying a powerful Turkish cigarette, whilst overhead the sound of approaching aircraft was clearly audible. "I'm sorry," she said, stifling a yawn, "but I never can take an interest in a foe I can't see."

"We shall have to shift the immobile cases, I'm afraid," said Mary, entering to her. "It's a bore, but we can't risk it in case they really mean business."

"Can you tell me," asked Johanna, as an explosion shook the windows, "whether that's a gun or a bomb?"

"Our new gun up on the hill, I should say," said Mary, doing up buttons wrong in a hurry.

"But that rude one was definitely something landing," said Johanna a moment later. "Hum! Big stuff somewhere."

"As you're dressed," said Mary, "I'd be glad if you'd help to call the day staff. Night Sister will take charge of the walking cases and Matron and I will stay with the immobiles."

"Matron's on holiday," Johanna reminded her employer.

"So she is! Well then, ask Sister Finan to come to the place under the stairs as soon as possible, and call the day staff at the double."

But it soon became apparent that doing anything at the double to-night would not be easy, for as Johanna left the room, a bang sounded which seemed to shake Woodside to the foundations, and in the same moment all the lights went out, leaving an auxiliary hospital somewhere in England in total darkness.

"Are you all right? Have you got a torch?" asked Johanna's voice, returning.

Yes. Get on, please," answered Mary, feeling her way back into her bedroom.

Downstairs some of the walking cases, under the guidance of Night Sister, were already heartily engaged pushing the immobiles, beds and all, out of the white saloon and across the pillared main hall to the "safe place" under the stairs. They called out "Make way, please," and "Yes, sir, that's my baby! Other men, who had been roused from innocent slumber upstairs by Lalage, were slippering down the main staircase. They had got on their blue trousers and, much incommoded by gas masks and tin hats, were struggling into their blue jackets. They looked unfamiliar and nightmarish, with roughened hair and eyes half-closed by sleep, and the meagre and swaying light afforded by candles, storm-lanterns and torches, cast wildly magnified shadows on eighteenth-century walls of fine plaster-work. From all over the dark and sun-drowsed house came sounds of doors clicking open, and voices complaining in every accent of Great Britain that the lights were gone. The banging overhead persisted, but everyone was busy.

"Take care of that patient, please," said Night Sister sharply. "You're not launching a lifeboat. Five—six—there's room for one more if you pack them closer. Nurse! I need you!"

Afterwards, looking back, Mary decided that Sister Finan must sleep in her teeth, a starched cap and a clean apron. The incredible woman was on the spot, with her teeth in her head and not a hair out of place, within five minutes of her summons, though she must have been, if not asleep, certainly in bed.

The drone of aircraft overhead settled down and drew closer and closer until the drumming in her ears reminded Mary of the last moment before you go under an anaesthetic. She remembered that on the night a fortnight before the hospital opened, all the windows on the garden-front had gone, and she remembered that there were now seventy-two people under her roof, not counting the head gardener and the ex-chauffeur who, as wardens, would be outside, keeping an eye lifted for incendiaries.

A walking-case, wearing a tin hat at a halo-like angle, strolled in presently to say that the flares and incendiaries were dropping like a snowstorm on the woods up behind. "Fairy-land!" said he romantically. Somebody ghoulish said that that would be his lordship's new plantation above Went Park, and somebody else remembered that poor Miss Masquerier lived in a street in Went. Everyone, it soon appeared, knew someone in Went to-night.

Gradually the drone decreased in volume, though the gun-fire did not, and public opinion decided that "They" were after Went to-night.

And two hours of uneasy boredom succeeded before the strange noises died, and the sirens sounded "All Clear," and the

wardens came in regretfully to say that poor old Went was burning like the fiery furnace. "They've got it proper, this time."

CHAPTER VII
POOR OLD WENT
(May 5th, May 9th, July 4th)

I

FROM THE MOMENT that she woke on the morning of Tuesday,
May 5th, Mary Hungerford saw that this was to be a quite perfect
May day. She had slept, for the first time in years, until ten a.m.
The sun was well up, and the cloudless sky and soft green world
beneath seemed to be swimming in light and warmth. A gentle
hum, which had nothing to do with aircraft, sounded in her ears
as she threw up the lower sash of her window and looked forth.

The view from her bedroom window at this season was
lightly screened by the picturesque boughs of an old locust tree,
planted in the middle of the north lawn when the house was
built. The old Robinia was the laziest tree in Mary's garden, the
last, in spring, to put out its delicate pale leaves and the first,
in autumn, to say "Ugh" and shed every leaf overnight. For
much the greater part of the year it stood, gaunt and elegant,
silhouetted against the Higher Merle plantations, saying, "It
wasn't kind to bring me from America." Light and shade danced
amongst its recently unfolded oval leaflets. Soon it would be in
flower, and hundreds of sprays of fragrant pea blossoms would
dangle from its branches. Except that they were white and
smaller, they might have been wistaria or laburnum flowers.
Mary always quite saw why it was also called White Laburnum
and Chain Flower and False Acacia.

As she dressed and slowly made her way downstairs, she told
herself that this morning, so obviously set fine, and wholly prosperous, seemed, like her Robinia, to belong to an earlier age. It

reminded her of Georgian England, and haycocks and smock-frocks—or perhaps even more, of mid-Victorian England, and family processions by field-paths to church; and gauze crino-lines and wreaths of camellias fluttering on the lawns between the dances. It was even possible to fancy the wail of violins and the throb of the big bassoon, for this morning the wireless at Woodside was mute. But, unfortunately, since the date was May 5th, 1942, a cloud of smoke still hung over the cathedral city of Went. Poor old Went had been blitzed on two successive nights.

In the west garden, a group of men in hospital blue were drowsing under a cherry-tree, and white petals powdered the grass beneath and the path beyond. On the east lawn, a pink peony and a Persian lilac were making a sentimental back-ground for men exercising under the supervision of the physical training instructor. There could be no post this morning and no telephone, so Mrs. Hungerford need not hurry. By the time that she turned back towards the house, the basket on her arm held lilies of the valley and large scentless white violets, and she felt better. When she was told that an air-raid warden was asking for her she did not at once recognize Godfrey Gibson, dressed in navy-blue uniform, and looking much younger in figure but older in face. He said, wringing her hand and speaking a little jerkily, "Good morning! I wanted to come over yesterday but couldn't manage it. I've seen Diana. How are all the rest of you?"

"We're all right to-day after a good night's sleep," answered Mary, also sounding a little jerky. "We didn't get our hit until the second night, as you probably heard, and it was only on the West Pavilion—the Orangery. It was the wing that my husband had done up."

"I'm sure," said Mrs. Hungerford, not quite herself yet, even after a good night's sleep, "that my husband would have preferred any damage to be to that wing."

"That's bad luck, though! Not the library—his books— I hope?" said Godfrey, glancing across sunlit and discoloured gravel towards an area surrounded by interested inhabitants.

"No, the library only lost windows, and, as you see, the men have swept up the glass and most of the earth. The two bombs landed on the end of the West Pavilion and in a border outside."

"I've brought a message for you from your Quartermaster," began Godfrey, giving up the attempt to see how much the west wing had suffered.

"Yes. Do tell me about her," interrupted Mary eagerly. "We've been waiting and wondering when she didn't turn up yesterday morning. But one had been asked not to try to go into Went, and of course we've had no telephone or light, though luckily we've still got water, as ours didn't come from there. We hoped that she was just finding it impossible to get here."

"Well, she was, you see," explained Godfrey, "because she was in her cellar."

"You can't mean that poor Miss Masquerier was trapped?" exclaimed Mary, staring at him.

"French Row is flat," said Godfrey, "and Rosanna Masquerier's house came down on the top of her. But, as you know, it had an eleventh-century cellar capable of housing twelve horses. I remembered that when I heard that French Row was flat. We got her out," he ended grimly, "at six o'clock yesterday evening."

"Then she had been there alone—for how long?" asked Mary.

"She was in there from eleven-thirty on Saturday night, when the house collapsed, until six on Monday evening," said Godfrey. "She heard the second night's raid, and thought it was worse than the first; wherein she was wrong. She had candle-light, and she didn't starve, because her ancient retainer, who is a radio fan, had long since laid in stores of all the little supplies one has been told to put in an air-raid shelter. Actually, they had sardines, soda water and a seven-pound tin of chocolate biscuits, and a more revolting menu I shouldn't care to imagine. But our poor authoress was not alone. She had for company her two spaniels, the old maid (who has quite gone off the deep end), a perfectly strange female in pyjamas, who had fled from the Victoria Hotel on the corner after the first bomb fell, rightly declaring that the place was a death-trap, and a child of four, who had also run in from the street, after seeing both his parents killed. Eleven people have been to our house already wanting to adopt him, but he appears to have an aunty. He's quite calm."

"How is poor Miss Masquerier?" asked Mary, still staring.

"Well, she is in pretty good heart, considering that she's lost every worldly possession," said Godfrey, "and what I was wanting to ask you is will it be all right if I bring her out here after tea this evening? She's at our house, but my wife has got fourteen people sleeping on the dining-room floor and we've got no water, though we hope for some to-morrow. We thought she'd be better out of the town after the shock, and she says she ought to be back at work. You won't need to have the old retainer, as she's having fits in the Infirmary."

"Of course we will have Miss Masquerier," said Mary, with vigour. "We must have her, but we couldn't have anyone else, even if we wanted. You see, we got a message yesterday morning, to ask us our Bed State, and we answered that we had ten empty beds, and were told to expect ten patients in an hour's time. It did the staff good, I think, to have to bustle round, and we got water boiling and instruments ready, all prepared for bad casualties, as the message had come from Went. When they arrived they were ten old men, pre-blitz civilian patients from the General Hospital, who had been moved out to us to make room there.

"I forgot to say that on the Sunday afternoon, one of our own patient's wives arrived in great distress, having hitch-hiked from Went with eight children. She gave birth to a ninth, twenty minutes after she arrived, in our head gardener's cottage, and is doing Sister Finan credit."

"It has all been so extraordinary," sighed Mrs. Hungerford, pushing the hair back from her forehead and blinking at her visitor, "so extraordinary, I mean, to be cut off from the outer world as if we were back in medieval days of storm and siege. Tell me, if you're not frightfully rushed—we've heard nothing. Or rather, we've heard the most deplorable things. Is it true that the Market Square was hit—the Dudmans' shop?"

"Yes," nodded Godfrey, "that's correct, I'm sorry to say. The entire Dudman family went together—widowed Mrs., two daughters and three children of married daughter. The husband's in Libya—tragic! Nice little old-fashioned shop. My mother always got her tapestry wools there."

"Reeny Dudman worked here," said Mary, with a catch in her voice. "We'd heard, but we'd hoped. . . . I saw her only on Saturday morning. She sold me a doll."

"They all went together," repeated Godfrey. "I don't know if that's any comfort. Personally, it's what we have always hoped for—why we decided not to send our youngest overseas. . . ."

"Silver Street?" asked Mary presently.

"Badly smashed, but that ghastly block of Moote's is standing up absolutely as bad as new. And the County Hotel got nothing either."

"Nor the cathedral, we've heard."

"You've heard wrong," said Godfrey. "But Hovenden of the Museum tells me that what's gone doesn't matter. It was, by the grace of Allah, the west door and window. I say! I believe I ought not to have said that, for I believe we owe their restoration to the generosity of your grandfather."

"I know. They were frightful," agreed Mary absently.

"The worst hit, as far as casualties are concerned," said Godfrey, "is the poor old Victoria Hotel. It appears to have been absolutely packed with everyone's elderly acquaintances. Dolly Yarrow had two old aunts, and the Wilsons a brother-in-law from Oxford, an arthritic clergyman. Pathetic! Well, now I've seen you, and it's all right about Miss Masquerier, I must be off."

"I suppose poor Miss Masquerier has got nothing—no luggage?" asked Mary, as her companion prepared to mount into a small car, with a windscreen which looked curiously rain-splashed for so fine a morning.

"She's got a green siren suit, and a deck chair, and a history of the Crusades, I gather," said Godfrey. "She'll get fifty pounds for her clothes, quite soon, and so will the old retainer. But for the rest I'm afraid she'll just have to put in her claim and wait, probably till the end of the war. Oh! by the way, I'm afraid she's got two spaniels who are accustomed to sleeping on her bed." He added, as he took his seat, "Aggie Sherman asked to be remembered to you, too. She's been perfectly splendid."

"Stop!" cried Mary. "Shall you be seeing her again?"

"At every so-called meal," said Godfrey. "She's helping my wife."

"Then I wish to heaven you'd give her this," said Mary, producing from her pocket a collapsible timepiece.

She toiled up to her office and shed a tear, together with Johanna Pratt, for Reeny Dudman. In the end, she decided that by moving little Johnson into Lalage's room they could provide the refugee with a quiet suite, complete with bathroom. "I want everything as nice as possible," she said.

"I know—flowers on the dressing-table and calming bedside books," agreed Johanna gruffly. "I'll see to it. The Dusty Millers are out in the kitchen-garden, I've noticed. They're old-world and homely. And there's honeysuckle on the summer-house thatch. I'll get some of that. I believe one of the taps in the bathroom needs a washer. Night Sister says the pipes gurgle, but little Johnson has never complained. There's a sofa in my room which I never use. I'll get that moved in—and some silly pink silk cushions which a relative sent when I broke my hip. They look pretty soft—but they are soft."

Miss Masquerier arrived at six o'clock, exactly twenty-four hours since her release from her eleventh-century cellar. Mrs. Gibson and friends, all of whom had evidently been large women, had lent her some clothes, and she was very bright going up the stairs followed by her frisking spaniels. She sat down rather suddenly on the sofa when she reached her room, and held up a clenched fist in front of her features for a moment, and said apologetically, "It's just the stairs—and seeing everything look so bright in the sunshine."

Sister Finan, with a keen look of professional interest in her eye, running, thought Mary, like a dotted line to the figure of a prospective patient, said firmly, "Now put your feet up and just relax, Quartermaster." A knock sounded on the door, and a timely cup of tea warded off, in the opinion of Sister Finan, pronounced at supper, a Collapse.

Mary drew up a chair and seated herself, while Miss Masquerier and the spaniels enjoyed their tea and biscuits. She had felt Miss Masquerier's hand, on arrival, and it had struck cold as the cellar in which she had sat for two nights and two days. Mrs. Hungerford said in leisurely fashion, "'Cast your bread upon the waters,' you know. Do you remember lending me the *de luxe* edition of the poet Duke's works? They're waiting for you—all safe and sound."

But even as she spoke she had a sudden vision, quick as a cinema-shot, of Miss Masquerier in her own bedroom at "Fleur-de-Lys" on Saturday morning. Through the slit of open door, as she had waited in the sitting-room, Mary had been able to see shiny shell-pink walls and bookshelves loaded with heavy-looking books, and a Czechoslovak pink glass powder-bowl on a skirted dressing-table with a triple mirror. It seemed unbelievable that all this was now what Godfrey Gibson called "flat." "It was all so old—and so lovely," thought Mrs. Hungerford.

II

"I just thought I'd call in to say that I can take the boy," smiled Mrs. Bates. "He'll be quite all right up at my place. I thought you might be worrying."

For her visit to Mrs. Hungerford's auxiliary hospital, Mrs. Bates had discreetly discarded her bell-bottomed trousers in favour of a tussore suit which had distinctly the air of being officer's tropical outfit. Mary almost expected to see a green-lined topee above her friend's warm, good-humoured features. But as she had come on her bicycle, Mrs. Bates carried on her arm the flapping panama with a Liberty scarf which had, for some ten seasons, been her headgear for Barsetshire hot weather.

"I thought you might be worrying," she repeated expectantly.

"I have been worrying," agreed Mary, "but only for an hour, since the post came in with Rosemary's letter. She had forgotten, in her hurry I expect, that posts are still odd. I see this is dated Wednesday, and it's Saturday now."

Mrs. Rosemary Morrison's letter, which Mrs. Bates had rightly imagined might cause Mrs. Hungerford anxiety, simply said that the Went blitz had settled matters as far as she was concerned. The place of every able-bodied woman was at the Front now. "I am leaving a note for Mummy, pointing out that I think it is time both of us began to do our duty."

Mrs. Thomas Morrison had not, as Mrs. Bates soon disclosed, taken at all kindly to the notion that, as one of riper years, her duty for the duration would be to stay in someone else's furnished house in the country looking after her daughter's child.

"Marcelle was in bed when Millie Harker brought in Rosemary's farewell note with her morning tea, and she's stayed there ever since," recounted Mrs. Bates. "She says that she's ill, but Dr. Greatbatch has not been sent for, I heard from Mrs. Harker. I ought to have guessed, when I saw Rosemary setting out with a walking-stick for Lower Merle, to order the village taxi on Tuesday afternoon. She's not a walker. It called for her at five-thirty on Thursday morning, and she caught the early train for London, with four suitcases. My Mrs. Higgs's landlord's son, who works on the railway, saw her. As soon as I got back from morning duty at my Post, the Harkers very sensibly brought Ferdinand-Africa straight round to me. He's been there ever since. He says that his Mummy told him, as a secret, that she was going to be a soldier. I suppose that means the A.T.S. I suppose she didn't give you any address?"

"She only says she's going to the Front," said Mary.

"She must mean the Home Front, not the Second Front, poor girl," said Mrs. Bates, frowning. "However, I say it's all for the best. For perhaps now (who knows?) she might meet someone and marry again. Then she wouldn't be wanting Ferdinand-Africa."

"I think I had better go over to Willows and try to see my sister-in-law," said Mary, startled at the rapid pace of events.

"I wish you would," said Mrs. Bates. "I'd have gone myself before now, but I know Marcelle can't bear the sight of me, and

I don't want to put her off the idea of shedding the boy when she returns to London."

"Is she returning to London?" asked Mary, even more startled.

"She told Mrs. Harker that it wasn't worth while ordering in any more anthracite, as she wouldn't be here when the leaves began to fall," quoted Mrs. Bates.

"Hum. That would mean that I should have to look out for another tenant for Willows," mused Mary.

"You wouldn't need to look out for long, in these days," Mrs. Bates told her.

On taking her leave, Mrs. Bates asked if Mary would mind if she looked at the West Pavilion as she passed down the drive on her bicycle. She was not one of those who enjoyed staring at blitz damage, but the fact was that several friends on the Green had known that she was coming here to-day, and they would be so disappointed and anxious if she could not tell them how much Mrs. Hungerford's hospital had suffered.

"Oh, certainly look at it," agreed Mary. "I'll ring the staffroom and get Diana to go with you. I know she's just coming off duty. But you'll find the men have swept up nearly all the mess. I'm sorry that I can't leave the office myself this morning, but my Sec. has gone over to Nettlerash for the day."

"Is that where Pippa Johnson's connection, Professor Beadon, is working?" asked Mrs. Bates.

"Yes, and she's lunching with him, and he's taking her to see a Roman Camp, or, to be exact, she's taken a picnic for two, prepared by her own hands, as she's afraid his landlady starves him."

"What a shame! Such a distinguished man, too!" Mrs. Bates looked as if she longed to get her claws into the Professor's land-lady. "Did Johanna know him at Oxford?"

"She can't have, because he is Cambridge," said Mary. "But he's been over here several times to see our plaster-work. Kit was in touch with him before the war upon the subject. Johanna took History at Oxford, so she's naturally interested in Roman remains."

Before delivering Mrs. Bates to the care of Diana, Mary told her, for the benefit of all at Westbury-on-the-Green, that the damage to the West Pavilion had been very slight, that the crater in the herbaceous border had been officially inspected before being filled in, and that she was not going to attempt to replace glass in the library windows. Mrs. Bates, for her part, detailed the temporary arrangements which she had made for the comfort of Ferdinand-Africa.

"As my Mrs. Higgs only comes four afternoons, and I don't consider the Harkers' suitable women, I've been to see Miss Whewell, who keeps the school for tinies in Westbury Bottom. Some quite nice children go there—the Yarrow twins and two of Lady Muriel Gidding's nieces. And I've bought a carrier basket for my bicycle, second-hand from Norah Hill, who got it for her dachshund when he was a puppy and used to chase hens. Ferdinand's quite taken to it, and I've given him a corner of my garden for his own, and two of my ducks, and he is to call me Aunt Sally. I sent a message to Marcelle, telling her what I proposed doing, but all the answer I got was that she was very unwell and must not be disturbed. Would you believe it, Ferdinand had scarcely seen his gas mask? Millie Harker says he has not been allowed to know that there is a war on. I drop the child at Miss Whewell's on my way to duty at my Post, and on the days when I'm late and Mrs. Higgs doesn't come, he's to get his main meal at the school and just wait for me. Most days, I pick him up in time for dinner at home, and we've come to an arrangement at the school about his rations. By the way, I wish you would ask Marcelle to send me his points. Millie Harker brought round his buff and yellow books with his little clothes and gas mask, and I've had to go and see the grocer about them already. I mean the ration books, which are in a hopeless muddle. So were the clothes, if it comes to that. Not a woman in that house seems to have had the use of a needle."

Diana now entered and greeted her old friend. As they prepared to depart, Mary arrested them by asking, "What has happened to Dame Sarah Lys?"

"Oh, she returned to London before Rosemary left," explained Mrs. Bates. "She got so many telegrams from friends and admirers, who had heard from the wireless and papers that Went had been blitzed, that she hurried back to London to reassure them. After all, her postal address had been 'Willows, Westbury-on-the-Green, Went.' A wonderful old lady. Did you meet her? Do you know that on the morning after the second blitz she made her way into Went, all alone, to see if her friend Miss Masquerier was safe? It appears that she had known Miss Masquerier quite well in London—in stage and literary circles, I suppose—and she set off without telling anyone, and got a lift from a milk van, and arrived on the scene just after your parents" (nodding at Diana) "had taken Miss Masquerier to their house. I heard all about it, because Marcelle sent Millie Harker round to my house to say that Dame Sarah was missing—not in her room, where she was supposed to be taking her afternoon nap— and had I seen her? I hadn't, but I happened to be down at the 'bus stop when the Went 'bus came in, and we walked back to the Green together, and she told me about Miss Masquerier's escape, of which I was very glad to hear. Dame Sarah had been much affected by the destruction of so many of our beautiful buildings, and told me that she hadn't seen anything worse in London, which I thought very broad-minded of her."

"Did she manage to get down French Row?" asked Mary. "Your father," she explained to Diana, "told me that it was flat."

"No, she couldn't get down because it was railed off and sopping with water and people asked her her business," said Mrs. Bates. "But she explained that a dearest friend had a house there called 'Fleur-de-Lys,' and someone pointed out the site to her, and she said that there wasn't a house any more, but that she noticed a beautiful bit of old balustrading hanging like a piece of stage scenery from a shattered wall, and it had dying wistaria still clinging to it."

"That would be the back of the courtyard," sighed Mary. "Poor Miss Masquerier is working here again, as you've probably heard, but we haven't liked to ask anything about her house."

"In the 'bus on her way home," recounted Mrs. Bates, "Dame Sarah had travelled with an old lady, a refugee from Went, who was carrying a parrot in a basket. And the parrot was wearing a white fur cape. Dame Sarah kept on saying, in her inimitable way, 'Where, where, except in an English cathedral city, could you find an old lady who possessed a parrot that wore a white fur cape?'"

"Father said that Aggie Sherman had been perfectly splendid during the blitz," said Diana, with a light in her eye.

"I know. I was so glad," murmured Mary. "I mean, I was sure she would be."

"And the man who brings the papers said that he believed that was the name of the lady who had been recommended for a very high decoration," continued Diana. "But when I asked Mummy on the telephone she only snorted."

"I haven't heard anything reliable," said Mrs. Bates, setting her mouth, while her eyes looked even brighter than those of Diana, "but in my opinion Aggie Sherman is a rolling stone. If she had still been attached to the Went Fire Services—which I hear did do remarkable work and have been commended as particularly efficient—she might have had an opportunity to be splendid. Of course," said Mrs. Bates, her voice echoing cheerfully on the dim but majestic staircase, "I acknowledge it's dull sitting at one's Post year in and year out. But unless one does, then how is one to be efficient and on the spot when the trouble begins?"

III

Lord Merle was on leave, doing what he rather incoherently described on the telephone as "settling up just a few things at home, don't you know." He had come over to Woodside to see his daughter. As they had not met since his domestic tragedy, Mrs. Hungerford imagined that he would prefer to see Lalage alone, not in the staff-room, where they would be liable to continual interruption. For this, and other reasons, she had given Lalage the key of the library, and told her to give her father tea in there, and Lalage had seemed grateful, but had said would Mary have tea with them, as Daddy had said that he was coming at three and he never had much to say.

Lord Merle had arrived at three, in a car belonging to, and driven by, his old friend, Colonel Albany Mimms. The gentlemen had been at school together. Colonel Mimms, who numbered amongst his benevolent activities the chairmanship of the Barsetshire Comforts for the Troops Fund, had brought to Woodside, as well as his old schoolmate, a ping-pong table, twelve packs of playing cards, two dart boards and several heavy bundles of old illustrated magazines and works of fiction, tied up with string. The two middle- aged gentlemen looked very odd in a bird's-eye view from Mary's window—Lord Merle, short and stout, staggering beneath the weight of printed matter, topped by a lurid picture of a grinning Land Girl driving a tractor, and Colonel Mimms, faded but still elegant, hopelessly involved with the collapsible legs of the games table. Mary rang a bell, a thing which had seemingly never occurred to the visitors, and almost immediately the sunlit scene below sprang into fresh life with a much augmented cast. Nurse Elizabeth appeared, look-ing very trim, with her white veil and apron fluttering, and a number of the patients, under her direction, firmly removed the comforts from their donors. More and more young men, with bright hair and faces, and one leg or arm muffled in plaster and bandages, came swinging out of the wings. Two dashingly hand-some Polish sailors came, arm in arm and singing a melancholy ditty of their own land. They carried Miss Masquerier's spaniels buttoned into the fronts of their jackets, and they considerately set down the spaniels to join in the fun, and Lord Merle, step-ping out of stagy sunlight into the dimness of a pillared hall, trod on one of the fatuous pets. It all looked rather like a scene from a ballet, thought Mrs. Hungerford, with the pirouetting, arm-waving Elizabeth as Columbine.

Elizabeth had brought the visitors up to the office, and Mrs. Hungerford had delivered Lord Merle to his daughter, and Colo-nel Mimms to the Quartermaster, and now she was apparently at peace again and holding her brow while she read a typewritten letter, but actually wondering with much inward sinking whether the time had not come to do something drastic about Matron.

The date was July 4th, and down in the kitchens of Woodside strawberry jam-making was in progress. The appetizing, unmistakable smell, and the sight of the highly coloured fruits seething in burnished copper bowls, attended by jealous high-priestesses, backed by a glittering array of greenish glass jars and cellophane covers, reminded the mistress of Woodside strongly of her schoolroom days, and past summers. In the lanes of Barsetshire now, dog-roses abounded, looking, complained Johanna Pratt, depressingly like a flag day. Dust and horseflies also abounded, and straws, swept from saffron and scarlet-wheeled hay wains, decorated the lower branches of overhanging trees. The narrow Lower Merle road was a green tunnel, sheltering foxgloves and scabious, and to-day's dinner had been roast lamb with new potatoes, green peas and mint sauce, followed by gooseberry tart. On the kitchen-garden walls peaches, plums and nectarines were well formed and plentiful. The orchard promised many apples. Everyone agreed that 1942 looked like being a bumper year, and that, except for the news on the wireless and in the papers, one had nothing of which to complain. But to Mrs. Hungerford, holding her brow in the sticky heat of three-thirty p.m., Saturday, the 4th of July, 1942, was fall of cares. For either Mrs. Hungerford was becoming fanciful in her old age or her staff was at sixes and sevens.

"I wonder if one person in a house being what Sally Bates calls 'a trouble-maker' is enough to upset the whole show," she thought. "I wonder if I've really been wrong in putting up with so much for so long. It was not kind or polite of her to say that she could work *with* the lady of a house given up for a hospital, but never *under* her. And she repeated it, as I took no notice. I was firm about Diana and Lalage being allowed to keep on their wedding-rings, and that passed off quietly. But I had printed authority for being firm about that. On paper I've got nothing against her. There's no doubt that she's efficient. But she's tried, at one time or another, to make me sack every single member of my staff. And now she's making an absolute condition of my sacking little Johnson."

Mrs. Hungerford reviewed her staff, one by one.

"I don't honestly think that Sister Finan is quite out of touch with modern methods. She's been retired for seven years, it's true, and had two children, but I think that's rather an advantage. She took a refresher course before rejoining, and Dr. Greatbatch and the army medical officers have never said anything. And she's such a nice woman, and so nice with the patients, and understanding with the younger members of the staff. . . .

"I know that Johanna Pratt ought not to have a page-boy bob. I know her manners are brusque. But she's first-rate at her work and will take responsibility, and has never let me down until quite recently, when she's done one or two quite daft things. Oh, dear!

"Poor Miss Masquerier is not herself yet after her dreadful experience, and is really at heart an historical authoress. But I have never known her silly or thought that she's too old to be doing a full-time war job. And she's devoted to the patients. I wish she wouldn't come and weep at me, though, and say that she's never been so rudely spoken to in her life.

"Diana Gibson's going away—for family reasons," as she proudly but blushfully asserted after her interview with Dr. Greatbatch this morning. Bless her heart! It does make me feel old when I remember calling with mother to inquire for Godfrey's wife and hearing that the baby was to be called Diana. Dr. Greatbatch says that this will be the third generation of that family that he's brought into the world. He attended Godfrey's mother. He's awfully spry, and Barsetshire people think the world of him and raised a perfect howl when he talked of retiring before the war, whatever Matron may hint. And he's got two boys serving, so is well able to deal with the ones here. I think I'd better have a quiet word with him about my difficulties. . . .

"I wonder if Diana's younger sister will be too young for here. She's given Diana all her civilian clothes to be converted into maternity wear in exchange for her uniform. And she's got proficiency certificates in every subject. That sounds as if she was keen. The Gibsons are what Rex calls 'a good stable.' I can't remember a thing about the child, except that she was striking as Nell Gwyn in the Women's Institute Pageant, which doesn't sound a recommendation. She had a sweet singing voice. . . .

"I don't really want another very young thing on my staff. . . .

"I wonder if little Johnson is really all that Matron hints. I could not help noticing, when I went to her room to see if it was suitable for Miss Masquerier, and whether it was true that the pipes next door gurgled. . . . There was a large signed photograph of an Air Force officer on the bedside table. She's been to dances at the hangar more than once—but always with someone else, and punctually home again. And I recognized the photograph. It was Derek Young, whom I know and like. I don't know anything about little Johnson, though, except that her parents differed, and her mother remarried and went to Australia, and her father, who is a very grim Methodist Major with the Middle East forces, got the custody of the child. She has been parked as a paying guest on an old friend of Sally Bates, and dragged up in a suburb. In view of her mother's record, I think I had better have a word with Sally Bates about little Johnson. She's quiet, but I shouldn't call her sly, and children of broken homes generally react the other way, I've heard.

"Elizabeth's a problem, I acknowledge. . . . I'm in a cleft stick there. Sometimes I wake in the night and wonder how I can ever have got myself into such a position. After her outburst over the baked beans at supper that night, I sent for her and told her that that sort of thing could happen once only. Her tears nearly washed me away. She has nowhere else to go if I turn her out, and her parents entrusted her to me when they were ordered to India, and her mother is one of my oldest friends. But the circumstances were quite different then. Catha wanted to take Elizabeth with her, and Elizabeth did not want to go, because she was engaged to be married to a naval captain. Her coming here was quite a temporary arrangement. She was to be married from here on her fiancé's first leave. He was such a good officer, all the obituaries said. . . . Not quite young, just right for her, I dare say. I think I'd better write to her father about Elizabeth staying on here. Tim is sensible. Catha is not sensible. It's folly to fill four pages of a letter with regrets that Elizabeth can't join her parents in India and go to tennis and sherry parties. Granny Merle was right. She said, in 1939, that Catha Rollo was a pleasant but quite futile woman. . . . Elizabeth was such a sweet little debutante in 1939. I never shall forget seeing her dressed for going to court, and having to feed her with barley sugar because she felt so sick. She was sickening for a very bad appendicitis. She's not strong. Catha once told me that Elizabeth was naturally sweet-tempered. She's not sweet now. She's as hard as nails. Lalage, on the other hand, from being a very sulky girl, looks like becoming a fine woman. Lalage says that Elizabeth is horrid nowadays, because she's feeling horrid.

"I think I had better have a quiet word with Granny Merle about all of them. Now that I come to think of it, Granny Merle has had every one of them to the Dower House as part of her war effort."

I V

Mrs. Hungerford's office clock told her that the hour was four-forty-five, so she descended to her husband's library, and discovered that, in spite of all her precautions, the tea party there consisted of a middle-aged peer, who had recently figured in the divorce courts as a guilty party, and a debutante of 1939, entrusted to her care by doting parents ordered to India. It was true that the company included Lalage, looking at once solid and nervous, and Colonel Albany Mimms, the picture of dignified reserve. But they were obviously taking little part in the gaiety.

As Mary entered, Elizabeth was answering Lord Merle, who had evidently just asked if they would have him as a patient there. "Yes, if you'll make your bed, and do out your room, and shave in time for breakfast at eight-thirty," said Elizabeth.

The library, with nine of its full-length windows filled in with oiled cloth, was flooded by diffused sunlight, which glowed in the gilding of picture-frames. It was very close, and the scent of old calf bindings mingled with that of a bowl of sweet peas, painstakingly imported by Lalage to a mantelpiece for which it was too large.

Lord Merle opened conversation with his hostess by saying that he heard she was needing a tenant for Willows.

Looking at this guest, Mary realized again from what source Lalage got her solidity, and also why Kit had always kept a warm corner in his heart for this cousin. Mary herself would have liked to have liked her connection by marriage much more. But since she could hardly ever make out more than half of what he said, even when he was present in the flesh, and could never decipher his handwriting, their acquaintance had failed to ripen.

"Yes, I am looking for a tenant for Willows," she agreed. "Or rather, I want a very nice one. A number of people have been to see it and to see me. I don't know whether it is the result of lack of transport. Perhaps it was easier for people to look neat and calm when they arrived in cars. But all that I've seen so far seem to be unnecessarily fierce and grubby. And I can't help remembering that if it's really going to be impossible, after the war, to run a house of this size, Kit and I may have to make our home at Willows, for a time, at any rate."

Colonel Mimms groaned deploringly, and Lord Merle growled—"Nice little house."

"I'm fond of it," admitted Mary. "I don't want to be a dog in the manger, but one of the women who came to see me wanted to paint the staircase scarlet. She said that she had the paint and would do it herself."

"Shouldn't stand for any of that," advised Lord Merle, drinking largely of boiling tea and looking as if he might explode at any moment.

"I wonder," said Colonel Mimms, his gentle tones contrasting strongly with Lord Merle's explosive mutterings, "I wonder whether the sister-in-law of an old friend of mine has come to see you. I should think that she would be a desirable tenant. That is to say," he corrected himself, "I have never seen the lady, but she is the wife of an officer who has been ordered down here—a Major Whichcord—and I know that she is looking for a temporary home for a young family. . . ." He stifled a sigh.

"I don't think that anyone called Whichcord has come as yet," said Mary.

"You, Merle, will remember her brother-in-law—Wilson," said Colonel Mimms to his neighbour.

"Never heard of the fellow in my life," replied Lord Merle, sinking deeply but not comfortably into a capacious wine-coloured wing chair.

"Oh, nonsense!" interrupted Elizabeth. "You must have heard of at least a hundred fellows called Wilson in your life."

Lord Merle, without changing his position, rolled a sleepy blue eye in the direction of the ex-debutante, and acknowledged, "I dare say you're right."

"But you must remember 'Puppy' Wilson," protested Colonel Mimms plaintively. "He was the fellow who got a double hat-trick in the junior house match against Thompson's in 1904."

Lord Merle repeated, with increasing firmness, that he had never heard of the fellow in his life.

"I don't see why you should be expected to remember him," said Elizabeth, coming to the rescue. "Especially if you weren't a cricketer. And anyway, it was so long ago that you've probably forgotten. Personally, I think that cricket is the slowest game in the world to watch."

"Daddy got his Blue," said Lalage, quickly for her.

"Ha! H'mm! Well, the slow games aren't the worst to watch," pronounced Lord Merle, looking at Elizabeth as if he meant to imprint at least one youthful figure on his failing memory.

Colonel Mimms returned to the charge.

"But I really can't understand your saying that you don't remember 'Puppy' Wilson. Why, I could show you half a dozen house-groups hanging on my dressing-room walls. . . . His father had a charming place in Oxfordshire," he continued, drawing the remainder of the audience into the fray. "You and I stayed there together more than once," he insisted, wagging a bony forefinger at Lord Merle. "It's sold now, alas, I heard from Whichcord."

"Sold, is it?" asked Lord Merle, showing a spark of interest.

"I was wanting to ask, Daddy," said Lalage, seizing the opportunity to escape from an unprofitable topic, "now that you're down here, do you think that I might bring another of the nurses to see over Went? It's Pippa Johnson," she explained to Mrs. Hungerford. "She's never seen any English country houses, though she's read quite a bit about them; and I've told her about home. I know she'd appreciate it. But I haven't liked to telephone to the Matron, as I don't know her."

Lord Merle was understood to say that he hadn't been inside his house yet himself, and wouldn't be going till Tuesday. He thought his daughter had better telephone to the Matron.

"I will, then," said Lalage resolutely, "and I'll tell her that we'd like to come on Tuesday, as I believe that my father is coming on that day. Then she can kill two birds with one stone."

"I'm off on Tuesday, too," reflected Elizabeth, "and I've never been inside Went either, although I believe Mummy took me to a sherry-party in the garden there in the summer before the war, when we'd just arrived at Crossgrove. I remember I thought it was divine."

"Crossgrove!" ejaculated Lord Merle. "How's your father?" he asked abruptly. "Haven't seen him since I was taken to a dance at Crossgrove in 1939."

"Yes, that was my coming-out dance," smiled Elizabeth. "Everyone in Barsetshire remembers it, as all the lights fused. My people are in India again," she added, the brilliance dying out of her small piquante countenance.

"How does your father like that?" asked Lord Merle with real interest.

"He loathes it, thank you," said Elizabeth. "And he's fighting with everyone, I gather. But he always does, even in peace-time."

"Ha—hum! Bad luck," commented Lord Merle, levering himself out of the wing chair as his hostess rose.

"I am sorry that I must leave you now," announced Mrs. Hungerford. "I always go round the wards and speak to all the bed cases between the six o'clock news and supper. Kit will be glad to hear that you've been here," she gently said to Kit's first cousin in farewell.

"Had a line from Kit the other day. I was meaning to tell you," muttered Lord Merle, the colour deepening in his pendant cheeks. "Nothing in it—all business. Sounded fighting fit, though. Got a step up, I see. Wish I had his job. Interesting job. But Kit's a clever fellow. Well, he'll be glad to hear that you're all so well here." His eye swept the handsome but not undamaged room. "Very glad if you'd come too, with your staff, on Tuesday," he added cordially. "I'm not staying in the house but I can see that you get tea. Round about five o'clock," he proposed with surprising brightness.

Mrs. Hungerford explained that she had an engagement for Tuesday afternoon, a Local Defence Committee at Westbury-on-the-Green. She smiled to Lalage, who was piling tea-cups on a tray, removed Nurse Elizabeth for return to duty, and said good-bye to Colonel Mimms, never a speedy business. Poor Colonel Mimms looked quite dejected, as he said, for the last time, that he would not have believed that his neighbour could have entirely forgotten an old and now distinguished school friend.

As he released his hostess's hand, a new clue suggested itself to the Colonel's brain. Hurrying out of female earshot, he urgently breathed—"'Puppy' Wilson—got ringworm in his second term!"

Lord Merle, although at the door, heard this perfectly.

"Who's that you're whispering about, Mimms?" he asked, returning to the hearthrug. "Little Wilson? I remember him. Father collected moths in Oxfordshire. Had an elder brother—not there in our time, though—went into the City. . . . Well, no use going into all that now—very sad business. 'Puppy' Wilson, as we used to call him, got ringworm in his second term. . . ."

"That's just what I was saying," protested Colonel Mimms's voice aggrievedly.

As Mrs. Hungerford passed from the staircase, through the baize door, back into her hospital, she dimly heard the happiest of reminiscent conversations proceeding between two gentlemen who had been at school together.

V

There were only five bed cases to be visited, and none of them needed anything more difficult than information as to where he could hire a room in the village for the wife, who was coming from the North on Tuesday next, and not a great one with the pen. A very young anxiety case, with a fractured ankle, rolled enormous blue eyes at the lady of Woodside, and then said the food here was nice enough, thank you, but somehow nowadays he couldn't fancy a bite. He expected it was because he never slept a wink at nights. Mrs. Hungerford made inquiries from Sister Finan, who reported that this patient had sent for more buttered eggs at supper last night and that his neighbour in bed had complained of his snoring. She would ask the night nurse, on duty on this floor, for further information.

Mrs. Hungerford generally enjoyed her quiet evening progress from ward to ward of her converted home, and this evening the spacious rooms of the stately Georgian house, flooded with sunshine and with every window open, were looking their best. Bees were busy in the lavender bed and the lime-walk outside the white saloon, and the view from the staircase window was of fading haycocks, neatly ranged like rows of boiled puddings on newly shorn bright green lawns. Nevertheless, at six-forty, Mrs. Hungerford mounted the main staircase with flagging footsteps. A worry which had haunted her brain since the Went blitz, had recurred with vehemence, as she sat at tea in the library; an apartment much darkened by oiled cloth in nine windows. There was no blinking the fact that her house had now twice suffered air-raid damage. On the first occasion the bombs, which had shattered the glass of the garden-front, had been dropped by a stray enemy plane, unloading at random and in a hurry to get home. It was sheer bad luck that Woodside had twice lost windows. It was a good eight miles outside Went, even as the crow flies, and although Went undeniably possessed large aircraft factories, these were on the far side of the town. The new bomber station was less than five miles distant, but the Went blitz had not touched that site. It seemed to have been deliberately aimed at the historic buildings of the cathedral city.

"I don't want to put the idea into anyone's head by asking questions," thought Mrs. Hungerford. "When I asked Dr. Greatbatch, he pooh-poohed the notion. . . ." For, in spite of the fact that she was almost driven mad by the eccentricities of her staff, Mrs. Hungerford had become devoted to her hospital. The thought that it might be closed down, because it was in too exposed a position, was almost more than she could bear.

Johanna Pratt, who had flown off early this morning, forgetting two matters of importance, should have returned by now, but no click of the typewriter sounded as Mrs. Hungerford opened her office door.

Mrs. Hungerford opened the door of her silent office and beheld a spectacle which made her doubt her eyesight and feel as if someone had emptied a bucket of cold water over her form. The sensation of an ice-cold douche was quickly succeeded by that of one direct from a boiling geyser.

Her office, though silent, was not unoccupied. Two tall figures, standing in the very centre of the floor, were locked in what any constant film-goer would instantly have recognized as a passionate embrace of the first order. Mrs. Hungerford saw, with dreadful clarity, a pair of blue serge arms, evidently belonging to a female, but at present wound tightly around the back of a grey tweed suit.

With a feeling of utter stupefaction she gradually realised that the arms belonged to her invaluable secretary, Johanna Pratt. But if she had been given a dozen guesses she would never have suspected that the very competent Romeo, who slowly raised his head and returned a stare equalling her own in horror, would have possessed the features of Professor Abbadie Beadon.

CHAPTER VIII

"I AM MAKING SOME CHANGES"
(July 20th, August 7th, August 10th)

MRS. MACDOUGALL, *née* Norah Hill, had come to tea with Mrs. Bates. Norah had brought her baby in its pram, and her dachshund, who had arrived attached to the pram-handle by an amber patent leather lead, but was now lying on a faded cretonne cushion at his mistress's feet. Otto, who was not as young as he had been, had a great idea of comfort and despised babies.

The ladies were seated in Mrs. Bates's front garden in full view of the village green and separated from it only by black-painted metal chains hanging from white-painted wooden posts. But their tea-table and chairs were set under a carefully trained weeping ash, which at this season formed a lofty green tent. Its lower branches swept the grass, and only through the point of entry, on which Mrs. Bates kept a jealous eye, could be seen a vista of village life. Mrs. Bates's front garden, which occupied the foreground of this view, was of strictly conventional design. It had a lawn of pocket handkerchief shape, and fortunately of limited dimensions, as its owner was now obliged to quell its growth with shears and a hand-mower. Not a single daisy or dandelion raised its head in the lawn, which contained a single round bed, filled at present with tufts of ageratum, encircling white and scarlet begonias. After a holiday at a West Country port in 1940, Mrs. Bates had been filled with emulation of a summer bedding effect in public gardens there, which had spelt the words "God Bless our Fighting Forces."

"It's Red, White and Blue," she proudly explained to Norah, who had just made the expected compliments on her own patriotic effort. "The ageratums are not the right blue, but with my duty at the Post, and now little Ferdinand, I really haven't the time for lobelias. Ferdinand has been asked to tea by Mrs. Yarrow to-day, and I'm not fetching him till six, so we shall have time for a nice chat. One sees so few people nowadays. Or rather I see the same old lot over and over again."

Norah, who had been mildly thinking that she wouldn't like to be a begonia that didn't do as Mrs. Bates told it, began the nice chat by asking, "Weren't you awfully surprised to hear that Mrs. Hungerford's secretary is going to marry an Oxford Don?"

"Oddly enough," replied Mrs. Bates, with complacency, "I seem to have been the only person on the Green not taken by surprise by that engagement. Mary Hungerford herself, when she dropped in to see me the other day, admitted that she had been kept quite in the dark. In fact, I believe that it came as an absolute shock to her, for I've heard from Johanna that in the end the poor Professor came to the point in Mary's office, and under her eyes.

"They had been for a long day's expedition together, to inspect Roman remains. Johanna's naturally interested in remains, as she took History at Oxford. By the way the Professor is not an Oxford man. He's Cambridge, and they're being married in his old college chapel on the Saturday after Bank Holiday, and he gets a fortnight's leave. . . . But, as I was saying, they had been for a long expedition together, on a perfect summer's day, and thoroughly enjoyed themselves, and he had accompanied Johanna back to Woodside, seeming unable to take his leave, but his feelings didn't overmaster him until the moment came when he must depart. Mary entered her office at that moment."

Mrs. Bates, who was equally fond of a romance with a happy ending, and a good tea, literally smacked her lips as she reached this point in her narrative.

"It had been a case of love at first sight," she proceeded. "My dear, that butter has been put out for you to eat. Please don't annoy me by having bread and scrape under my roof. And I have plenty of honey. My Mrs. Higgs made those little cakes on her own when she heard you were coming, so I can't answer for them, but the Swiss roll I made myself."

"Has the Professor known Miss Pratt up at Oxford?" asked Norah, who did not readily assimilate a new idea.

"No, nor in London, although of course they both have many London friends," answered Mrs. Bates, who liked everything about an engaged couple to be magnificent. "He met her first at Woodside this spring, when he came over to look at the staircase. Colonel Hungerford had been in communication with him about the staircase before the war."

"Is he an architect?" asked Norah. "I can't imagine Miss Pratt married to an architect. Drains are so awful."

"Well, you needn't trouble, my dear," said Mrs. Bates, "for he's not. Still, I see what you mean. She's such a beautiful girl, and so modern. But she's very capable, too, you know, and amusing though this is, I don't really believe that it was their historical tastes that turned the scale."

"What was it?" asked Norah eagerly.

"Food," announced Mrs. Bates, with matronly satisfaction. "The poor Professor was not getting his rations from his landlady. Johanna found this out. With her opportunities and looks, she must have had many other chances, but I don't think she had ever been sorry for a suitor before. When she discovered that the Professor, who has no idea of comfort (I'm so glad it's not me), was being starved, she determined to give him at least one good meal. So she took a picnic, made by her own hands. She's an excellent cook. She's keeping on the Harkers, I hear, but not to sleep in. She's going to get their breakfasts herself. Then the Professor and she will bicycle daily to the station, and he will take the early train to his office, and she will go on to Woodside."

"I should think Mrs. Hungerford must be delighted to have got such nice tenants for Willows," reflected Norah.

"I believe she considers it an answer to prayer," agreed Mrs. Bates. "She's been looking very tired recently. She sounded almost overcome as she said to me, 'Now Willows will be a happy house again.'"

"And a tidy one," Norah pointed out. "All that lovely antique furniture! It used to make me want to cry when I saw the condition into which Marcelle and Rosemary were letting it get. And I know I'm not artistic, but didn't you sometimes think that things like that cuckoo clock which Marcelle brought from' her London flat, looked quite wrong for a house like Willows? I expect," continued Norah, sounding shy, "that the Abbadie Beadons will be very artistic. I've never met a Professor. Will you come with me, the first time, when I go to call? Or won't they expect one to call?"

"Johanna is going to give a small party on the Sunday after their return, to introduce her bridegroom to her Barsetshire friends," announced Mrs. Bates. "The Professor doesn't know yet, but I know that you and your husband are being asked. The wedding is to be absolutely quiet—no bouquets or brides-maids, and eleven-thirty a.m. I'm afraid that may have been a disappointment to little Pippa Johnson, who might reasonably have expected to be asked. But not even Mrs. Hungerford was asked. She's going, all the same, because Johanna has explained to her that when the Professor kept on saying that of course he couldn't think of inviting anyone to make such an expedition, and it would be a quite unrewarding exertion, he was secretly hoping she would make the effort, and would be deeply touched if she just turned up. So she's combining it with a day in London on hospital business.

"Johanna herself was a little difficult about having to get what she called a wedding garment. She said that she saw she could not be married in her uniform, because her regulations say that uniform is not to be worn on unnecessary occasions. She possessed a divided tennis skirt and pullover, but had never owned a hat, and wondered if it would be all right if she borrowed a veil from Sister Finan, and just twisted it round her head for the time she was actually in the chapel. That," said Mrs. Bates, with swelling eyes, "made me mad. I told her outright that, for a lovely British girl to be married in shorts, an old pullover, and somebody else's headgear, was cheapening herself for life. I appealed to the Professor, whom she had brought with her, and he said that females in his office wore what he described as their heads tied up in bits of cloth, and he did not admire the fashion. He waved an arm, and fell off the fender, on which he'd been balancing himself, and said that he thought Johanna ought to have a white gown and a large black hat."

"Good gracious! Poor Miss Pratt! It sounds like 1904!" exclaimed Norah.

"So I thought," nodded Mrs. Bates, "but Johanna's clever. She's been up to London, and she's ordered something which she says looks like 1804. The hat sounds very *outré*—a black velvet cart-wheel, tied under the chin with long ribbons. But Mrs. Yarrow, who went with her, says that the effect is pure Romney. Johanna didn't want to go to London. She said, how could she face the posters on the station, asking, 'Is your journey absolutely necessary?' Luckily, her father, on seeing the announcement in the papers, and getting a letter from the Professor, telegraphed, saying he must see both of them in London. Johanna had not written to her father."

"How very modern of her," thought Norah. "I hope he won't forbid the banns, out of spite."

"He can't forbid anything," chuckled Mrs. Bates, "because Johanna is twenty-six and the Professor is thirty-nine. I gather any trouble is rather the other way. Lord Billingsgate is insisting on going up to Cambridge to give his daughter away. He wanted everything to be what he called 'slap-up.' But Johanna has explained that she will be working until the last moment, and that the Head of her fiancé's college is kindly putting her up for the night before. They were going to East Anglia for the honeymoon because the Professor had never before had a peaceful opportunity to obtain rubbings of some notable brasses in country churches down there. But it turns out that the churches are now in a Defence Area, and the brasses are under sandbags, so they're just going to the Lakes."

"Jimmy and I went to the Lakes for our honeymoon," cried Norah in tones of relief. "It rained every day. But it will be something to begin upon when I'm introduced to the Professor."

I I

Mrs. Hungerford, who had successfully attained a corner seat in the eight-fifty London express from Went Junction, unfolded the newspaper which she had prudently brought with her from Woodside Auxiliary Hospital. "Threatening German Drive from Tsymlyanskaya," she read. "Puppet Rulers for Burma." "More Bombs on the Ruhr." "Artillery Duels in Egypt." There was an interesting article about Turkey's neutrality. Mrs. Hungerford refolded her newspaper with a gentle sigh, and resigned herself to the most soothing occupation in this life—watching English countryside in high summer, fly past the windows of a railway carriage. Going up to London by the eight-fifty was not what it had been. In pre-war days, Mrs. Hungerford had generally known nearly every occupant of her carriage. This morning, although the carriage contained ten people, all were strangers to her.

"This is a very interesting world," thought Mrs. Hungerford doggedly. "I never should have guessed that I should have to thank Aggie Sherman for removing Matron from Woodside."

Miss Agatha Sherman, like everyone else in Barsetshire country-house circles, had read with pleasure the announcement that the marriage arranged between Professor Abbadie Beadon and Mrs. Hungerford's beautiful secretary, would take place quietly at Cambridge on Saturday, August 8th.

Barsetshire was looking wonderfully prosperous under grey skies on Friday, August 7th. Every available acre was under cultivation, and the tomato houses of the valley—in pre-war days a dying industry—were brim-full of swelling produce, and as smart as paint. It did not seem to matter that light rain was falling. The past week had been one of rain and shine—good growing weather.

Miss Agatha Sherman, who was apt to put two and two together and make five, had arrived at Woodside Auxiliary Hospital within an hour of reading the paragraph so deeply interesting to her. Since Mrs. Hungerford was not present, she had been received by Matron, who alone of the inhabitants of this building, had been in no placid mood since Cupid had shot his dart into its midst. For the first five minutes of the interview which had followed, two powerful personalities had conversed with urgent amiability. But by the time that Mrs. Hungerford had entered her staff-room, a quarter of an hour later, a shouting match had been in progress. Miss Sherman was in the act of shaking from her feet for ever, the dust of an establishment controlled by a female Führer, and Matron had hardly waited for the guest's departure, to inform Mrs. Hungerford that if that woman came here as secretary, she must ask to be allowed to resign from her post, a step she had long contemplated.

So Mrs. Hungerford had not been obliged to have a quiet word with Dr. Greatbatch, and almost regretted having made a diplomatic call upon Sally Bates, to ask whether she knew if little Johnson seemed happy at Woodside. For Mrs. Bates, who combined with mother-wit a vast innocence, had answered promptly, "Happy! My dear Mary, the last time the little creature was here, she told me that every night, as she kneels down to say her prayers, she feels she ought to mention my name for having got her the job!"

The Dowager Lady Merle, who knew all the cast in this serio-comedy, and never asked awkward questions, had confirmed Mrs. Bates's unconscious testimony to the character of little Johnson, and mentioned during the course of the conversation that had followed, that if her grandson's wife was looking for anyone to undertake an administrative post in her hospital, she believed that the highly proficient trained nurse, imported by a London specialist to attend her in her critical illness last winter, might be available. This character, who had been Assistant Matron at an establishment with a famous name, was, said Lady Merle, a great tranquillizer in a household.

The Dowager concluded by recollecting that poor Miss Nightingale had experienced much trouble from her staff at Scutari.

So now Mrs. Hungerford was going up to London, on hospital business, and on to Cambridge to attend the nuptials of her secretary, and last night, before she had left home, she had quietly removed no less than twenty-four handwritten notices, attached to the doors and passages of her house by surgical plaster, all of which forbade patients and staff to do things which would at once suggest themselves as desirable to any normal person.

"Except for having to explain, at my interview, why Matron left, and having Marcelle to dine," she thought, as she gazed at fast-fleeing Barsetshire scenery, "I haven't got a big bogy in my path at the moment. Oh, I'd forgotten poor old Went's Warship Week coming on in a fortnight's time. Well, I suppose there's always something. Oh, and there's Elizabeth. . . ."

III

"Come in," called Mrs. Hungerford, and Nurse Elizabeth entered, and as the resident N.C.O. was present, collecting the men's passes for the day, Nurse Elizabeth said, "Good morning, Madam. Matron told me that you wanted to see me."

The N.C.O., who suffered from rheumatism, picked up those of the passes which had fluttered to the floor, closed the door behind him, and clumped down the stairs. Mrs. Hungerford rose from her desk with a smile, seated herself in an arm-chair by the fire, and waved her companion to a twin chair opposite. Still, anyone could see that Auntie Button had not sent for the ex-debutante daughter of one of her oldest friends just to enjoy a pleasant chat.

"I am making some changes in my staff here," began Mrs. Hungerford, sounding as if she was quoting from a script well known to her. After an effort, she went on, "I wanted to discuss your own future with you. I am afraid that you're not very happy here."

Eighteen months ago Elizabeth would have replied, "Are you sacking me, Auntie Bee?" She now merely said, staring at the floor, "No, I'm not happy."

"I am sorry," said Mrs. Hungerford, sounding as if she meant it. "Do you think that you would be happier in fresh surroundings? I realize that it is sad for you to be so near your own home here, but with no relations in England."

"I've got Tony," Elizabeth pointed out. "I saw him when I was on leave in London, and he was awfully sweet and understanding."

Mrs. Hungerford, who could not imagine Elizabeth's elder brother ever being sweet, said again that she was sorry. "I had forgotten Tony. Was he able to suggest anything helpful?"

"Oh, no," admitted Elizabeth, "But he hates everything he's having to do just as much as I do."

"Still, I imagine that both of you realize that you have got to do something," said Mrs. Hungerford, keeping calm.

"Oh, yes," said Elizabeth resentfully. "We realize that."

"If you took up work in London, you might be able to see more of your brother," mused Mrs. Hungerford.

"It's not worth considering," said Elizabeth. "Tony's even more unsettled than I am. Besides, I should loathe all his medical student friends. They're all scruffy."

Mrs. Hungerford was so much relieved to gather that her godson was still pursuing his medical studies, a fact unknown to her, as he did not reply to letters, that she looked quite bright as she asked, "Don't you think that a complete change of scene and company might help you to feel more settled?"

"It might," murmured Elizabeth grudgingly.

"I know," said Mrs. Hungerford hesitantly, "that when you first came here it was only as a temporary measure, and that you have had a great grief. . . . I had hoped that being with Lalage might be a comfort. . . ."

"Lalage and I are different," said Elizabeth.

"What would you like to do?" asked Mrs. Hungerford outright.

"Like!" exclaimed Elizabeth, looking up, and looking dangerous. "Well, I'm about to enter my twenty-third year. I'd like to marry, and have a lovely house, and one or two babies, and lots of servants to look after them so that I could have a good time."

Mrs. Hungerford had come out in 1914, when it was not the fashion for young ladies to admit that they would like to marry and have one or two babies. But she replied valiantly after a moment, "Yes. Well, I don't see why you should not be able to do all of these things some day. I hope that you may, for as you know, I am interested in your happiness. And I know that you won't be a happy woman unless you are a useful one. But I expect you realize that at present some of these things are not possible."

"I'm about to enter my twenty-third year," repeated Elizabeth, her dark eyes filling with tears. "It's not natural, the life I'm living here—a housemaid without even any fun on my evening off."

"A very wise friend of mine said to me the other day, in a letter," remembered Mrs. Hungerford, "I think that this should be called 'The Lonely War.' Most people are separated from those they love best just now. Nearly all are having to contend with some difficulties, and some with very great difficulties. . . . Would you rather do something else than nursing—which is a vocation, not only a profession?"

"No, thank you," said Elizabeth quickly. "I might like them worse."

"Well, then," began Mrs. Hungerford, speaking very slowly and distinctly, "on my visit to London the other day, I met a cousin of your father, who is, like myself, running a War hospital in a country house. Her hospital is not her own home, although she knows it well, for she was brought up there. But it was your grandfather's house, the house in which your father was born."

Mrs. Hungerford flushed slightly as she tried to draw the most attractive picture possible of a mansion known to her only by an enlarged photograph which used to hang above Sir Daubeney Rollo's study mantelpiece at Crossgrove. The photograph had been taken on a shiny wet day, when there was not a single leaf on a tree, and the birthplace of Elizabeth's father was evidently built of the local red sandstone, which only blackens with age. Lady Rollo had never looked at the enlarged photograph without shuddering, and had dubbed it, "And no bird sings!" On the death of her father-in-law, Lady Rollo had suffered agonies of apprehension lest her husband might feel drawn to settle there, in the cradle of his race. She had not rested until the Welsh property was sold, and her family was happily established in rural Barsetshire.

"We spoke about the possibility of your making a change," continued Mrs. Hungerford, "and your cousin, who says that you won't remember her except as 'Aunt Douglas' was very will-ing to have you. She seemed to me a particularly nice woman. She reminded me of your father."

"Oh, she's strict, is she?" asked Elizabeth.

"It was her appearance principally. She's got your colouring and build," smiled Mrs. Hungerford. "I should say she was strict and a good organizer. But there is no reason why you should mind that—quite the other way."

"It's in North Wales, isn't it?" asked Elizabeth.

"Yes, and near a large garrison town and a base hospital, so you should get plenty of interesting work," said Mrs. Hungerford.

"Do you know the address?" persisted Elizabeth.

"I have it here," said Mrs. Hungerford, handing her a paper.

Elizabeth read her cousin's letter carefully, and some colour rose in her cheeks as she did so, which made her look much younger and prettier. She looked very young and pathetically incompetent, seated in the big armchair, in a child's attitude, with one leg drawn up beneath her and the other dangling, and a hand propping her brow. Presently she produced a ball of damp handkerchief, and wiped her eyes and sniffed. The note was quite brief, but she took a long time reading it, as if she was being called upon to make a weighty decision. At twenty-one, Mrs. Hungerford remembered, all decisions seem to be for life, and life sounds endless. "She's much older in some ways than I was at her age," she thought. "And yet in other ways she's infan-tile. I wish I could get in touch with her—poor little creature. Having to learn by experience is so hard."

But Elizabeth sounded perfectly decided as she returned the letter, saying, "Yes, I'd like to go there."

"I'm so glad!" escaped Mrs. Hungerford.

"How soon can I go?" asked Elizabeth, looking round the room.

"In a month's time, possibly sooner," said Mrs, Hungerford, chilled again.

Elizabeth seemed to realize some of her ungraciousness as she rose to depart. "I expect it may be all for the best," she said with a hard little laugh.

"I hope it may be very much for the best," said Mrs. Hungerford gravely. "For when anyone tells me that they have not been happy here, I feel that I, too, have failed."

But after Elizabeth had gone, she told herself, "There is something here I do not understand."

Chapter IX
GRAND FÊTE
(August 29th)

I

WESTBURY-ON-THE-HILL, Westbury-on-the-Green, and Upper and Lower Merle had decided in committee that they ought to do Something Big to help Went Warship Week.

When Mrs. McDougall, the highly embarrassed Chairman for Westbury-on-the-Green, had muttered that she was sure all here would agree that the time had come for the Westburys and Merles to do Their Bit for Those at Sea, "and, as I served for eleven months in a naval hospital, and my husband is a Surgeon-Commander, I know what I'm speaking about when I say that I think Our Sailors are perfectly splendid," the cheers raised by the largely female audience gathered in Lower Merle Women's Institute hut were mistaken by old Sir James Wilson, at the Old Mill House, for an air-raid warning.

The Bit soon swelled to include a Grand Fête, to be held on Westbury Green on the Saturday preceding the third anniversary of the Declaration of War, and the Committee, represented by Mrs. Taylor, Chairman for Westbury-on-the-Hill, thereupon invited Mrs Hungerford to open the Fête with a few rousing words. But Mrs. Hungerford's craven suggestion that Mrs. Crispin Rollo would be in every way a more suitable recipient for this honour, was, to her enormous satisfaction, adopted.

"I suppose it must always rain in Barsetshire for a Grand Fête," thought Mrs. Hungerford on the morning of Saturday, August 29th, as she looked forth from her office window.

One of the loveliest summers in her memory was fast slipping away. This morning it seemed definitely to have retired. "By the end of August one's beginning to go down the other side of the hill," she thought. "Oh, dear, that's what I said to Kit, in the library here, that night after our return from our honeymoon, when he'd just told me that he was giving me Woodside as a hospital for my wedding present. I burst into tears, and said that I was forty-three, and beginning to go down the other side of the hill. I was a donkey! And he was so bracing, saying, "My dear, I'm forty-five, and just beginning to cut my wisdom teeth. By seventy or so, I expect to be in my prime. I shouldn't wonder if by ninety I'm ready to undertake big responsibilities. Provided I'm not doubtful whether I'm not still too junior to carry much weight.'"

But there was no denying that this morning a gale was blowing, and Mrs. Hungerford shuddered sympathetically, as she pictured the Fête Ground on Westbury Green, which she had visited last night. The tents had been up, and the platform for the band. At this very moment, without doubt, ancient stalwarts were marking out with red, white and blue pennons, the courses for the sports and the sacred cricket pitch. High Summer was gone. The cuckoo's note would not sound for another eight months. August, the birdless month, was almost ended. Patients in blue uniforms no longer lolled in golden sunshine outside the house, shelling green peas and broad beans, or shredding runner beans with knives. . . . In Miss Masquerier's store a glittering array of jam-pots testified that 1942 had been a good year in the kitchen-garden. Mrs. Hungerford pictured complacently the serried rows labelled, "Strawberry," "Raspberry," "Cherry," "Black Currant," "Plum," "Blackberry and Apple," and the less popular "Rhubarb and Ginger," "Quince," and "Marrow."

Mrs. Hungerford drew a typewritten sheet towards her, and read with sinking spirits—

GRAND FÊTE

AT

THE CRICKET FIELD, WESTBURY-ON-THE-GREEN, SATURDAY, AUGUST 29TH, 1942

2.45 p.m. Arrival on the Field of members of H.M. Forces and Local Civil Defence Personnel.

3.0 p.m. Opening Ceremony: Speech by the Hon. Mrs. Crispin Rollo

3.20 p.m. Arrival on the Field of Model Warship

EVENTS

3.30 p.m. Children's Fancy Dress Parade

3.50 p.m. Pitching a Camp. Display by Boy Scouts

4.0 p.m. Children's Riding Class (under 15 years)

ATHLETIC SPORTS

(1) 100 yards

(2) 60 yards

(3) Egg and Spoon Race

(4) Wheelbarrow Race

(5) Skipping Race

(6) Slow Bicycle Race

(7) Obstacle Course

(8) Relay Race

(9) Sack Race

(10) Tug-of-War

TEAS and REFRESHMENTS will be sold during the afternoon.

6.30-8.30 p.m. Open-air Dancing. Royal Air Force Band

SIDE SHOWS

Produce Stall

Treasure Hunt

Clock Golf

"Bring and Buy" Stall

"Target for To-day"

Fortune Teller

Hoop-La!

Skittles, etc.

PLEASE DO NOT WALK ON THE CRICKET PITCH
Please do not throw away this Programme. Put it in the Salvage
Sack by the Entrance.

"Come in," called Mrs. Hungerford, and Lalage entered,
bearing in her hand a twin of the typewritten sheet which Mrs.
Hungerford had just mastered.

"I wonder," said Lalage, speaking as if she had been running,
"if I might use the typewriter in here, just for five minutes."

"But, of course," said Mrs. Hungerford.

"It's for My Speech," explained Lalage, her brown eyes more
than ever like those of a well-trained sporting dog. "I've learnt
it really, and I had hoped to be able to speak it *extempore*, like
Bottom, But this morning, when I woke, and saw that it was
raining and blowing, and I remembered that I should have to
wear my gas mask, which always gets in the way of my hands,
and that I haven't got the legs for a platform, I thought, just for
my own peace of mind, I'd better type the thing, so as to have it
in my pocket if I got stuck."

"Sit down here," suggested Mrs. Hungerford soothingly.

"My fortune, in the newspaper this morning," said Lalage
over her shoulder, as she began to dab at the machine with three
fingers, "says, 'Neighbours will be critical.'"

"Neighbours always are," said Mrs. Hungerford. "It's because
they are really interested."

When Lalage concentrated, it was clear that she had inherited her father's unfortunate gift of looking about to burst, and
Mrs. Hungerford consulted an article in a horticultural magazine
until she heard the noise of a sheet being rolled off the machine.

"I've got to order some more wall-fruit trees for here," she
opened presently. "Listen! This article tells one what Queen
Anne planted in her Royal Gardens. The names are too lovely—'*Peaches and Nectrons:* "Violet Musk," "White Nutmeg,"
"Belgrade," "Royall," "Persique," "Aromatick."' But it's no
use thinking of peaches. However, the plums are even more
gorgeous—'St. Catherine,' 'Reine Claude,' 'Imperatrice,'
'Queen Mother,' 'Pomegranate,' 'Virginall . . .' I wish we were

needing vines, I'd love to order a 'Grizly Frontiniack' or 'Blew from Windsor.'"

"Did she have a Muscatel of Alexandria?" asked Lalage, taking polite interest.

"'Muscatel from Jerusalem,'" quoted Mrs. Hungerford. "Ah! *Cherries*—that's what I need. 'Carnation,' 'Red Heart,' 'Morocco,' 'Morello' . . ."

"Birds don't like Morello," said Lalage helpfully.

"Neither do people, except with lots and lots of sugar," remembered Mrs. Hungerford. "Oh, she had an unnamed cherry, 'sent down by my Lord Duke from St. Albans.' How charming!"

"The Lord Duke was Marlborough, I suppose," said Lalage.

"We made a little cherry jam while you were away on your holiday," continued Mrs. Hungerford. "Did you know that it's impossible to stone cherries without becoming like Lady Macbeth? We had to do it ourselves, because the patients ate four for every one they stoned. They complained of the taste, too."

"I know. I got back to find the kitchen all freaked with gore, and you sitting in your scarlet dress with scarlet hands," remembered Lalage. "I say, if I'm not interrupting you at your work, would you mind looking at this?"

"Your Speech?" inquired Mrs. Hungerford, stretching out a hand.

"Yes, I'd like your opinion," said Lalage humbly. "For instance, how long do you think I ought to take?"

"How long does this take?" asked Mary, reading it.

"Twenty minutes, if I do it properly," said Lalage, with gloomy pride.

"Too long!" said Mary, shaking her head.

"Oh, do you think so? I thought that less would be pusillanimous."

"Fifteen would be ample."

"What would you cut?"

But Mrs. Hungerford had the sense to know that an orator does not love the friend who kindly cuts her first public utterance.

"I think it's quite excellent, especially the third paragraph," she said, returning it. "Do you think that you could put that at the end, or the beginning, or both? Rather plug it. I mean, I'm sure that's the right note to strike."

"I see what you mean," said Lalage, in whose fingers the sheet trembled. "My conclusion is rather tame. By the way, do I have to thank the organizing committee?"

"No, John will be doing that before he introduces you," said Mary, alluding to her cousin Pamela's husband, the Rector of Westbury-on-the-Hill.

"Does John have to talk before I can begin? He'll be ages! To be perfectly honest," said Lalage, as if she was ever anything else, "that paragraph you liked was Dolly Yarrow's. I thought that as her husband had been an M.P. she might be able to give me a few hints. She made me go down to the hall and do it while she sat in the drawing-room. She made me do it three times, and then she said that I should get on better when I could forget that I was making a speech. It's bad luck that she won't be able to turn up to hear me putting her stuff across."

"Why won't she?" asked Mary.

"The evacuated infants at Hydden Hall have got mumps, so now she and her children are in quarantine," recounted Lalage. "It's rotten luck on poor Rolfe, who went into camp for the first fortnight of the holidays, so was only due home last week. Granny Merle's taken him in, I hear. Well, thank you so much."

"Just one thing more," cried Mary, recalling her. "I mean, I'm sure you haven't forgotten, but as you hadn't typed it, I thought I'd just remind you that you must end by saying, 'I have much pleasure in declaring this fête open.'"

"I had quite forgotten!" exclaimed Lalage, striking her brow.

"I shouldn't worry for a moment," Mary advised her. "I've known it happen again and again. . . . Only, it is better the other way."

"I see. Splendid speech, but fête still firmly closed," commented Lalage. "In fact, I suppose that I might well have sat down where there was no seat, as nobody would have imagined that I could have finished. . . . Thank you so much!"

II

Staff dinner, with half the staff, who were going to walk to the Grand Fête, already dressed for the journey, was rather a morbid affair. Through the windows could be seen a steady downpour, but also a steady stream of plodding villagers, using the right of way. Dinner, in order that the kitchen staff might be released as soon as possible, was cold meat and salad, followed by a trembling and still lukewarm shape and custard. Miss Masquerier and Sister Finan, who were going to hold the fort while their juniors frolicked, talked hopefully in low voices of the clearing shower, and reminded one another that although the clock said one-fifteen, it was really only twelve-fifteen by the sun. On the whole, Mrs. Hungerford was the most cheerful person present. For, in the middle of the morning, Mrs. Hungerford had discovered an air-mail letter from Lisbon, which should have been put amongst her personal post, but owing to the absence of her secretary had got between two business circulars at the bottom of the hospital pile. Colonel Hungerford, who had received his wife's letter dated May 2nd, said that he was sorry to hear that her probationers were beginning to see him at Woodside. One never could tell, but they might have to face the reality before long.

As news spreads quickly in a community, every member at the staff dinner-table soon knew that Madam had heard from the Colonel, and that he had been in Turkey, but had reached Lisbon safely.

"But is Lisbon safe?" hissed Daphne Gibson, aged seventeen, to Pippa Johnson. "I saw in some paper the other day that British officials there had been obliged to complain strongly of the activities of Nazi agents."

Pippa, who was devouring the *Greenmantle* omnibus volume in her bedroom every night at present, longed to hint that Nazi agents were probably objecting even more strongly to the activities of Colonel Hungerford. But since witnessing a recent film, she had been particularly careful of what she said regarding the movements of her military friends. She exclaimed loudly, "Look! the sun!"

Everyone looked, and she was quite right. Through heavy grey clouds, brilliant rays were beginning to struggle. The wind had dropped, and although the trees were still dripping mournfully, the afternoon was not cold.

The plodding procession of villagers through the park was succeeded by a frieze-like effect of men in hospital blue. By two it was obvious that the afternoon was going to be very hot indeed. A steamy haze arose from the landscape, as Mrs. Hungerford brought the utility van round to the door, and prepared to embark Night Sister and six naval plaster cases. "It's a pity that it's bound to be still sopping underfoot for the dancing," she said to Night Sister, as they turned on to the Lower Merle road, "but I shouldn't wonder if at this time of year, it still turned into a perfect Victorian summer day."

"'Queen's weather,' didn't they use to call it, Madam?" inquired Night Sister, rather meanly shifting the responsibility for such memories on to her employer.

More than the weather reminded Mrs. Hungerford of Victorian days, when she arrived on the cricket ground. The Grand Fête, given in aid of a popular object at a date when outings were few, had attracted company from far farther afield than the Westburys and Merles. The utility van had to proceed at a funereal pace for many yards amongst dismounted cyclists. "If I'd known there was going to be such a mob, I'd have started earlier," said Mrs. Hungerford apologetically to her front-seat companion. Her prestige was soon to be enhanced, however, for Mrs. Sidney Crippen, niece by marriage of the postmistress of Westbury-on-the-Green, who was in charge of the "gate," waved the Woodside party in without demanding the "sixpence, please," which she was receiving from other sources quicker than her two pig-tailed daughters could punch the tickets. It had been arranged in committee that, as Mrs. Hungerford had paid for the band, promised to give away the prizes, and provided the speaker, her contingent should pass in free.

"There are some odd turn-outs here to-day," remarked Mrs. Taylor, striding up in a white coat, with a crimson ribbon inscribed in gold letters "Umpire" across her breast.

"Has Lalage arrived?" asked Mrs. Hungerford, sounding much like a nervous bride in the porch. "She wouldn't come with us in the van; I didn't press her, as I know what it is."

"She's come alone on her bicycle, and she's gone into the tent where the Home Guard are displaying enemy bombs and leaflets dropped on the neighbourhood, to cool off," said Mrs. Taylor. "John's got his eye on her. Did you hear, by the way, that yesterday John found old Mrs. Bunch from the Mill cottage waltzing about at the corner outside our house, where we've put the salvage bins? The one labelled BONES had been turned half round, and as she could only read BO and the first leg of the N, nothing would persuade her that it wasn't full of BOMBS. Hallo!"

Mrs. Taylor's voice changed, and Mrs. Hungerford, following her cousin's gaze, saw the most Victorian thing yet in a scene already reminiscent of Frith's "Derby Day." An equipage of the type named after the Queen-Empress was converging upon the ground from the direction of Upper Merle. It could not truthfully be said to be moving fast, and the two old hunters who drew it evidently felt their position acutely. The old coachman, on the other hand, had satisfaction written on every feature, as he approached a large and enthusiastic gathering, which did not seem to have heard the hated word "automobile." The vehicle, which bore a lozenged coat of arms, rather larger than would be deemed necessary by moderns of average sight, was in good condition, and showed signs of much recent attention. The harness had clearly never ceased to be a source of loving care. But even without considering its occupants, no one could have pronounced this turn-out anything but a genuine antique. Its passengers were five. In the seat of honour, an ancient lady with a hook nose, reclined happily beneath the shade of a black-and-white striped parasol with a long, yellowing ivory handle. The Dowager Lady Merle had come to the Fête in her Victoria, and to increase the historic resemblance, she had brought with her a docile-looking married daughter, who was wearing a toque. On the back-to-the-horses seat opposite them, which was so narrow that its occupants were gripping tight with their hands in the correct position for a backwards somersault, sat a skinny

stripling in Boy Scout's uniform, and a sombre figure, unmistakably the Dowager's faithful Scots retainer. On the floor reposed
a Scout's pole, and a white bull-terrier, who was accustomed to
take a nap after his luncheon.

"Did you know Granny Merle meant to come?" asked Mrs.
Taylor fiercely, and without waiting for an answer, fled towards
the new attraction.

Looking back on the scene that followed, Mrs. Hungerford
was quite certain that the band of the Royal Air Force had not
chosen this moment to strike up with the National Anthem.
Dolly Yarrow, who had experience of female voices piping in
the open-air, as well as a kind heart, had taken the trouble last
night to telephone to the Rector of Westbury-on-the-Hill, and
tell him not to allow those strong young men to play a single
note until after poor Lalage had got through. All that the band
did before the speakers mounted the platform, was to sound
a prolonged roll to attract the company nearer. Nevertheless,
the atmosphere, as the Dowager's equipage bowled on to the
Green, was exactly as if the curtain was now at liberty to rise.
The Dowager, who did not believe that punctuality consisted in
arriving twenty minutes before the advertised hour, had chosen
her moment with her customary efficiency, so Mrs. Hungerford did not attempt greetings until after the opening ceremony
should have been achieved. This, however, now seemed to be
indefinitely postponed, and she was presently surprised to see
the Vicar of Lower Merle clambering towards her through a
heavy sea of small children, who had been pushed into the front
row of the audience by their unselfish owners. The Rev. Cuth-
bert Mallet, after wiping his countenance with a large white silk
handkerchief, perceived the figure of which he was in quest,
and inquired of Mrs. Hungerford in a stage whisper, "Will Lady
Merle go on the platform?"

"I don't know, but I can find out," said Mrs. Hungerford
obligingly.

"The platform is very slippery, after such a quantity of rain,
and the steps up to it are, alas, insecure," explained old Mr.
Mallet, "but a couple of churchwardens will be holding them

steady while Mrs. Rollo mounts. The big drum has already had to be removed until after the speakers have finished," he continued wildly, "but, of course . . ."

"Granny Merle won't go on to the platform because of her rheumatism. She's just taken the Green on her drive, so as to wish us all well, but she may go for a short stroll after the opening," gabbled Mrs. Taylor, appearing from nowhere. "You might tell John to get on with it."

Looking back on the opening ceremony, Mrs. Hungerford could not truthfully say that she remembered or recognized a single word of Lalage's discourse. For Mrs. Hungerford was one of those unfortunate persons who are paralysed by sympathetic nervousness, if they are even seated next to an after-dinner speaker. It was, she knew, useless for her to assure herself that her neighbour at table had been responsible for the lives of thousands in a distant clime, or even that he was a Minister of the Crown, accustomed to throw off brilliant after-dinner speeches as medieval feasters threw gobbets to their waiting hounds.

Mrs. Hungerford saw the churchwardens holding down the steps borrowed from Willows, which were the only decorous means of reaching the slippery platform. (Later in the day, infants who had escaped from their mothers, instituted an unlicensed event in the sports by storming the platform; and the stalwart members of the band systematically scorned the steps.) She saw that the ascending procession included the incumbents of Westbury-on-the-Hill and Lower Merle, and Mrs. Rollo, all walking with bent heads. Somehow, the presence of two attendant clergy gave the *cortège* more than ever the air of an execution.

I I I

The sun shone and the band played, and above damp and patched grey tents, drooping national flags, and much warm humanity, the sky deepened in colour to an ultramarine hue. Pippa Johnson, walking between her Auntie Prue and Mrs. Bates, thought that the scene, allowing for the difference in costume, was exactly like the opening chapter of *The Scarlet*

Pimpernel. Or was she meaning *The Elusive Pimpernel*? She couldn't remember. Anyway, as she had tried to explain to her audience, it was the one which began with a fête on an English green, and awful things going on across the water, in France, and robust British rustics speaking broad dialect to giggling village maidens, and affable Quality secretly harassed by affairs of state and heart. And there had been a lovely phrase, descriptive of the time of year, which kept on recurring—*fin d'été*, "the ending of the summer."

"Yes, dear," said Auntie Prue. "I remember the film. I took Michael and you to see it in the Christmas holidays of 1935. And you both developed whooping-cough exactly a fortnight later. You were so much luckier than Michael, who retained all his meals. . . . So when I discovered that I couldn't get a room in the place, except over a dentist's in the main street," she continued, resuming her conversation with Mrs. Bates, across the form of Pippa, "I gave up the idea of the West Country, and I tried the Yorkshire coast—and then the Cotswolds. . . . One night I spent literally two hours on the telephone, trunk-calling hotels. Shouldn't you have thought," she asked with feeling, "that by the end of August there must have been a single room for a weary war-worker somewhere in England, in a place which hadn't got the sea-front tied up in rusty barbed wire, or a large new flying-ground just opening, or a schoolboys' timber camp, or an evacuated fever hospital. Good old May was a little irritating—pluming herself that she was taking her entire holiday this year staying with friends. But I happen to know that she's having to do out her own room at one place, as they've got no help. May and I are paying for the rooms in the private hotel at Bournemouth to which we have sent our Free French cook for a fortnight's complete rest, together with her sister-in-law. I must remember to say 'Fighting French.'"

"It really wasn't any trouble," said Mrs. Bates, vigorous as ever. "Pippa's telephone message, telling me that you had wired, saying that you would like to come down here for ten days while Michael was under canvas, caught me just as I was mounting my bicycle to go to my Post. I simply asked everyone on duty what they could suggest. I must say that I regretted I had not known sooner, then I could have told Mrs. Thomas Morrison that I was very sorry I could not put her up while she saw to the removal of her bits and pieces from Willows, as I had long kept this date for a very dear friend. Being the Fête week-end made it rather difficult. But I believe the Squirls are decent people, and the girl, Amy, can cook."

"Oh, yes," agreed Auntie Prue, "I couldn't be more comfortable. It's just what I needed—a real retreat. Of course, I should have preferred to stay at The Pheasant, with its memories of Hazlitt and the Lambs, and lovely old panelling. But I can well believe that it has been packed with officers' wives ever since the War began. And the Squirls' cottage is so picturesque, with the clematis on the porch, and the old green pond and cows in front, and the pigsties behind. Last night, when I opened my bedroom window—tiny, I admit— and stuck my head out, and smelt the rich country air, I felt a new woman already. Now that all the younger women have been removed from my Post—and quite rightly . . ."

"How extraordinary people are, talking about fighting cooks and their Posts, when they needn't," thought Pippa. "I thought the opening ceremony went off awfully well, didn't you?" she appealed.

"I couldn't hear all that your friend said, because of a baby next door to me," admitted Auntie Prue, "but I thought she had a very nice expression. I suppose that, as the only daughter of Lord Merle, she's well accustomed to public speaking. I suppose that was her mother, in the Parma violet toque, who arrived in the carriage with the Dowager."

Mrs. Bates, staring fixedly at the Hoop-la! stall, promptly showed Mrs. Beal how wrong she was in both surmises, especially the second; and before they paused, at a safe distance from "Target for To-night," she had divulged in hushed tones and absolute confidence that Lalage's mother was about to be married again.

"A young man who does up people's houses for them in the Empire style—a Mr. Tony ffolliott. . . . He's been down here and stayed with Mary Hungerford, when she had a house-party for Elizabeth Rollo's coming-out dance, in 1939. I don't think Mary really knew him. He was brought by Elizabeth's brother, as a dancing man. They were up at Oxford together. That makes him only about twenty-three now. Marcelle says that he's quite captivating, and of Byronic appearance. I remember I thought he looked rather ratty. He's not in khaki, I hear, but I believe he's doing war work of some kind in an office in London. That's why Lady Merle is going up to Scotland for the autumn, I dare say. Until January, when the decree becomes absolute, she daren't even go out to supper with him, Marcelle says. She thinks it's so romantic. It's all settled, although, of course, a dead secret. It sounds quite mad to me, but then I'm old-fashioned."

IV

The skinny small boy, with a rust-coloured forelock and terrible freckles, who had been brought to the Grand Fête by the Dowager Lady Merle, was straying from stall to stall like a questing hound. He had taken part in the Scouts' display, and watched the children's fancy dress parade with benevolent interest. Now his public duties for die day were at an end, and he was at leisure to enjoy himself. No stranger would have guessed from his expression and gait that he was spending an ideal after-noon. But not many of those present to-day were strangers to Rolfe Yarrow, aged twelve, son of the late M.P. for the Went Division. And Rolfe had, as his mother tenderly noted, inherited his father's perfectly unaffected kindly interest in other people's concerns.

"Hallo, Rolfe," said a voice far above him. "I was so sorry to hear about your people being in quarantine."

"Hallo, Mrs. Hungerford!" said Rolfe smiling, which suddenly made him look a very attractive, instead of a very hide-ous, small boy. "Yes, it's rotten luck for them, isn't it? I wonder if they'll get it. I was awfully miserable when I got Mummy's letter, telling me I mustn't go near them. But Lady Merle's butler is letting me work the soda-water machine, and her maid, Miss McNaughton, is awfully nice. Did you know she'd got second-sight? Lady Merle has given me a ferret, and two-and-six to spend at the side-shows. The ferret generally lives up my sleeve, and her name is 'Secret.' But I couldn't bring her to-day. I've taken a ticket in the raffle for a goose, and done the treasure hunt, and hoop-la! three times. I very nearly won a pearl neck-lace, only Amy Squirl said my hoop hadn't completely encircled the wooden block. The Exhibition of Bombs is sixpence, which I think rather a lot, don't you?"

"Shall we do the hoop-la! again, together?" suggested Mrs. Hungerford.

"You only get three tries for tuppence," Rolfe warned her.

Mrs. Hungerford lavishly paid for twelve tries, and with his second-last hoop Rolfe won a white china cat wearing a mauve artificial silk necktie. He handsomely offered it to Mrs. Hunger-ford, and when she had denied herself the pleasure, admitted that he had really been hoping all along that she would say "No," so that he could give it to his mother for her birthday, which had actually happened on May 20th.

"Mummy told me, in her last letter," continued Rolfe, his wary grey eyes searching his companion's face, "that she's got to register on October 3rd. I don't know exactly how old she is. At least, she told me once, but I've forgotten. She said it quite cheerfully, but do you think she'll be called up to do something?"

"I don't think she could possibly be called upon to do anything more than she is doing already," Mary assured him.

"I should simply hate having no home for the holidays," admitted Rolfe, "and Dick and Jemima and the twins would miss her. But that tiny little boy who got the first prize in the children's fancy dress parade told me that his mother was a soldier. Did you notice him—awfully well done? He's dressed as an air-raid warden, and he's got blue overalls, and a tin hat, and a whistle, and a scarlet ladder. Mrs. Bates, who looks after him, made everything, except the ladder, in the evenings, when she was off-duty from her Post. She got old Mr. Wookey, who keeps the antique-shop on the hill, to make the ladder, in exchange for some dahlias, but she had to paint it herself."

"I missed the parade, as I was talking to Lady Merle," said Mary. "But I've seen several of the competitors walking about. Little Barbara Crippen, in nurse's uniform, and carrying a dressing tray and instruments, looked sweet, I thought, and the curly-haired boy as a rabbit, with 'Not rationed' on his front. I didn't know him."

"He was one of the 'vaccies from Highbridge," said Rolfe. "Lady Wilson and Mrs. Gibson did the judging, and they gave second prize to a Harker, who was 'Dig for Victory,' in a smock, with a frightfully sharp spade over his shoulder, and a string of carrots round his neck. He's eaten them all now. How's Colonel Hungerford?"

"Very well, thank you," smiled Mary. "I had a letter from him from Lisbon to-day."

"Did he say if he'd be able to get home in time for the Fête?" asked Rolfe.

"He didn't even know it was taking place," said Mary apologetically. "You see, he's been in Turkey, and he'd only just got a letter from me dated May 2nd."

"Can one still get Turkish Delight in Turkey?" wondered Rolfe, with a seraphic look. "I wish Colonel Hungerford was going to be here to-day. I would have liked to ask his opinion about something private. Look!" He delved into his pocket. "I found this in the potting shed at home, when I was there unexpectedly on Tuesday. I wasn't going anywhere in particular, and I suddenly found myself on my bike, quite near, and I couldn't resist snooping inside to see if old Barguss was there. Do you know him? He's our gardener, and he's frightfully old, about sixty, I dare say. I shouldn't think he could possibly be infectious."

Mary stared at the treasure which Rolfe laid in her palm. It was a well-worn silver pocket-knife, with one broken blade. . . . She turned it over, and read the initials R. H. Y.

"Should you think it had belonged to my father?" breathed Rolfe.

Yes," nodded Mary. "Quite certainly. Where did you find it?"

"Tumbled down behind a bundle of bamboos," said Rolfe. "The rays of the setting sun struck upon it, just as I was glancing round the shed in farewell, as Barguss wasn't there. It must have been there years and years. It's got one bust blade, as you may have noticed, but the other two are quite all right, and there's a screwdriver—and an instrument for removing flints from horse's hoofs," he concluded yearningly.

"I should keep it," advised Mary briskly.

"Should you really?" asked Rolfe, his face alight. "That was just what I was wanting to ask. You see, I should terribly like to have it, because of it having belonged to my father, and also because of its general usefulness in my future life. But I was so afraid that perhaps Mummy might want it more, and I suppose it really is hers. And I didn't like to ask her on the telephone, as she never can hear what I say, because I speak too fast; and I thought that a letter about it would be rather difficult."

"I shall be speaking to your mother on the telephone to-night," said kind Mrs. Hungerford. "I'll explain, and ask her. But I'm quite sure she'll say 'yes.'"

"Will you really? Oh, thank you so much," said Rolfe, delighted. "I say, are you quite sure you wouldn't like my cat, I won? I could quite easily get something else for Mummy, as I've still got ninepence left of Lady Merle's money."

Mrs. Hungerford reassured him, and he drifted away, after returning a greeting from Lady Wilson.

"It is so disappointing for poor Dolly Yarrow, not being able to come to-day," said Lady Wilson, who was resting under a spreading chestnut, after the exertion of judging the Children's Dress Parade. "She had made fancy dresses for the twins, too. However, their competing would only have increased my difficulties. Dolly always has such original ideas. Have you see her recently?"

"Not for more than a word," said Mary. "We had made a plan to go for a picnic together, on her birthday, but when May 20th came it was the only day on which the Dean could officiate at a little memorial service in the cathedral, for her poor old aunts. So I went to that instead."

"I hear that Pippa Johnson has an aunt staying down here on annual leave from war work," said Lady Wilson. "Do you know

211 | SOMEWHERE IN ENGLAND

where she has found rooms? I should like to show her some civility, as we have seen so much of her engaging little niece."

Mary told her neighbour where Mrs. Beal was to be found, and Lady Wilson continued, "Do you know—of course, I shall not mention this to the aunt, unless she herself opens the subject— but I believe that we have such a romance going on between your little probationer and a very suitable military admirer?"

"Military!" echoed Mary.

"My husband knew his grandparents out in India—a thoroughly sound Service family," said Lady Wilson, "and we have both known David since he was at Woolwich. Such a steady fellow! I am sure that he has 'good husband and father' written all over his countenance. I am almost sure that he has made up his mind, but equally sure that he has not said anything as yet. If he gives me the opportunity, and asks my advice, I shall advise him to mention his feelings frankly, and without delay. I am a little afraid lest perhaps he is deterred by ideas of it being hardly fair for a regular officer on active service to engage the affections of a very young girl."

"What about her feelings?" inquired Mary.

"If she has lost her mother—and in the saddest way—as I believe is the case," said Lady Wilson, "it would be an excellent thing for her to settle as early as possible. She is a little young, and looks even less than her age. But my grandmother married at sixteen, and never regretted it."

"I mean, do you think she likes him?" probed Mrs. Hungerford.

This suggestion seemed to be novel and unpleasing to her neighbour.

"She cannot fail to do so," decided Lady Wilson, rallying. "And I know that she takes an intelligent interest in the progress of the War on the various fronts. She has always listened to the bulletins with rapt attention, when we have turned on the news at six or nine o'clock, during her visits. (I was horrified to hear from our good Mrs. Bates that some of the younger women at her Post seem to regard the wireless as nothing more than an accompaniment to light conversation and loud laughter!) I remember that Pippa was supping with us on the night after the first thousand-bomber raid on Cologne. Such a hot night! We heard the bulletin—sad losses, of course, and all highly trained men—but as Captain Cox pointed out, as far as numbers went, nothing compared to the casualty lists which we used to expect as the fortune of war, after a big trench raid in 1917. I did not notice her slip from the room later, but when I went into our scullery, to hasten our Austrian maid with the grog tray, I happened to look out of the window, and there I saw our little guest, standing up to her waist amongst wet cabbages, staring upwards at the darkening sky. She had clasped her hands behind the nape of her neck, and her face was as white as a flower in the moonlight. Some aircraft, from one of our local stations, I imagine, were drawing near overhead, moving in formation—a beautiful sight—such an impression of power and efficiency! Young ears are very quick. I had not heard anything, although my hearing is above the average. I called out to ask her whether these were some of our Went bombers returning from the raid. She answered, sounding quite shocked, 'Oh, no! Not coming home. Cologne is only two and a half to three flying hours from here, under favourable conditions. This must mean that they're going out again to-night.'

"Quite extraordinary, it still seems to me, to be able to dine in Went and return for breakfast, having bombed Cologne! I cannot imagine that the young people of to-day will reach such years as my husband and myself. John Taylor, who had called, in after supper that evening, said sadly that he feared that *spirits* were responsible for much of the high spirits of our airmen to-day. Can one be surprised? But I was quite surprised by the sharpness with which my youngest guest took him up, on that point. Captain Cox took her home, by the field path across the Park, and said, on his return, that she had seemed to him much tired. I am almost sure that he said nothing to worry her further."

V

Two khaki-clad female figures were proudly leading between them a very small boy dressed as an air-raid warden, and clasping in his hand a ticket, announcing "First Prize." One of the ladies was tall, fair and rosy, and might well, thought Mary, have been photographed for a recruiting poster, for anything smarter than Aileen, *née* Hill, in uniform, Mary had not yet seen. Aileen, who had been the youngest and much the handsomest of the three Hills, had left for Vancouver in a hurry, in August 1939, to marry a young engineer of Scottish extraction, a few months younger than herself, on whom nobody at Westbury had ever set eyes. She now bore the word "Canada" on her shoulder-straps, and as she had an upright carriage, glossy, honey-coloured locks and splendid teeth, she looked the picture of jubilant health. Poor Rosemary, Mary noticed, although she had obviously taken pains over her appearance, had already a button hanging loose. Khaki did not suit her complexion, and she had adopted, together with her new profession, a severe Joan of Arc coiffure.

"Aileen, my dear," exclaimed Mary, holding out both hands. "Rosemary! This is a splendid surprise!"

As she had not met Aileen since 1939, she made her first inquiries in that direction.

Aileen did not in the least mind detailing in a rather loud, clear voice, that she would have been in England before now, only by the time that her husband had finished his training as an air-pilot, she had started a baby. However, with the fuss of saying good-bye to him when he was ordered abroad, and all that, although she was usually as strong as a horse, and everyone at Home had been more than kind, things had gone wrong, but perhaps it was all for the best, as she'd then been able to follow her husband as soon as possible, She was awfully glad to see everyone at Westbury again, but, although this might sound crackers, she was already nearly crazy with homesickness for British Columbia. She said, stooping and picking up Ferdinand-Africa by the scruff of his neck, as if he were a puppy, and setting him astride her shoulders, "He's cute, isn't he? The first thing I mean to do as soon as I get right back Home, is to order another exactly like him."

Mary, who had been making sympathetic noises at appropriate points in Aileen's narrative, could not help thinking that Nature had made a mistake when she had presented the spindly and erratic Rosemary—and for that part, Rosemary's mother—with not greatly desired offspring. But Rosemary, as soon appeared, was now taking unwonted interest in Ferdinand-Africa. She told Mary that, honestly, he was much better off with Mrs. Bates, and that Mrs. Bates was behaving very decently.

"When I got down last night—quite unexpectedly—I found that he'd got the photograph I had sent, of me, with my unit, beside his bed. And he's able to point out which is his Mummy—aren't you, Ferdinand? Sally and my mother were in the middle of a thundering row about his going to the Fête dressed as an air-raid warden, so it was lucky I turned up, to lay down the law as his mother. After all, it had taken poor old Sally ages to make the costume, and he wanted to go, and as Sally tactfully pointed out, an air-raid warden is practically a healer.

"Did you hear that Mummy and I met, quite by chance, each gripping suitcases, on the doorstep of her flat in London? But I had never intended to do more than spend the night there, so it wasn't the least use her ordering me off the premises. I was a bit furious when I found that she'd run away from what was clearly her duty. But, as I said before, Ferdinand is much better off with old Sally, and she quite understands that when the War is over, I shall be needing him again, and she's told me that when my mother asked him whether he liked being at Willows or Flagstaff House best, he said, 'Flagstaff House, except that I'd like my Mummy too.'"

Ferdinand, thumping Aileen's chest with his heels, now demanded to be taken to see the model warship again, so they departed, and Rosemary proceeded to give details of her Spartan life, and expectations of being sent to Scotland, to an officers' cadet training unit. She said, following the figures of Aileen and her son with a possessive eye, "Didn't it make your blood run cold when poor Aileen spoke so glibly of ordering another just like Ferdinand? I couldn't help remembering that Mrs. Taylor's never had a second chance, and simply got more than previously snappish."

""Dear Pamela was quite ten years older than Aileen," said Mary, absently.

A shade of melancholy was stealing over her. She could not help seeing that Aileen, of whom she had always been fond, was now entirely lost to the Westbury community, whereas Rosemary did not as yet show signs of seeing other people's point of view much, and presently even went so far as to suggest that it was high time Amy Squirl went mobile.

But Mrs. Hungerford's worst moment of this afternoon was yet to come.

Leaving Rosemary with the Albany Mimms, whom she greeted as if she had not seen them for many years, Mrs. Hungerford betook herself to the vicinity of the Dowager.

Old Lady Merle, on her daughter's arm, was about to remount her Victoria. Her exit was imminent. She had made a purchase at every stall, and was now, as Mary could see, the owner of a rose-pink guest-towel, embroidered with orange hollyhocks, a tin of insecticide, a basket of rather tough-looking artichokes from Willows kitchen-garden, and a volume of Scottish war-songs.

"One of the most successful fêtes we have ever had at Westbury," was the Dowager's gracious comment. "I congratulate you all."

"I'm afraid I've done very little, except supply the speaker from my staff," confessed Mary.

"All of your staff seem to me well occupied," said the Dowager. "I had a word with Sister Finan and little Nurse Johnson. They are organising the children's relay races, together with some helpful Air Force officers. Violet"— indicating her attendant daughter—"was quite upset to see what she imagined to be Diana Gibson, winning both the sack race and the slow bicycle race. But I was able to assure her that it was Daphne, a younger sister, who is now, I think, employed at Woodside."

"Yes, Daphne came three days ago, when Elisabeth Rollo had to leave rather sooner than we expected," explained Mary. "Elisabeth has gone to a hospital in North Wales, run by a cousin of her father. But I am quite settled again now, for Dolly Yarrow's niece comes to-morrow, to take Diana's place. Lalage was good, wasn't she?"

"She has much to learn," pronounced the Dowager, with devastating honesty. "Still, I wish that her father could have been present to hear her first effort. In what part of North Wales is the hospital of which you spoke? I ask, because I have just heard from my son that he has been ordered up there."

VI

When Mrs. Hungerford realized that, with the best intentions in the world, she had dispatched the ex-débutante entrusted to her care, to the one place in Great Britain where she could see more of a suitor who was hardly as yet in a position to be considered as a suitor, and to whom her parents might reasonably object, she felt so shaken that she had to sit down as soon as possible. The grey tents, brilliant flags, hard azure sky and level landscape, rocked in her gaze. Her one desire was to get out of hearing of babies crying, a band braying, and adults roaring with laughter.

She found a seat on an empty but very hard bench, beneath a row of whispering Lombardy poplars, and collapsed gratefully. Its view was of the children's competitions, now drawing to a close, and the teams mustering for the Tug-of-War. The band was undoubtedly earning its keep. Mrs. Hungerford closed her eyes, and removed her hat. Her watch had told her that the hour was now four-forty-five, and she knew that she had no prospect of retiring until after the prize-giving at seven. She told herself that she always felt ghastly after having to listen to someone she knew making a speech, and that Rosemary and her mother always lowered her resistance, and made her foresee the worst. As soon as she had enjoyed a short rest, she would arise and join the queue outside the cricket pavilion; and after a cup of urn tea and a bun, she would probably feel much better able to visit the Exhibition of Bombs, and distribute the prizes, and generally look on the brighter side. It was not possible to sleep while seated on the backless bench and listening to the Air Force band, but she was wrapped in profound reverie when a satisfied voice startled her with the words, "Mrs. Hungerford! Just the lady we're looking for."

Opening her eyes, she at first received a quite false impression that she was Macbeth, surrounded by the three witches. In front of her, all scanning her unguarded features with glittering orbs, stood Mrs. Bracket, Miss Crouch, and bearded Miss Copper, from Lower Merle Dairy Farm. Mrs. Hungerford well knew the first two figures, as the most formidable collectors for the Westbury and Merle District Nursing Association. She decided that poor Miss Copper's beard must have suggested the Macbeth theory to her fevered brain. But there was no denying that all three elderly females had, at the moment, the look of vultures about to attack their prey. Mrs. Hungerford assured them that they weren't disturbing her, and that she had not been asleep, which was quite true. She said, forcing a smile, "Were you all looking for me? I'm so sorry, I'm afraid I was woolgathering. It's such a warm day, isn't it? Lady Merle," she added, "has just told me she thinks this is one of the most successful fêtes we have ever had on the Green."

This opening was fatal to her future peace of mind, for it gave Mrs. Bracket exactly the cue for which she was waiting. With the feelings of a spent swimmer, attempting to strike out amongst heavy weeds, Mrs. Hungerford heard her companions unfold that, as to-day's fête for Warship Week had been such an unqualified success, what we all felt we ought to do now, was to have another fête.

"Another fête?" gasped Mrs. Hungerford, groping for her hat.

The three witches thereupon proceeded to cap one another's utterances in precisely the Shakespearian manner.

"In aid of Russia," announced Mrs. Bracket, with a sinister smile.

"On Saturday, September the 26th," contributed Miss Crouch on a higher note.

"The Rector and Mrs. Taylor are ever so keen," chanted Miss Copper.

"Do sit down," said Mrs. Hungerford faintly, and the three witches swooped, and the band, as if it realized that the situation was now serious, ceased to play.

"Mrs. Taylor said that it would be best for us to ask your opinion first of all," reopened Mrs. Bracket diplomatically.

"She was sure that you would be interested," murmured Miss Crouch.

"Without your help, we really feel we couldn't make the attempt, ma'am," crooned Miss Copper.

"Oh, nonsense," said Mrs. Hungerford, rousing herself. "I know you'd get on marvellously. Of course," she added weakly, "I think it's a splendid idea, and I'm ready to do anything I possibly can to help. But I'm afraid that I shall be able to give very little time."

"That we quite understood," nodded Mrs. Bracket.

"Mrs. Taylor warned us," said Miss Crouch, sounding awful.

"That we couldn't ask you to do more than just speak the few opening words," slipped in Miss Copper triumphantly.

"Knowing Colonel Hungerford's deep interest in Russia," proceeded Mrs. Bracket, with fiendish cunning.

"Having Mrs. Hungerford to open the Russian Fête," began Miss Crouch,

"Would be just as suitable as having had the Honourable Mrs. Rollo to open the Warship Fête," ended Miss Copper, cutting off Mary's last hope of escape.

The band began to play pot-pourri from *The Mikado*, and by the time that it had reached "The Flowers that bloom in the Spring, tra-la!" Mrs. Hungerford was opening the Aid to Russia Fête, and Mrs. Bracket, who knew when to let well alone, had said, "That's settled then!" and, with ever so many thanks, had gathered her confederates around her, and swept them off towards the cricket pavilion and a nice cup of tea.

Mrs. Hungerford, feeling that a cup of poison was what she now needed, rose unsteadily, and prepared to follow them.

She was surprised, when she emerged from her comparatively cool retreat, to observe that the Dowager's equipage had not yet withdrawn. Pamela must have succeeded in her plot to get Lady Merle to present the cup to the winning Tug-of-War team at four-thirty. Mrs. Hungerford, shading her eyes with a hand, as she re-entered a scene of glaring colour and tumult, which was momentarily becoming more and more like Frith's "Derby Day," gave an involuntary start, and then stood rooted.

A new and evidently welcome guest had joined the family group drooping about the Dowager's Victoria. Judging by the angle of the handsome newcomer's headgear, he was in the best of spirits, and something which he had just said was making the black-and-white striped parasol rock.

"It can't be!" escaped Mrs. Hungerford, as a string of five children, running hand-in-hand towards the Treasure Hunt, but all looking at the Hoop-la! collided violently with her stationary form, and simultaneously a timid voice asked in vain would she like a ticket for the Goose?

But it was indeed, and he had asked a question, and turned his head, and was looking straight in her direction.

And in the three minutes which elapsed before the striding late arrival had covered with speed and elegance the stretch of faded grass which was now all that lay between him and his wife, Mrs. Hungerford realized with a rush that it was a perfect English summer's day, and this was certainly going to be one of the most successful fêtes ever held on the Green.

She was looking ready for anything, when Colonel Hungerford halted in front of her, and asked indulgently, "Giving a party, m'dear?"

THE END

FURROWED MIDDLEBROW

Made in the USA
Middletown, DE
09 January 2021

31172554R00129